PIN

'I was glued to the pages from start to finish.
Children will be spellbound by this tale'
ABI ELPHINSTONE ON *A PINCH OF MAGIC*

'The wry enchantment of an E. Nesbit classic'
DAILY MAIL ON *A PINCH OF MAGIC*

'This delightful tale fizzes with magic.
It completely charmed my socks off!'
ALEX BELL ON *A PINCH OF MAGIC*

'An eerie adventure sure to enchant readers'
SOPHIE ANDERSON ON *A SPRINKLE OF SORCERY*

'A spellbinding story with feisty characters
that spring to life on the page'
SUNDAY EXPRESS ON *A SPRINKLE OF SORCERY*

'Totally brilliant . . . with a killer twist that I
didn't see coming at all!'
EMMA CARROLL ON *A TANGLE OF SPELLS*

'A stunner, with such great writing'
PETER BUNZL ON *A TANGLE OF SPELLS*

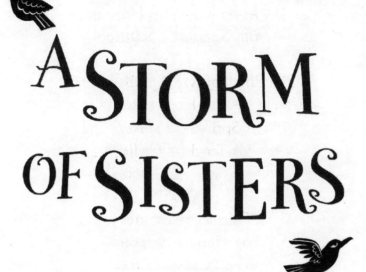

A STORM
OF SISTERS

MICHELLE
HARRISON

SIMON & SCHUSTER

First published in Great Britain in 2022 by Simon & Schuster UK Ltd

Text, map and chapter illustrations © Michelle Harrison 2022

1 3 5 7 9 10 8 6 4 2

Simon & Schuster UK Ltd
1st Floor
222 Gray's Inn Road
London WC1X 8HB

www.simonandschuster.co.uk
www.simonandschuster.com.au
www.simonandschuster.co.in

Simon & Schuster Australia, Sydney
Simon & Schuster India, New Delhi

A CIP catalogue record for this book
is available from the British Library.

PB ISBN 978-1-4711-9765-9
eBook ISBN 978-1-4711-9766-6
eAudio ISBN 978-1-3985-1605-2

This book is a work of fiction. Names, characters, places
and incidents are either the product of the author's imagination
or are used fictitiously. Any resemblance to actual people
living or dead, events or locales is entirely coincidental.

Typeset in Goudy by M Rules
Printed and bound by CPI Group (UK) Ltd, Croydon, CR0 4YY

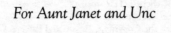

For Aunt Janet and Unc

Dear Reader

Growing up as the youngest of three girls there were plenty of stories, adventures (and squabbles!) in our household. As most siblings know, you can be the best of friends or the worst of enemies in a heartbeat. That's why my three Widdershins sisters, Betty, Fliss and Charlie, feel so real to me – because they're inspired by my own experiences as a sister. Their Pinch of Magic Adventures take them from breaking a curse in misty Crowstone to outwitting pirates on the high seas, and even to a witch-infested village.

Now, in deepest winter, the Widdershins sisters and Granny are visiting cousin Clarissa in far away Wilderness and one by one they fall under its icy spell. For explorer Betty it's the festive market, animal-loving Charlie is drawn to Echo Hall's resident wolf-dog, and romantic Fliss is enchanted by the ghostly tale of a doomed highwayman.

But the legend, and its hauntings, are closer than the sisters realise. Soon they find themselves skating on thin ice where the highwayman's loot – a magical crystal ball – is said to lie at the bottom of a frozen lake. And someone dangerous is searching for it . . .

Come a little closer and wrap up warm . . . things are about to get chilly!

Wishing you a spine-tingling read.

Michelle Harrison

Prologue

The crystal ball lay hidden, as it had for many years: its smooth surface untouched, and any secrets it had to impart, unknown. It had once rested in its own wooden box inscribed with strange silver symbols, but the box was long gone and the two would never meet again. Yet time had not changed the crystal ball in any way. It was still as perfect, as beautiful and as mesmerising as it had always been.

And it had lost none of its magic.

The crystal ball had once belonged to a family of famous fortune tellers. Within its glassy depths, visions of the future and even the past had been revealed. It had glimpsed births, money, marriages and deaths, and had earned its owners many a pretty penny. But while the fortune tellers were the ones with the fame and glory, they were only as good as the crystal ball allowed them to be. Without it, they would be powerless and penniless, reduced to tricks and clever illusions.

At first, the crystal ball had filled with a furious black fog when it had been stolen. It had been rather attached to its owner and missed her attention and soft murmurs of encouragement. Gradually, the fog faded and the crystal cleared, and it found that it quite liked being alone without curious eyes peering into it and constant demands to show the future. But occasionally, when it sensed people were near, it could not resist conjuring a vision to look into their lives and see what lay in store for them.

One day, almost forty years after it had been stolen, the crystal ball sensed a new presence and it was an intriguing one. The glassy orb swirled with such a vision of white snowflakes that for a moment it seemed as though the crystal itself was a formation of carved ice. Then, from within the depths, an image of three girls appeared within swirling snow. Three girls who were no strangers to enchanted objects.

Three sisters with their own pinch of magic . . .

Chapter One
Winter in Pendlewick

I T WAS A CRISP FEBRUARY MORNING WHEN THE
letter arrived at Blackbird Cottage. Betty Widdershins
saw it first as she galloped down the crooked stairs
towards the smell of breakfast. She scooped up the white
envelope from the doormat and read the small, neat writing
before heading into the kitchen where her grandmother was
pouring tea from a large pot.

'Letter for you, Granny,' she said, handing over the
envelope while taking in the smudged postmark. The
Widdershins didn't get much post, and the stamp suggested
this hadn't come from anywhere local, which immediately
got Betty's attention.

Granny puffed a wisp of grey hair out of her eyes and put
the teapot down with a bang. She wasn't cross, merely heavy-
handed and inclined to clatter about and stamp instead of
walking. Wiping her hands on her apron, she took the letter
and inspected the handwriting. 'Looks like it's from Clarissa,'

3

she said, placing it to one side with a groan. 'I'll open it in a minute.'

Betty rolled her eyes, her interest in the letter vanishing. Her father's cousin Clarissa didn't write often, but when she did her letters were usually a very long moan.

Betty's father, a large, red-faced man, was toasting bread over a crackling fire. He looked up and winked, holding out the toasting fork towards her.

'Hungry?'

'Starving.' Betty took the toast and a plate, sitting down to slather on butter. She sank her teeth into it hungrily. 'Where are Charlie and Fliss?' she asked. It wasn't like her two sisters to miss breakfast but she knew they couldn't have gone far. There wasn't a great deal to do in Pendlewick unless you liked tea rooms and meadows, which Betty *did*, but there was only so much tea and cake you could eat. Lovely as the village was, Betty found herself bored all too frequently these days, and wishing that something, *anything* would happen.

'Charlie's out on that swing of hers, you know what she's like,' said Father. 'And Fliss just popped into the garden.'

Betty's eyebrows shot up into her bushy hair. '*Garden? In this weather?*' Toast in hand she marched towards a small door at the back of the kitchen that led to Fliss's room. This was in a newer part of the house which didn't slope like the rest of the cottage. Because of this, her older sister Felicity – or Fliss, as she was better known – had claimed it as her own, as it was the only room which didn't make her feel 'seasick'.

At the back of Fliss's bedroom, which she had named 'the Nest', was another door that led to the garden. Betty went towards it, breathing in the faint smell of her sister's rosewater perfume. Through the window she could see down the path through a leafy archway and past the garden walls. There, in the meadow beyond, her little sister Charlie was swinging high in the air from a large tree, her pigtails streaming out behind her in the wintry brightness.

A swish of chilled air wrapped itself round Betty as a shivering Fliss, who was bundled up in several layers of clothing, burst in from outside. 'Brrrr!' she said. Then, 'Oh, Betty! I was just on my way to get you. Come and look!' Her dark brown eyes shone with excitement as she beckoned Betty outside.

Betty followed without even bothering to grab a coat. Her sister's excitement was catching – had she found something important?

'Close that door!' Granny hollered. 'Yer letting all the cold in!'

Giggling, Betty and Fliss darted outside and snapped the door closed behind them.

'What did you want to show me?' Betty asked as Fliss led her to a neat little flowerbed overlooked by the kitchen window. Each of the sisters had been given their own small patch of the garden to grow things as they pleased, but only Fliss had bothered to. She had planted several rose bushes along with plenty of lavender which she'd pruned back at the

5

end of summer. Next to a swept-up pile of dead leaves lay a dirt-covered trowel, and Betty's tummy did an excited flip. Blackbird Cottage was over two hundred years old and had already proved to hold several secrets – all sorts of things might have been lost or hidden in its grounds. Images flashed into her head: an old key, a necklace, an ancient weapon . . . whatever could Fliss have unearthed?

'Look!' Fliss pointed eagerly.

'What?' Betty asked, not sure what she was supposed to be seeing.

Fliss kneeled down and poked at the earth with the trowel, where a few small green shoots were nosing out of the dirt. 'These, silly. See? They're golden trumpets coming up, and I think those ones are tulips!'

Betty stared back blankly, her anticipation whooshing away like a blown-out candle. '*Flowers?* I thought you'd found something exciting, like treasure, or . . . or—'

'Flowers *are* exciting,' Fliss insisted, not put off by Betty's lack of interest. 'Because they mean spring's on the way!' She flung out her arm happily, sending a shower of earth over Betty's ankles. 'Oh, I can't wait. Everything coming to life again. Soon there'll be blossom on the trees, new lambs over at Peckahen Farm . . . and then it'll be summer,' she added dreamily. 'Long, lazy picnics in the garden, butterflies and bees humming round the lavender . . .'

'Wasps attacking your ice cream,' Betty added, shaking dirt off her boots. 'Sunburn, and frizzy hair.' She eyed Fliss's glossy dark locks wistfully. 'Not that you've got that problem.' Her sister had the sort of hair that no kind of weather could ruin, and clear, rosy skin that was always pretty even when streaked with dirt. Fortunately Fliss was as lovely inside as she was on the outside which made her difficult to envy but easy to tease.

Betty was startled out of her thoughts by a shriek.

'Jumping jackdaws, she's done it again!' Fliss cried, scrabbling to her feet. She dropped the trowel and cupped her hands round her mouth to yell across the garden. 'CHARLOTTE WIDDERSHINS! COME HERE THIS INSTANT!'

'EH?' Charlie hollered back from the swing. 'Ain't done nothing!'

'You know exactly what you've done!' Fliss shouted. 'If you're going to bury things, do it in your own patch!'

Betty glanced at the flowerbed, finally understanding. There, poking out of the earth, was the thin little tail of a half-buried mouse.

Charlie leapt off the swing while it was still alarmingly high in the air, landing perfectly on her feet. She ran up the garden path, pausing only to make a couple of soft *chook-chook* noises to the chickens.

'Oh, no!' she exclaimed as she reached her sisters. 'You dug up Mr Whiffles!' She shot Fliss an accusing look.

'Never mind that,' Fliss said huffily. 'Will you *please* stop burying animals over here? I don't want dead mice under my tulips, thank you. If you want to make a graveyard, there's

7

plenty of space.' She pointed. 'What about over there?'

'That's full of weeds,' Charlie said, wrinkling her upturned nose. 'It's ugly. This bit's pretty.'

'Yes, because I've worked hard on it!' Fliss retorted.

Charlie's large green eyes filled with tears. 'I just thought he'd be happier over here, under the chew lips.'

Fliss softened at once. 'Oh, Charlie,' she said. 'I'll help you plant some tulips of your own, and we'll make it nice together. Just . . . no more corpses in my lavender, deal?'

'Deal.' Charlie nodded, cheering up. 'It'll be the best graveyard ever!'

Fliss eyed the little tail and shuddered, handing Betty the trowel. 'Betty, you do it. I don't think I can.'

'Give it here,' said Charlie, rolling her eyes. She dug up the dead mouse and, with Betty's help, cleared a small space on the other side of the path to rebury it in. 'May he rest in cheese,' she said solemnly, patting down the earth with the trowel.

'Er, it's rest in *peace*, Charlie,' Betty said gently.

'I know,' Charlie replied. 'But I think he'd like cheese better, don't you?'

'I suppose he would,' Betty said, ruffling her little sister's untidy hair. 'Ooh, your cheeks are cold – let's get inside.'

'It's not that cold,' Charlie said. 'Is it?' She sniffed the air hopefully. 'Can you smell snow, Betty? Do you reckon we might get some?'

Betty lifted her nose. 'Dunno.' All she could smell now

was a faint whiff of burnt toast. A few days ago it had been colder, and Granny had insisted she could detect the scent of snow on the air which had thrilled Charlie to bits, but so far it had failed to appear. Betty doubted it would at all, for winter in Pendlewick was far kinder than they were used to.

The Widdershins had moved to the village during the summer. Before this they'd lived on the gloomy island of Crowstone, a prison town surrounded by grey marshes which were forever swamped in cold, damp fog, the kind that made old bones creak and clothes feel permanently clammy. Here, further inland, it was drier and milder, which Betty was glad of, not least because the damp weather played havoc with her frizz-prone hair. But while she loved their new home with its wonky cottage and charming meadows, she found that now the thrill of a new place had worn off Pendlewick was possibly a bit *too* nice.

They turned to go back indoors, but then Fliss gave a cross squeak. 'Oi!'

A scruffy black cat was squatting in the freshly turned earth. It straightened up, sniffed, and then began raking over the dirt with its paws.

'I don't know why I bother.' Fliss brushed the dirt from her knees and flounced indoors.

Betty and Charlie followed, Oi shooting past their ankles to secure the best place in front of the fire. Inside, the kitchen was warm and hazy with their grandmother's pipe smoke.

'I must say,' said Granny while Fliss grumbled about mice

graveyards and cat toilets, 'it's nice to see you looking grubby for once, Felicity.'

'Bit of dirt under the fingernails never hurt anyone,' Father agreed.

'P'raps it ain't dirt,' Charlie suggested wickedly, with a nod in Oi's direction.

Alarmed, Fliss got up and began scrubbing her nails over the sink.

'What's old Bossy Boots got to say, then?' Father asked, nodding at Granny's letter, which was still on the flowery tablecloth, unopened.

'Probably just wants a whinge, as usual,' Granny muttered. She picked up the envelope and sliced it open with her butter knife. 'I do hope she's not going to pester us to visit her again.' Her eyes narrowed. 'Or worse, be planning on visiting us.'

Betty poured herself some tea and sat back to listen. She wasn't especially interested in cousin Clarissa's whingeing, but the lure of a new place was something Betty couldn't resist. She, Fliss and Charlie had never visited Clarissa. They had met her only a handful of times when she had turned up either unannounced or at very short notice at the Poacher's Pocket – the pub the family had lived in back in Crowstone – and proceeded to lecture Granny about everything that was wrong with the place.

'Perhaps we *should* visit her,' Betty suggested, watching as Charlie spooned jam straight into her mouth from the jar while Granny wasn't looking.

10

'I think not,' Granny said at once, her eyes racing down the letter. 'You know she lives way up north in Wilderness, one of the bitterest places in the country. My creaky old bones can't take that sort of chill.'

'Have you ever been there?' asked Betty.

'Once,' said Granny, with a scowl. 'And never again. I can't imagine why she'd want to live in that eerie place, cut off from everywhere. I told her she was mad, but if you ask me, she did it to make life difficult for herself. All the more for her to moan about.'

'Well, if we went *there* it'd save her coming here,' Betty persisted. She was intrigued by the sound of Wilderness; it was hard to imagine anywhere colder or bleaker than Crowstone. She thought she remembered Clarissa telling them something interesting about the place, too. Something about an old legend ...

Father snorted. 'Any excuse, eh, Betty Widdershins? You and those itchy feet of yours, unable to keep still. We've only been in Pendlewick for five minutes!'

Betty grinned. It was true: she loved discovering new and thrilling places more than anything. A few months ago Pendlewick had been one such place with its mysterious landmarks and whispers of village witches, but of course, any place that became home eventually became familiar. Her craving for excitement, the 'itch' that her father described, had started to tickle once more.

Betty was sipping her tea, wondering if she could convince

Granny and Father to take them on holiday, when Granny let out a gasp and slapped the letter down on the table.

'Bats and broomsticks! The daft boot's only gone and broken her ankle!'

'Daft boot,' Charlie said at once, clearly squirrelling this away for future use.

'Poor Clarissa!' Fliss said.

'How's she managed that?' Father asked.

'Slipped on some ice, she says,' Granny snapped, clearly irritated. 'And our Clarissa's no string bean. She would've gone down with a bang, that's for sure. Of all the things to happen! Now we'll have to go and look after her.'

'Wait,' said Betty, feeling a spark of excitement. 'We're visiting cousin Clarissa?'

'But you said we couldn't,' Charlie reminded Granny. 'Because of your creepy bones.'

'She's family,' Granny said firmly, as if this explained everything. She gave an especially wrinkly scowl. 'We're going, *creaky* bones or not.'

'Hold on,' Father interjected. 'We can't just up and leave. We've jobs to do, a house to run, animals to feed. Not to mention Betty and Charlie's schooling.'

'You're right, Barney,' Granny said, pursing her lips. 'You stay here and take care of things with Betty and Charlie. Fliss can come with me. She's good at looking after people.'

'But that's not fair!' Betty and Fliss said in unison, exchanging glances.

12

'You know I like seeing new places, Granny,' said Betty, jumping in. '*I* should be the one to come with you – it'd only mean missing a day or two of school. Next week is half-term!'

Charlie folded her arms fiercely. 'I ain't going to school if Betty ain't.'

'Betty's right,' Fliss said soothingly. 'They won't miss much at school. The three of us will come with you, and that way we can all help out. We know Clarissa can be a little, um . . . demanding.'

'That's putting it politely,' Father said under his breath. 'But I'm still not happy about all four of you heading off up—'

Granny gave a crisp nod. 'Good, that's settled then. Barney, fetch my bag down from the attic. You girls, go and start packing some things. We won't make today's ferry, so we'll have to be on the first one tomorrow if we're to make it by nightfall.'

Betty put down her teacup, utterly thrilled. They were really going!

'Ooh,' said Charlie, sucking jam off the end of one of her pigtails. 'Will it be *very* cold there, Granny?'

'Extremely, so bring your warmest clothes.' She took out her pipe and began stuffing it with tobacco. 'You wanted snow, Charlie. Well, now you're going to get some – and a good dollop of it, too.'

'*Yes!*' Charlie whooped. 'SNOW!'

A whispery shiver tingled down the back of Betty's neck. 'Wilderness,' she said, imagining icicles and tasting

13

snowflakes. It was exactly the sort of name that invited you to explore . . .

'Betty,' said Granny, with a warning tone in her voice. 'You've got that look in your eyes.'

'What look, Granny?' Betty asked innocently, swatting Charlie out of the way as her little sister immediately peered into her face.

'You know what look.' Granny puffed on her pipe and watched her shrewdly. 'We're going on this trip to help Clarissa, not so you can go off gallivanting.'

'Who, *me?*' Betty grinned and placed her cup neatly in the sink before skipping across the kitchen to the stairs.

'Yes, you, Betty Widdershins,' Granny called after her. 'This is family business, not an excuse for you to sniff out an adventure!'

Betty, however, had raced upstairs and was throwing things higgledy-piggledy into her trunk. The only word of her grandmother's that remained in her head, spinning around it giddily, was 'adventure'.

Chapter Two
Dead Man's Curve

T HE JOURNEY WAS AS LONG AS IT WAS COLD. The next morning, after much squabbling, Father was finally persuaded (or rather, ordered by Granny) to remain in Pendlewick and allow Granny and the girls to leave for Wilderness. They packed as lightly as possible, though Granny had told Charlie to put in more than one pair of clean socks and a bar of soap and made Fliss take out her perfume and a book of poetry which, Fliss complained, was hardly fair seeing as Granny had insisted on bringing her lucky horseshoe.

'Always good to have a little luck when we travel,' she'd said crisply, knocking back a nip of whiskey to 'keep her warm'. 'And you girls remember, this isn't a holiday. We're going to nurse Clarissa and that's that.'

Betty, the most practical of the three sisters, had not had her packing inspected too closely. But had Granny bothered to look properly, she would have found a curious set of wooden nesting dolls tucked up tightly in Betty's clothes. These were no ordinary trinkets, and Betty had not brought them along for sentimental reasons. The dolls, unbeknown to anyone except the three sisters, were magical. By hiding a personal object inside them, the owner of that object would vanish from sight. The girls had used the dolls to get out of scrapes (and into mischief) several times, and Betty would not be parted from them. *Our pinch of magic*, she'd thought to herself as she wrapped the dolls carefully in her stockings. Whatever Granny had said, Betty knew that adventures usually popped up when you least expected them to. The best she could do was make sure she was prepared.

Following thorough goodbyes to the chickens and Oi from Charlie, the pony trap had been loaded up and they'd set off up Bread-and-Cheese Hill in the direction of the harbour. It took longer than it should have because the pony, whom Charlie had named Pumpkin, kept stopping by the roadside to chomp on the grass and refusing to budge until she was ready. Every time it happened, Betty fizzed with impatience and excitement. She just wanted to get there!

At the harbour they parted with Father, who swept them all into crushing hugs. Betty squeezed him back, smiling as his bristly chin tickled her cheek.

'I don't see why we can't take *The Travelling Bag*,' she pestered, eyeing the Widdershins' jewel-green fishing boat bobbing on the water in the distance. 'You know I can sail it.'

16

'Yes,' Father agreed. 'But a winter storm could change everything. I want you all to be safe.'

With no time to spare they boarded a waiting passenger ship and minutes later, set sail. The next three hours were spent taking turns to be on deck with a seasick Fliss as she threw up over the side. Below deck, Betty peered out from her woollen travelling cloak, her nose pressed to the window to watch as the landscape shifted and changed. Light, open meadows slipped away and in their place came unfamiliar islands and strange new landmarks. Betty took it all in greedily, determined to miss nothing.

'Are we nearly there yet?' Charlie moaned, as they eventually trudged off the ship and on to another horse-drawn carriage. 'I'm starving. Are there any more sandwiches?'

'Must you talk about food?' said Fliss, still wobbly and green in the face.

Granny poked around in her bags. 'You've already had two sandwiches, Charlie.'

'I shared one with Hoppit,' Charlie explained.

Granny rolled her eyes. 'It's astonishing how much that rat can eat.'

'Eh?' said the driver, a scrawny fellow with the spindliest fingers Betty had ever seen. He turned round in alarm. 'No rats in my carriage!'

'Oh, don't worry,' Granny said. 'It's an imaginary rat.'

'Yep. *Imaginary*,' Charlie repeated, as the driver turned to face the road again. 'He's only got three legs, too.' She

17

winked at Betty and Fliss who were watching in silence, and who both knew very well there was nothing imaginary about Charlie's rat. Thanks to the sisters' magical nesting dolls, Hoppit spent most of his time invisible and safely tucked in Charlie's pockets or snoozing in her collar. Neither Granny nor Father had a clue that the rat was real.

'Tricky journey, this one,' the driver said, friendlier now he'd been assured his carriage was rat-free. 'Don't get many people wanting to come to these parts.'

'Best keep your eyes on the road, then,' Granny replied, a warning glint in her eye. 'We'd be waiting a long time for help if there were any accidents.'

The carriage rumbled on, along with Charlie's tummy. It was late afternoon now, and the wintry grey sky was growing ever darker. Betty gazed out of the carriage window and listened to the sounds of the horses' hooves clip-clopping along the road at speed. Before leaving Pendlewick she'd unrolled one of her maps, barely managing to locate Wilderness before Granny hollered at her to hurry up. The quick glimpse had been enough for her to see that it was located at the very top of remote countryside, far away from even the nearest town and surrounded by blank, empty space, like a lost kite in a vast cloudless sky.

Betty wished they could stop to explore, or even have something to eat at one of the many quaint inns they'd passed, but Granny had been clear: they were heading straight for Clarissa's and there would be no stops. Already

Betty could imagine their carriage passing through that deserted space on the map, for there was less and less to see as the inns and landmarks rolled away into nothingness.

Soon Charlie was fast asleep in Granny's lap, occasionally muttering about sandwiches. Granny's head began nodding too, and before long she was snoring softly.

Without warning, a wooden sign loomed at the side of the road: WILDERNESS – 1 MILE.

'Nearly there,' Betty said with a shiver of excitement, more to herself than anyone else, for the only other person awake was Fliss. Betty craned her neck for a better view but the daylight was fading fast now and the window kept misting up from her breath.

Fliss squashed up closer to her and squinted out. 'Is it me,' she said through chattering teeth, 'or is it suddenly much, *much* colder?'

Betty felt the carriage dipping as it began a downward slope. Usually she would tell Fliss there was no such thing as bad weather, only the wrong clothes, but not this time. The hairs on Betty's arms were prickling and the temperature had definitely dropped. The moon was visible now, hanging like a pale orb in a clear sky. Bare branches clawed up to it like wizened fingers, and Betty could see the faint shimmer of frost on them.

The carriage continued its downward journey, slowing to a crawl. Betty's eyes fixed on the jagged branches. Now the carriage was travelling more slowly, it was easier to see them, easier to imagine them as gnarled fingers pointing. She wondered why the driver had slowed down.

'Surely we can't be there, yet?' she murmured. 'It still feels as though we're in the middle of nowhere.'

'I hope the horses aren't lame,' Fliss said, nibbling her lip nervously.

Betty hoped so, too. The last thing they needed was for the driver to turf them out on a lonely road in the bitter cold, with heavy luggage to carry. Glancing at Granny, who was still dozing, Betty lowered the window.

At once, freezing air swept around them. Granny and Charlie sat bolt upright, shuddering and blinking at the rude awakening. Betty leaned out of the window as far as she could bear to, her eyes streaming almost instantly from the cold.

'Why are we slowing down?' she called.

'Because the road's steep and the ground's icing up,' the driver shouted back. 'It's not called Dead Man's Curve for nothing!'

The words sent a thrill down Betty's spine. This was a place with history, with stories – she could almost *feel* it. The road began to twist sharply to one side, and the slope became steeper still. There was a moment of danger; the horses whinnying as their hooves skidded on ice. Betty closed the window and gripped the door handle, trying not to think of carriages sliding off roads and crashing to pieces, before the ground thankfully levelled out.

Dead Man's Curve. The words went through her head again. It was plain to see how this place might get such a name, and clearly her sister was having similar thoughts.

'Why would Clarissa choose to live somewhere like this?' Fliss muttered through gritted teeth, glancing up at the trees.

'There must be something good about it,' said Betty. This icy new landscape might be dangerous, but she couldn't help be mesmerised by its sharp edges and wild beauty. She hadn't had many chances to explore new places so she wanted to make the most of it.

'Look!' Charlie shouted suddenly. 'Oh, Betty, Fliss! Come and see!'

Betty and Fliss scrambled to the other window, squashing up to Charlie and Granny. Here, the trees lining the road had thinned away and before them lay a vision that Betty could never have expected.

'It's . . . it's like something from a fairy tale,' Fliss whispered.

All Betty could do was nod.

A wide sweep of open land lay before them. It was surrounded by high, snow-topped mountains that glowed silver in the moonlight. Lower down, dotted between copses of trees, a handful of lights glowed in tiny windows from what must have been homes, scattered like breadcrumbs in this frosty almost-wilderness. Each one appeared so isolated that Betty was reminded of will-o'-the-wisps, the little flickering lights of lost souls that could sometimes be seen over lonely marshland.

At the centre of the scattered lights a grand stone building rose up like a castle, its rooftops glittering with frost. Some way off to the left lay a huge lake, and even from a distance Betty could tell from its pale, milky surface that the water was frozen solid. Between the lake and the huge building was a wide area that looked like a deserted town square. The strange, frozen emptiness of this place took her breath away.

'Jumping jackdaws,' she whispered. Fliss was right. It really *was* like something from a fairy tale. A different kind of fairy tale to Pendlewick with its crystal-clear stream, buttery golden meadows and ice-cream parlour. While Pendlewick was a witches-in-gingerbread-cottages sort of place, Wilderness was somewhere that snow queens, wolves and ice dragons could easily be imagined.

'It's beautiful,' said Fliss, softly.

'It looks like everything's been dipped in sugar,' said Charlie, gazing at the snow-capped mountains as though they were slabs of iced cake she'd like to sink her teeth into. 'I'm *really* hungry now.'

The carriage sped up as the ground levelled out further, and suddenly they were no longer on the lonely lane. With Dead Man's Curve safely behind them, the horses trotted over the cobbled square which was sandwiched between the frozen lake and the large castle-like building. Betty wished they would slow down again to allow more time to take in the sights; everything was passing in a blur. As the carriage turned she moved to the other side to better see the grand stone building which was towering above them, windows lit. Who could possibly live *there*, she wondered? It must be someone very rich, for the only other place she had ever seen with so many windows was the prison back in Crowstone.

Now they were closer Betty saw that the cobbled area wasn't empty after all. It was full of little market stalls that were a mixture of wooden cabins and tents, some of which were empty and others covered over. A few had painted signs, though it was too dark to read them. She tried to look past them to the frozen lake on the opposite side, but too quickly the carriage had left the square and edged closer to another narrow road that twisted up into darkness.

Only a short way along it, the carriage halted.

'Here we are,' said the driver, opening the doors abruptly. 'Frostbite Lodge, Chill Hill.'

'Ooh,' said Charlie. 'Chilly Hilly. I like that name!'

'Not sure about Frostbite Lodge,' Fliss muttered, making a face at Betty as they clambered, stiff and achy, out of the carriage. 'Doesn't sound very inviting, does it?'

'Mmm,' said Betty, still bewitched by the snow-globe scene they had just seen and only half listening.

The girls' trunk and Granny's bags were heaved down from the carriage roof and placed at the side of the road.

'Careful,' said Fliss in alarm, almost losing her balance. 'The ground is rather icy.'

Betty barely heard her. She was looking about them in

confusion, for as far as she could see there was nothing but the treelined road in both directions – and they were the only people on it. 'Where's Clarissa's house?' she asked.

'Up there,' Granny said, jerking her head along the road. She turned to the driver with a stern, questioning stare and tapped her foot.

The driver looked apologetic. 'I can't get you any closer – it's too dangerous. The temperature's dropping fast and the roads are icing up.' He pointed a little way up the road to where Betty could now see a dimly lit window peeping through the trees. 'Frostbite Lodge is just over there.'

Granny muttered under her breath and slapped the money into the driver's hand. He climbed back on to the carriage, steering the horses around to turn in the opposite direction.

'Hup!' he said, and the horses began clip-clopping back down the hill with the carriage rumbling off into the dark night, leaving them alone on the road.

As Betty stared after it, a sudden sense of unease settled upon her, but she couldn't quite figure out why. It was more than the freezing air against her cheeks; more than the bare branches and lonely road. It was, she realised with a chill, something about the sound of horses' hooves thudding over the frozen ground.

'Do you hear that?' she murmured, reaching out to touch Fliss's arm. 'Those hoofbeats? There's something not right about them.'

'Maybe the horses are slipping on the ice again,' Fliss said through chattering teeth, pulling a shawl round her head. 'Oh, it's so very c-c-cold!'

'No,' said Betty. '*Listen.*' She tilted her head, her eyes fixed on the carriage which was growing smaller in the distance by the second. 'The sound doesn't match,' she breathed, realising as she said it that it was true. What she could hear was fast and urgent. A fierce gallop, not a slow trot like the horses pulling their carriage ... and this sounded like a single horse.

'It's getting louder,' Fliss said, frowning as the sound swelled around them.

Fliss was right. Betty whipped round to face the other way, half expecting to see another horse careering towards them, but all she saw was Granny rummaging in one of her bags and grumbling to herself. She couldn't work out where the sound was coming from. Up the hill, or down? It seemed to be all around them, echoing through the air, and she suddenly felt afraid.

'Granny,' said Betty urgently. 'Move off the road, quickly!'

Granny's head snapped up, her eyes widening ... but as she did so the sound vanished, leaving only silence.

'What?' Betty muttered, looking this way and that. 'Where did it go? How ... ?'

There was no one on the empty road but them. The carriage had disappeared from sight and the only movements were their own. Even the trees appeared frozen and the air, though bitter, seemed to be a held breath.

'Chop chop,' said Granny, buttoning up her bag. 'Before we freeze to death.'

'But Granny,' Betty began. 'Didn't you hear that? Those hoofbeats?'

'Of course I heard,' Granny replied. 'I'm not deaf. It was the wind carrying the sound of the horses back to us, that's all. These sorts of places play tricks with sound.' She took a deep swig of whiskey from her hipflask, hiccupped, then herded them towards the glow of the window. 'Why on earth Clarissa insists on living in this wretched place is beyond me.'

Between them, Fliss and Betty lifted the heavy trunk. Patches of ice glittered on the road and once or twice Betty felt her feet slide a little from under her. The strange galloping sound echoed in her head but she forced it away. Granny was right. It had to have been the horses moving away from them; it was the only explanation that made sense.

Wasn't it ... ?

Chapter Three
A Ghost Story

B Y THE TIME THEY HAD WALKED THE SHORT distance to the lit window they were all shivering and Charlie's teeth were beginning to chatter. A wooden sign hung above a door: *Frostbite Lodge*. In the window there was a handwritten note with a long list of people who *shouldn't* knock there. Granny raised an eyebrow at it and lifted her knuckles.

'I'm going to assume "family" isn't on that list,' she muttered, rapping smartly three times.

For a moment there was silence. Then, from somewhere inside, a shrill voice shouted, 'Can't you read? GO AWAY!'

Betty and Fliss exchanged glances. This wasn't the welcome they'd been expecting.

Granny gave an annoyed snort. 'Clarissa?' she boomed. 'Open up. It's Bunny!'

'You won't think it's funny when I get to the door!' the voice hollered back.

'It's *Bunny*!' Granny repeated. 'BUNNY!'

'Granny?' Betty said suspiciously. 'You *did* tell Clarissa we were coming, didn't you?'

'Of course I did,' said Granny. 'I wrote back to her straight away.'

'But we only received her letter yesterday,' Fliss reminded. 'And it was rather late by the time Father posted your reply . . .'

'Bunny?' a voice called from within. 'Is that really you?' The door was flung open and a woman stood blinking out at them. It had been a while since Betty had seen Clarissa but she never seemed to change a bit. She was stout and plump like Granny and shared the same bright red cheeks as the girls' father, Barney, and had unruly brown hair like Betty's. Unlike the rest of the Widdershins, whose noses were soft and slightly upturned, Clarissa's was pointed and beaky and the corners of her mouth were permanently turned down, which Father said was due to all the moaning she did. Her left leg was trussed up in bandages, and she leaned heavily on a wooden stick.

'It *is* you!' she exclaimed, her eyes widening as they swept past Granny and over the three girls. 'All of you! Well, I must say this *is* unexpected, if not overdue. Now, in you come, out of that cold, and away from that spooky old hill.'

Betty and Fliss lifted the trunk and followed Granny and Charlie as they stepped inside the lodge. A homely waft of woodsmoke curled round them like a hug, but Clarissa remained by the door peering out into the darkness.

'Where's Barney?'

'At home,' Granny replied. 'Taking care of things while we look after you.'

'Oh,' said Clarissa. An odd look flickered over her face but was gone so quickly that Betty couldn't quite work out what it was and was left wondering whether she had imagined it. Clarissa closed the door and stared at the heavy trunk as though seeing it for the first time.

'And it looks as though you're staying a while?'

'Just until you're on your feet again,' said Granny, peering around the place.

'But Granny,' said Charlie, staring at Clarissa. 'She *is* on her feet. One of them, anyway.'

'It's "Clarissa", not "she",' said Clarissa, pinching Charlie's cheek. 'My, haven't you grown? Your granny did mention that you never stop eating.'

'Granny says I've got a healthy appletite,' said Charlie, rubbing her cheek.

Clarissa didn't seem to have heard. She hobbled over to Fliss and Betty and for a moment Betty wondered if she was about to be pulled into a fierce hug like one of Granny's. Instead, Clarissa regarded them both and said, 'Penny pudding, penny pie, here I rest my beady eye,' while jabbing her walking stick at each of them in turn. It landed on Fliss. 'Kettle's through there, Felicity. Betty, you bring the biscuits.'

'Well, really!' Fliss whispered indignantly, once she and

Betty were through the kitchen door. 'I know we've come to help, but she might have let us take our coats off first.'

'Old Bossy Boots,' Betty murmured, remembering what Father had called his cousin. 'Living up to her nickname.'

Betty stared around the little kitchen they'd found themselves in. It was clean but sparse, the surfaces clear of clutter and knick-knacks. The few things on show were practical: pots and pans, the kettle on the hob and a bowl of fruit. There were no dried herbs hanging up, no lucky charms like in the kitchen at Blackbird Cottage.

Fliss filled the kettle with water and set it on the stove to boil, then arranged a teapot, cups, milk and sugar on a tray. Betty poked through the cupboards, finding three rather stale biscuits and four delicious-looking buns topped with white icing and sugar. She decided to leave the biscuits and bring the buns instead.

'Oh,' said Clarissa, disapprovingly. 'You found the sticky buns, then.'

They sipped their hot tea in a tiny sitting room which was almost as bare as the kitchen. Yet, despite the lack of ornaments, the room was cosy. The chairs had plump pillows and soft blankets, and a roaring fire crackled in the brick hearth with a basket of logs nearby. There had not been quite enough buns to go round, so Betty and Granny had a half each, as Clarissa had not offered to share hers with anyone.

'Delicious,' Fliss mumbled through a sugary mouthful.

'Sticky buns are my favourite,' Charlie agreed, sighing with pleasure. 'Hoppit's, too.'

'That's your imaginary rat, isn't it?' said Clarissa. 'Bunny's told me all about it in her letters. I do hope it'll be on its best behaviour while it's here, or I shall have to bring out my imaginary mousetrap.'

'It's "he",' said Charlie. 'Not "it".' She wiped sugar off her chin and smiled sweetly. Betty hid a grin and relaxed back into the armchair she and Fliss had squeezed into, the heat of the fire warming her through. Her fingertips and toes tingled and for a moment, while Granny and Clarissa chit-chatted about broken bones and slippery ice, she began to feel drowsy. It was the ticking of the clock that brought her back from the doze, for the rhythm of it made her think of the drumming hoofbeats she had heard on the hill in the moments before Clarissa had come to her door.

She sat up, squishing further into Fliss.

'Clarissa,' she began, 'why did you say the hill was spooky when we came in?'

Clarissa took a sip of tea and stared at the last piece of sticky bun in Fliss's hand. 'Oh, habit, really. Lots of people say it – you know what it's like living in a place with a dark history. It never gets forgotten.'

'Dark history?' Betty asked, sitting up straighter as her curiosity stirred. What had Clarissa told them before about this place? It tickled at her like a feather, just out of reach. 'What happened here?'

'You know.' Clarissa waved a hand. 'The story of Jack Frost, the highwayman.'

'That's right,' Betty said softly. 'I think it was a ghost story. I remember some of it now.'

'I don't,' Charlie said, puzzled. 'I haven't got a very good remembery.'

'Nothing wrong with your memory,' said Granny. 'You were playing up the last time Clarissa visited. Too busy trying to climb up the chimney as I recall.'

Charlie grinned. 'Was I?'

'Tell us again,' said Betty. 'Please?'

'And make it nice and scary,' Charlie added, scooching closer to the fire.

'Not *too* scary,' Granny said, giving Clarissa a warning look.

'Yes, not too scary,' Fliss agreed, snuggling closer to Betty. 'I think I remember some of it, too. Wasn't it a love story?'

At this, Betty groaned and Charlie made sick noises. Even Granny rolled her eyes. Fliss and romance went together like tea and cake.

'What?' Fliss said, offended. 'Well, *wasn't* it?'

'It was.' Clarissa topped up her cup and Granny's from the teapot. 'Bunny!' she said crossly, as Granny added a splosh of whiskey from her flask to both cups. 'You know I don't—'

'It's medicinal,' said Granny. 'It'll help dull the pain in your leg. Drink up.'

'Oh, all right, then.' Clarissa took a long swig and continued. 'This is a tale of mystery and magic, one that

32

continues to haunt Wilderness to this day.' She paused dramatically, the sharp edges of her face softened by the flickering firelight.

'It begins on a winter's night just like this one. A highway robber once prowled the roads of Wilderness after dark. They called him Jack Frost, but no one ever knew his true identity. He was king of the thieves, master of the shadows. Then one night – the coldest night of the year – he robbed the wrong person: a fortune teller with a magical, mesmerising crystal ball. It's said that the crystal ball came from a haunted lake, where a flooded town lay beneath. People all over the land had heard of its owner, Madam Divina, and her incredible predictions into the past, present and future. And because of this, people all over the land longed to own the crystal ball for themselves in the hopes of harnessing its power.

'As the highwayman snatched the crystal ball, he chuckled – but the fortune teller laughed harder.

'"Take it," she said. "For it has shown me your future – and it holds death."

'Sneering at her warning, the highwayman galloped off into the night to present this treasure to his secret love ... but he never arrived. Skidding on a patch of ice, he tumbled from his horse into the icy lake, taking the crystal with him. Waiting at her window, his love, Elora, saw his riderless horse and rushed out into the snow to search for him. That night the lake froze over. By morning, Elora too had perished in the cold. She was found the next day, as pale as the snow, surrounded by trees encased in the biggest icicles you ever saw. Today, that place is known as Elora's Tears.'

'Elora's Tears,' whispered Betty, bewitched by the ghostly tale. She could easily imagine Jack Frost's horse snorting hot breaths into cold air, a terrified face at a window. Her sisters, too, were captivated. Charlie's mouth was hanging open, and Fliss looked misty-eyed.

'Now they say the highway robber's ghost, and that of the heartbroken Elora, roam still, searching for each other on the coldest nights of the year. The magical crystal ball, however, was never seen again,' Clarissa added. She leaned closer, golden firelight flickering over her face. 'But there's a darker part to the story. For legend has it that a sighting of Elora's phantom at the window foretells death. The death of a loved one.'

Chapter Four
Echo Hall

'RIGHT, THAT'S QUITE ENOUGH OF THAT,' said Granny stiffly, putting down her cup and, for once, making no effort to refill it with whiskey. 'We don't want anyone having nightmares, do we?'

'I won't have nightmares,' Charlie said at once. She was still staring wide-eyed at Clarissa as the ghostly story hung in the air like a chill. Betty could tell from her expression that she was greedy for more. Though the tale had been short, all three sisters, including Fliss, had clung to every word of it.

'Hmm,' said Granny, clearly not believing that for a moment.

'But who *was* he?' Fliss asked earnestly. 'Jack Frost? They must have discovered his identity after he died, surely?'

'That's just it,' said Clarissa. 'They never found a body. The lake froze so deeply that night that there was no way to search it and no hope he'd be found alive. When the spring came and the lake thawed there were searches then, but no trace of him was ever found.'

Betty frowned. 'Someone apart from Elora had to have known *something*. Whoever he was, he must have had family and been reported missing. People don't just vanish without anyone noticing.'

'You could be right, Betty,' said Clarissa, wagging her finger. 'There was talk of a cover-up, but no one ever got to the bottom of it.'

A mystery, then. Betty's heart did a little hop, skip and jump. Already, Wilderness was proving very interesting indeed.

'Poor Elora, searching for her love in the cold night,' Fliss added. 'How dreadful!'

'Is it really true, about Elora's ghost?' Betty asked. 'That seeing her at the window leads to someone dying?'

'So people say,' said Clarissa darkly, and both she and Granny crossed their hands over their hearts to make the protective sign of the crow and ward off bad luck. 'Anyway,' Clarissa went on, 'I can see your granny is giving me "a look" so I shall change the subject. You've picked an excellent time to visit, what with the winter market just about to start.'

Fliss looked less mournful at once. 'A winter market? Is that why all those stalls are out in the square?'

Clarissa nodded. 'It comes every winter and has done for the past fifty years. It has every kind of wintry trinket you could imagine, all kinds of snacks—'

'Snacks!' Charlie repeated happily.

'And there's plenty to do and see,' Clarissa went on. 'It lasts for three days. People come from miles around – it's the highlight of the Wilderness calendar, apparently.'

'*Apparently?*' Betty questioned in surprise. 'You mean, you don't go to it?'

'Never.' Clarissa shuddered. 'All those people crowding round with bad breath and winter germs ... no, thank you. Still, I suppose it's all right if you're visiting,' she went on. 'And then on the final night there's the masked ball in the great chamber at Echo Hall.'

'A masked ball?' Fliss breathed. 'With costumes and everything? How utterly—'

'*Romantic!*' Betty and Charlie interrupted at once.

'Oh, shush,' said Fliss, going red. 'Granny, please can we go to that? I know we haven't brought costumes, but perhaps we could make something?'

'Don't fuss yourself,' said Clarissa. 'There's a cloakroom at the hall with costumes for hire, just for the night.'

'Ooh,' said Betty. 'What sort of costumes?'

'Anything and everything you could imagine,' Clarissa replied. 'Let's see: pirates, mermaids, goblins ... queens, kings, genies, all sorts of animals. I heard there was even someone dressed up as a giant toadstool one year! The only rule is you have to cover your face.'

'How *dreamy*,' said Fliss. 'Please say we can go, Granny?'

'I'll see,' said Granny sternly. 'I've already told you this isn't a holiday. We're here to help Clarissa, not to go off gallivanting to markets and dressing up as mushrooms.' Her voice softened a little as she took in their earnest faces. 'I suppose you can have a look round the winter market tomorrow morning, and if you all muck in and help over the next few days then *perhaps* you can go to the ball as a reward.'

'Yes!' said Betty, delighted at the prospect of exploring the winter market. She grinned at her sisters.

'I might even go to the ball myself,' Granny added with a mischievous glint in her eye. 'You never know, I could meet a tall, dark, handsome stranger.'

'*Granny!*' Fliss looked outraged. 'Behave!'

Clarissa gave a disapproving sniff.

Granny drained her cup and yawned pointedly. 'It's been a long journey, Clarissa, and this cold is playing my joints right up. Where are we all sleeping?'

Clarissa made a strange noise, something between a laugh and a hiccup. 'Oh, Bunny,' she said. 'Surely you didn't think you'd all fit in *here*? There's no room!'

Granny stared back at Clarissa wordlessly. Charlie gazed at the crackling fire longingly, her eyelids heavy now, while Fliss and Betty exchanged worried looks. They wouldn't have to return all the way home now, in the cold, would they?

'I can sleep on the rug,' said Charlie. 'It looks nice and warm.'

'You can't sleep on that old thing,' Clarissa said at once. 'You'll freeze once the fire goes out, and besides, it's very itchy.'

'I don't mind,' said Charlie, hopefully. 'I'm used to being itchy. I get nits all the time, don't I, Granny?' She gave her head a convincing scratch.

'Er, well ...' said Granny hurriedly, noting Clarissa's horrified face. 'Not for a good few months now.'

'There's room for one,' Clarissa said firmly. 'And that'll have to be in with me, as long as you don't mind a bit of snoring. The rest of you will have to take a room at Echo Hall, that's the old stone building overlooking the lake.'

'That's Echo Hall?' Betty asked, curious at once.

'I don't think so,' Granny cut in. 'It looks expensive. Is there somewhere else, a little inn, perhaps?'

'It won't cost a penny,' said Clarissa, sounding rather mysterious all of a sudden. 'If you mention you're relatives of mine they'll give you a room for nothing.'

'For *nothing*?' Granny enquired suspiciously. 'Why on earth would they do that?'

'Never you mind,' said Clarissa, waving a hand. 'Just a little agreement we once came to. You needn't carry that heavy trunk down the hill, either. One of the porters will collect it.'

'The owners must be very good friends of yours,' said Fliss, puzzled.

'Not exactly,' said Clarissa, with a thin smile.

Betty raised an eyebrow. According to what Granny always said, Clarissa didn't have many friends.

'You're in luck, too,' Clarissa went on. 'Finn Sharkey – that's the lake marshal – popped by earlier today and mentioned they still have rooms left which is highly unusual for this time of year. Normally it's booked solid for the winter market – they even bring in dozens of extra staff to help out every year, it gets so busy.'

'What if Granny stays here?' said Fliss, in her best responsible voice. 'I'll take care of Betty and Charlie over at the hall, and we can pop back tomorrow after we've looked round the market.' She winked at Betty, a silent way of acknowledging that at fourteen, Betty hardly needed looking after now.

'Hmm,' said Granny, uncertainly. 'I don't know about that, Felicity. The three of you on your own in that big old hall? Sounds like a recipe for mischief.'

'Come on, Granny,' said Fliss, flashing a disarming smile. 'I'm seventeen now, and you *know* I'm responsible.'

Granny's eyes flickered in Betty's direction. 'It's not you I'm worried about.'

'I can behave,' said Betty, her fingers crossed firmly behind her back. 'Really, Granny, I can! I promise I'll do whatever Fliss says. Besides, it'll give you and Clarissa time to catch up.' With its intriguing name, Echo Hall sounded like the kind of place she'd love to explore.

'That's right,' Clarissa added, 'I haven't told you the latest about my arthritis, Bunny. It *is* painful. And it's been such a long time since you visited last.'

Granny was looking less keen by the minute.

'I'm sure Clarissa would rather be looked after by you than

40

one of us,' Fliss persisted. 'We might do something wrong.'

'You make better tea, too,' Clarissa put in hopefully.

'And I'm sure your snores will be just as loud as Clarissa's, so it makes perfect sense,' Betty added.

'Fine,' Granny snapped. 'But don't let me regret this.'

'We won't,' the girls chorused. Betty grabbed Fliss's hand and squeezed it. Their very own room in a vast old hall, without any grown-ups telling them what to do!

And so it was settled. The three girls kissed Granny goodnight, then wrapped up warmly once more and stepped outside into the blistering cold to head down Chill Hill.

Betty could hardly wait for a better look at the large, majestic building they had seen from the carriage as they'd ridden through the square. As they approached, she found it even more thrilling a sight now that she knew she would be staying there. Stacked over three floors, it reminded Betty of castles she had read about in fairy tales. There was no moat, but rows of bushy evergreen trees stood around it like soldiers on guard. The walls were made from weathered white stone that looked strong enough to withhold any storm, and chimney stacks were dotted all over it from end to end. An enormous set of wooden doors sat at the top of several stone steps, with white stone pillars on either side. One of the doors was open a little way, evidently to allow guests in and out. Betty touched the cold iron handle, then with a deep breath of excitement, pushed the door open.

They emerged, raggle-taggle, into a large, dimly lit hallway.

Stepping inside into the warm felt like climbing into a hot bath on a cold night.

'Cor,' said Charlie, her mouth dropping open as she looked up.

The ceilings were high and vaulted, with ornate swirls and patterns carved into them. Huge mirrors and paintings had been bolted to the walls and, as they headed towards a faint hum of voices, their footsteps echoed on the marbled floor beneath them. Most remarkable, however, was the domed glass ceiling above their heads which showed the inky night sky.

They went through another set of doors and found themselves in a wide-open room with a flagstone floor and panelled walls. At the far end, a cosy fire crackled behind a large oak desk. A couple of people were already waiting at the desk: a smart man with a peculiar curling ginger moustache, and a striking-looking woman with long, glossy black hair and a dress of deep purple velvet. Both had luggage cases with them and stared with interest at the three new arrivals. Unusually for her, Betty felt her cheeks flushing. She wasn't nervous, exactly, but she'd never been to a place such as this before. The Widdershins were used to shabby, homely pubs and cottages, not grand sweeping halls, and Betty guessed that three young girls in tatty travelling cloaks with no possessions must look rather strange.

The black-haired woman gave a dramatic sigh and draped herself on a nearby chair. It wasn't hot, but she fanned herself with a gloved hand. Betty couldn't help staring at her. She had ivory pale skin and startling eyes that were rimmed in black, with gold glittery powder on her eyelids. Her lips were pale pink, and had a slight smirk about them. The man remained standing. His face was red – not ruddy and cheerful like Father's – but an angry red like a pimple ready to burst. He reached over to give a bell on the counter an impatient *ding!* and when this yielded no results, he thudded his fist on the wooden surface so hard that a vase of flowers moved across the counter.

Within seconds an ashen-faced woman appeared. She was tall and sturdy, and had dark eyes and fair, coppery hair with a few wisps of grey at her temples. The lines in her forehead seemed to be etched there like a well-worn apology and she had the fed-up look of someone who had worked too hard for too long. Though she was younger, she reminded Betty a little of Granny when they had lived and worked at the Poacher's Pocket inn. A small brass badge pinned to her lapel read: *Mrs Chambers*. In her hand she held a single woolly mitten, which she hurriedly pushed into a large wicker basket marked LOST PROPERTY, before stepping up to the desk.

'How can I help you, sir?' she asked, brushing a strand of hair out of her eyes.

'You could have helped by answering this blasted bell a bit sooner,' snapped the moustached man, giving the bell another heavy-handed *DING!* for good measure. 'Three times I've rung it now.'

'I do apologise,' said Mrs Chambers. 'We're extremely busy, what with the market—'

'Yes, yes, I know,' the man cut in rudely. 'Just show us to our rooms. The reservations are for Mr Rupert Sneed and Lady Fortuna.' He drummed his fingers on the counter until the flustered woman handed him two keys from an array of hooks on the wall behind her. At the same moment a heavyset porter appeared by the desk and, directed by Mrs Chambers, went to pick up the luggage.

'Not that one,' Mr Sneed said abruptly, waving the porter away from a large black case. He reached for it himself, muttering, 'That's Lady Fortuna's *personal* case.' He lifted it importantly, following the porter towards a large, curving staircase. As he turned, Betty saw a flash of silver. A round, moonlike orb and several stars had been painted in gleaming silver on the side of the case. The velvet-dressed woman – Lady Fortuna – got up from the chair and moved silently after the man, her gown rippling softly. A waft of rich scent drifted after her.

Charlie sneezed and rubbed her nose, while Fliss stared longingly at the dress until the elegant woman was out of sight.

'Wonder what was in the case?' Betty murmured, thinking of the silver globe and stars. It had looked very mysterious, and the name Lady Fortuna had aroused her curiosity even more.

'Did you see her dress?' Fliss whispered. 'What I wouldn't give for a dress like that.'

'Why?' asked Charlie. 'Dresses are stupid. You can't run or jump, they just get in the way. And they have silly itchy lacy bits—'

'What can I do for you girls?'

'Oh,' said Fliss, instantly blushing as they turned to face the woman at the desk. 'Well, we need a place to stay, and our father's cousin, Clarissa Widdershins, who lives in Wilderness, told us to ask here.'

Mrs Chambers' gaze swept over them, curious but kind. She took a black book from a drawer in the desk and checked something before raising her eyebrows and nodding. 'And do you have any luggage?'

Betty left Fliss to explain about the trunk at Clarissa's and followed Charlie, who had begun to wander away from the desk to investigate a couple of rooms nearby. One held a roaring fire and sparkling decanters that could have been glass or crystal. This was where the hum of voices came from, and a cloud of pipe smoke hung hazily in the air around a cluster of people.

To the left of Mrs Chambers' desk an open door led to a dining room with neatly laid tables and dazzling silverware. A table ran along the back wall, laden with baskets of bread, fruit and cheeses. Gravy spilled over the sides of a large black pot, its contents steaming and delicious-smelling. Beside it was a glass dome covering the fattest sponge cake Betty had ever seen, and next to that was a golden treacle tart. Betty's tummy rumbled with hunger and Charlie's growled back as though in reply. They hadn't eaten anything since Clarissa's iced buns, but just as Betty wondered if they were allowed to go in, Fliss caught them up.

'We're in room six,' she said breathlessly, a silver key dangling from her fingers. 'Our trunk will be collected and brought up to us, and we're to help ourselves to whatever we like from the dining room . . .'

'Yes!' said Charlie, charging towards the doors.

'. . . *after* we've washed and made ourselves presentable,' Fliss finished, grabbing Charlie's coattails and pulling her back. 'Come on, let's see what our room's like!'

Charlie's lip stuck out obstinately, but by the time they'd reached the stairs she had perked up. Like her sisters, she was too excited to sulk when there was an opportunity to explore.

The staircase rose up to a small landing, where a clock was set in a panelled wall. Here, the stairs forked into two and went in opposite directions and it was now, as they followed the arrow to rooms numbered one to twenty, that Charlie's mood changed once more. She stared, open-mouthed with horror, at the walls where rows of antlers – some with stags' heads and some without – were displayed. Immediately her eyes filled with tears.

'Oh, Charlie!' Fliss swooped to comfort her. 'There, there. I know it's sad but try not to look at them.'

'H-how can I not look?' Charlie wailed, her voice sounding alarmingly loud in the empty corridor. It was fascinating,

Betty thought, how Charlie's voice rang with a slight echo. *It must be the high ceilings and panelled walls*, she pondered. *No wonder it's called Echo Hall.*

'They're looking straight at me,' Charlie went on, sniffling. 'Like they want me to help them!'

Betty took her little sister's hand and squeezed it. Charlie was right. The poor creatures' brown eyes – which were rather like Fliss's, now she thought about it – seemed to be gazing at them.

'They've probably been here a very long time,' Fliss added, patting Charlie on the back.

'Doesn't make it right!' Charlie growled, and Betty and Fliss had to agree. It was a relief when the corridor ended and turned into another, and this one was far less gloomy. In fact, it was rather magical. Above them a row of glittering chandeliers hung all the way along the ceiling. As the girls moved below them, the light bounced off the glass prisms and dazzled their eyes.

'Do you think they're real crystals?' Fliss breathed.

'Probably,' Betty replied. Echo Hall didn't seem the kind of place where valuable-looking things wouldn't be real. Even though the hall was old, it had lost none of its splendour. She felt a surge of excitement and awe building up inside her. *Real* crystals! 'They must be worth a fortune.'

'Here we are,' said Fliss. 'This one is number seven, so we must be in – oh!'

Ahead of them a door was flung open and a figure came

hurrying out of the room Fliss had pointed to. It was a young girl, probably around the same age as Fliss. She wore a smart black pinafore dress with a white apron, black stockings and plain but sturdy shoes. A curl of long, golden hair had come loose from under a white cap. As she hurried away, she tried to poke her hair back into the cap with one pale hand. In the other, she carried a black coal scuttle with a dustpan and brush balanced on top. She moved quickly, in the way of someone used to always rushing and never having enough time.

Hearing the footsteps of the three sisters behind her, the girl glanced over her shoulder. Betty was ready with a friendly smile, but it froze on her lips when she realised the look on the girl's face was far from kind. Her eyes were narrowed and her mouth was drawn into a tight line, as though she were holding back some unpleasant word or thought. Just as quickly she turned her head and continued down the corridor away from them.

'Who was that?' Charlie asked between sniffles.

'One of the maids,' Fliss answered as they stared after the girl. 'She must have been helping get the room ready for us. Wonder why she didn't shut the door after her?'

Betty shrugged, eager to see inside the room. 'Maybe they leave the doors open in guest houses,' she said. 'Before the guests arrive in them, anyway.'

A brass number six hung on the door. Fliss pushed it wide open.

'She's left us a nice warm fire,' said Charlie, as they entered the room. 'Oooh, and snacks!'

A cosy fire glowed in the grate behind a guard, and the coal scuttle was nicely topped up. There were two iron-framed beds, one large and one smaller. Curiously, they hadn't been made up, but a pile of crisp white sheets and blankets had been placed at the foot of them, as though by someone in a hurry.

'Odd that she didn't make the beds,' said Fliss, frowning. She peered at the little washbasin and stand. 'No clean towels, either. Dear me!'

'Perhaps we were supposed to bring our own?' Betty suggested. 'Or maybe they were in a hurry and forgot. We did turn up rather unexpectedly.'

The walls were white and chalky, and another chandelier hung from the smooth ceiling above. A large wardrobe stood in one corner and under a criss-crossed leaded window was a set of drawers. On top of it was a basket containing some shortbread wrapped in paper, which Charlie was helping herself to, as well as a jug of water, a tray of glasses and a vase of fresh flowers. A large iron key had been left next to it. Betty picked it up and was surprised to notice that despite the cosiness of the room, the key was icy cold.

'Oh,' said Betty. 'That girl – the maid – she must have left her key here. I'd better give it back in case she gets into trouble for losing it.' She darted out of the door, leaving Fliss gazing out of the window and Charlie munching shortbread.

49

By the time Betty stepped out into the hall the girl was almost at the other end of the corridor. She'd moved quickly, and Betty suspected that if it hadn't been for the weight of the coal scuttle she'd have been long gone.

'Hey!' she called, then remembering her manners, 'Excuse me? You forgot your key.'

The girl halted for the briefest of moments. Betty waited for her to turn round, but instead she carried on walking and turned to her right, vanishing into what must be another corridor beside an old brass lamp.

'Bother,' Betty grumbled. Manners forgotten, she shouted, 'Oi!' and began to run down the hall to where she'd last seen the girl. But when she arrived out of breath at that very spot, her already-pounding heart began to thump even harder. For where the girl had disappeared there was no other corridor, or even a door. There was only a wall, with a thin hairline crack running from top to bottom. The girl had vanished entirely.

Chapter Five
The Wrong Key

BETTY STARED AT THE WALL, UTTERLY confused. Had she been mistaken? She was sure the girl had walked past the old lamp, but now she doubted herself. Perhaps, she thought, the maid had been further along. She walked on a little more, and sure enough another corridor appeared, although there were no lamps near it.

I must be tired after the journey, she told herself. *That's all.* She returned to the room where Charlie was now bouncing on the beds excitedly and Fliss had discovered a full-length mirror inside the wardrobe door and was preening in front of it.

'I couldn't find her,' Betty said, placing the key down on top of the drawers. She moved closer to the fire and lifted her hands to the heat. The coldness of the iron key had seeped into her fingers and now they felt stiff.

'Never mind,' said Fliss, closing the wardrobe. 'We can

hand it in when we go down for dinner. Look! The view up here is lovely – you can see for miles.' She urged Betty to come to the window, and the two of them peered out.

'It's too dark,' Betty complained. 'I can barely see a thing.' But as she cupped her hands to the chilled glass and allowed her eyes to adjust, things began to appear before her. There were market stalls below, set neatly in rows and covered over for the night in the cobbled square. Then there was the road leading up to Clarissa's – Chill Hill, and on the opposite side, Dead Man's Curve leading off into darkness.

And there, beyond the market, was the vast frozen lake. Its surface was misty with ice, and in the centre it glowed a pale grey-blue from the moon shining above it. Betty had never found anything so cold-looking to appear so inviting before, but something about the lake made her even more desperate to explore.

'It feels like we're really high up,' said Fliss. 'Maybe it's because we live in such a little cottage now. I've got an idea! Let's tie something to the window so we can see which one our room is when we're outside tomorrow. Otherwise we'll never be able to tell.'

'Good idea,' Betty agreed. 'What can we use?'

'What about my hair ribbon?' Fliss pulled a scrap of thin red fabric from her hair. 'It's nice and bright.' She opened the window and tied the ribbon to the catch on the outside. 'There!'

'Look at me!' Charlie called breathlessly, leaping from one

bed to the next. 'Come on, Betty. The beds are boats and the floor is a frozen lake. You can't fall in or you'll freeze to death! *Boing!*' She jumped to the smaller bed, her bird's nest hair wild around her head. 'You're on thin ice, you're on it, *quick!*'

Betty and Fliss exchanged a look that their little sister didn't see, but they dutifully sat down on the beds and lifted their feet up so no part of them was touching the floor.

'Broken ice, broken ice,' chanted Charlie. 'Falling through it isn't nice!'

A lump came to Betty's throat, and she saw that Fliss's eyes were damp all of a sudden. Charlie was too young to remember their mother, Grace Widdershins, but Betty and Fliss did. She had died after going off in search of a doctor for a sick Granny and Father. A fog had lain over Crowstone that night. A fog so thick that the girls' mother had failed to see that she had lost her way on the path and wandered on to a frozen pond over near Skinny Woods. Unable to find her way back, she'd ended up in the middle of it where the ice was thinnest. She'd slipped, hit her head, and drowned as the ice cracked around her.

Charlie, who'd still been just a baby when it happened, didn't really think of her much and even though she knew how their mother had died it was just a story to her. A story about someone she'd never know, and in her childish excitement, she'd forgotten.

'Oh, Charlie,' Fliss said briskly, wiping her nose on her sleeve in a very un-Fliss-like manner. 'Look what you've done to these bedsheets, they're all rumpled! Come on, enough of that now. Let's go down for something to eat – perhaps by the time we get back our trunk will have been collected.'

At the mention of food Charlie stopped bouncing and jumped on to the floor with an enormous bump. Betty swallowed the lump in her throat away as Fliss straightened out the piles of bedclothes and instructed them all to rinse their hands and faces in the little washbasin in the corner of the room. Once they were presentable and Fliss had tamed Charlie's wild hair the best she could, they collected the key Fliss had been given and exited the room.

'Oh,' said Fliss, as she turned the key. 'That's odd – the door won't lock. It's like it's stuck.' She fiddled with the key, removed it and tried again, shaking her head.

'Wait a minute,' said Betty, as a thought occurred to her. She went past Fliss and back into the room, grabbing the key that the maid had left. 'Try this one. Maybe that girl left the key for us on purpose.'

'Then why would they give us this one?' Fliss asked, waving the silver key.

'I don't know,' said Betty. She inserted the dark iron key into the door and twisted it. Instantly there was a click and the door locked. 'But look, I'm right.' She laughed at Fliss's perplexed face, then shrugged. 'Perhaps the woman on the desk realised she'd given us the wrong key and sent the girl up with the right one.'

'I suppose so,' Fliss conceded. They headed back down the

corridor and towards the impressive staircase, being careful this time to distract Charlie from the upsetting stags' heads.

'This is the best staircase I've ever seen,' said Betty, tapping the twisting wooden banister. 'Imagine how fast you'd whoosh along if you slid down it!'

As they approached the desk, they saw the tired-looking woman, Mrs Chambers, once again talking to the ginger-moustached man. An impatient queue of people were lined up with suitcases behind him, and Betty tried not to gawp as she realised that some of them were speaking with unfamiliar accents. A few even spoke a different language. It seemed that people were flocking from all over to visit the winter market.

'I'm telling you there are loud bumps and bangs coming from above,' Mr Sneed said rudely. 'Terrible racket – I demand that you move whoever is in that room at once, or give them a good talking to.'

'But sir,' Mrs Chambers said patiently. 'As I've already explained, the room above you is empty.'

'Madam, it *isn't*. I quite clearly heard noises . . .'

Unexpectedly, Betty caught sight of a movement. A shadowy outline of a person was visible through the frosted glass panel in a door behind Mrs Chambers. For a moment it stilled as they appeared to listen, then it shifted and moved away.

Betty gave the woman on the desk a sympathetic look as they passed her and went into the dining room. What this place needed, she thought, was someone like Granny. When they had lived at the Poacher's Pocket pub back in Crowstone, Bunny Widdershins had been the toughest landlady the place had ever known. Anyone who got on the wrong side of her got marched out by their collar. She had even thrown horseshoes at customers a few times, too.

But one thing Echo Hall *did* have that the Poacher's Pocket didn't was a decent cook. This much was obvious from the delicious smells wafting about and the speed at which the serving staff were refilling the rapidly emptying bread baskets, trays full of tarts and jugs of custard and gravy.

'Ooh,' said Charlie, her eyes the size of wagon wheels. 'I want to try everything!'

While Fliss took a tray and began ladling thick onion stew into bowls, and Charlie raided the bread baskets, Betty looked around the room. It was rowdy and crowded, full of voices and the sound of cutlery scraping china. Most of the tables were full already. Like the Widdershins, many guests appeared to be newly arrived for the winter market and still in their travelling clothes. Even from a distance, however, it was plain to see that they were different from the folk Betty and her sisters were used to. Their clothes were new and smart, not the patched-up hand-me-downs that the Widdershins went through, and they were using the elegant silver tongs to pick up the pastries and bread – unlike Charlie, who was using her fingers and licking them in between.

Betty spied a small table against the far wall that was

unoccupied. As she headed for it, she noticed the glamorous woman, Lady Fortuna, whom they had seen earlier with Mr Sneed. She was sitting alone and sipping from a gold-rimmed teacup. She had changed out of the purple velvet dress into a black one which was covered in tiny silver stars. A steaming teapot sat on the table before her, beside an enormous scone heaped with thick cream and jam. She hadn't taken a single bite, but instead was staring at it very hard with intense, glittering eyes that were almost as dark as her dress. Once or twice her lips moved behind the teacup, as though she were muttering a silent spell to herself. Betty couldn't help being fascinated, for there was definitely something a little spooky about her.

Evidently, Charlie agreed, for when she and Fliss joined Betty at the table, carrying plates that were piled ridiculously high, she glanced back at Lady Fortuna with narrowed eyes.

'There's something funny about her.'

Betty dunked a chunk of warm, soft bread into her stew then sank her teeth into it ravenously. 'She does stand out a bit.'

'Who?' asked Fliss, brushing crumbs from the tabletop. Her eyes fixed admiringly on the glamorous guest. 'Oh, yes. She is rather eye-catching in that dress, isn't she?'

Betty wasn't one for frocks, not like Fliss, but she had to agree it was pretty. It seemed many of the other guests did, too, for lots of curious glances were thrown her way. However, there were just as many admiring looks being directed at

Fliss, whose lovely face attracted attention everywhere she went. Even, thought Betty with a rush of pride, dressed as she was: smartly but simply in a plain brown frock.

Betty glanced around the room. There were lots of other people who had come to dine, and though they weren't quite as striking as Lady Fortuna, many were still interesting: a round, bald-headed man with pink nose and cheeks carefully examined the scones and treats; a woman with fair hair so pale it was almost white was pecking at a bun the way a duck might peck at bread. Another man did not seem to want to sit, but instead was pacing up and down, eyeing the food, the staff and the tables. He was grey and twisty like a gnarled old tree, with a spiky white beard and eyebrows. He drew such nervous glances from the servants, who fumbled and quickened their pace around him, that Betty wondered if he was the owner of Echo Hall. After muttering something to one of the serving staff, the man hobbled out on his walking stick with a crotchety look on his face.

And then a fair, freckly boy with coppery hair entered the dining room and made straight for the food. He was alone, which Betty thought was odd considering he was only about her age. Was he a guest, she wondered? Before the boy could reach the table, Mrs Chambers stepped in front of him. She could tell by the woman's expression that the boy was being scolded, and from the boy's sullen face it was clearly something he'd heard before. He turned and skulked out.

'Oh, look,' said Fliss, interrupting her thoughts. She was

pointing to the wall above where Betty sat. 'Next to you Betty – it's something about the highway robber! What does it say?'

Betty twisted round in her seat. Above her was a framed cut-out from a newspaper. It showed a pen and ink drawing of a highwayman galloping on a huge black horse. His figure was in silhouette, and he wore a tricorn hat and a cloak which streaked behind him, leaving a trail of snowflakes. 'JACK FROST,' she read from the headline. 'JUST WHO WAS THE NOTORIOUS HIGHWAYMAN OF WILDERNESS?'

The story outlined what Betty and her sisters had already heard from Clarissa: the doomed love affair between the robber and Elora, the theft of the magical crystal ball and the death of the pair on the coldest night of the year. But then it got even more interesting.

'The robber's identity remains a mystery,' Betty read. 'Will the truth ever be known? Nearly four decades have passed since Wilderness was plagued by a notorious highwayman known only as Jack Frost, but despite clues and several theories, all attempts to unmask the notorious robber have failed. Only one suspect was ever identified in what was to become Wilderness's most enduring tale. Duggan Trent, a stableboy at Echo Hall, was known to have been in love with Elora Goode, who worked there as a servant.

'It was from a first-floor window of the hall that Elora was believed to have seen the highwayman fall from his horse into the freezing lake.*

59

Betty paused, her heart galloping with excitement at this revelation. 'It happened *here*,' she exclaimed. 'Right here at Echo Hall!'

'Keep reading,' said Fliss, gazing at the silhouette of the highwayman. There was a hazy look in her eyes which Betty suspected was her lovesick face, but it could have been a touch of indigestion.

To this day no more is known about the doomed pair, nor the whereabouts of the missing crystal ball. Did Jack Frost take it with him to his watery grave? The only answers to the mystery lie in the depths of Shivershock Lake – which shows no sign of letting go of its secrets.'

Betty finished reading, enthralled. A real-life highwayman just like the ones she read about in books! And though it had all happened nearly forty years ago, it wasn't exactly ancient. 'Granny would have been alive then,' she said, thinking out loud. 'She would have been young, but it's exciting to think that it wasn't *that* long ago . . . not really.'

'They'd probably still be alive today,' Fliss said softly, her brown eyes roaming over the frames next to her side of the table.

'What's that one?' Betty asked, nodding to something handwritten in a scrawl.

'It's a letter from a servant of the hall,' said Fliss, peering at it. 'Handing in their notice. Oh,' she added, reading the first few lines. 'Listen to this – the servant left their job because of the haunting! It says there were sightings of Elora's ghost on the stairs, and up on the first floor . . .' She trailed off, her face paling a little.

'Excellent,' said Betty, feeling another thrill. 'An unsolved mystery – and a ghost story, too – all in this very place! We might even see something ourselves . . . or hear a bump in the night . . .'

'That'd probably just be me falling out of bed,' said Charlie cheerfully, cramming another spoonful of apple tart in her mouth.

'Oh, Betty, I don't think I want to stay somewhere that's haunted,' said Fliss, looking anxious now. 'Don't forget what Clarissa said.' She lowered her voice. 'You know, about seeing Elora's ghost and the . . . the death of a loved one.'

'I'm sure she was just exaggerating,' Betty suggested, suddenly worried that Fliss might want to leave. Without her there, Granny definitely wouldn't let Betty and Charlie stay. 'You know how Father gets carried away when he's telling a story. Anyway,' she added, determined to win Fliss over, 'what if we were the ones to unmask the highwayman after all these years? I bet you'd love to know who he was!'

'Well, maybe,' Fliss conceded. 'As long as we don't come face to face with any ghosts.'

'Perhaps we should do some sniffing around,' Betty said. 'Ask some questions and find out if there really is any truth in it, or if it's just silly gossip.'

'Hmm,' said Fliss unenthusiastically. 'Well, you can sniff on your own.' She eyed a grainy photograph just behind her shoulder. It showed three people on the steps of Echo Hall. Betty couldn't see it clearly from where she sat, but from the way Fliss shuddered she suddenly had an idea of who it might be.

'Is that her?' she asked. 'Elora?'

Fliss nodded and pushed her plate away, too creeped out to eat. 'And her parents. None of them look very happy.'

Betty was about to get up to take a closer look when a bloodcurdling scream locked her in place. A clatter of crockery followed, and as Betty whipped round she knew immediately who it had come from. Lady Fortuna had reared back from her table, one hand clasped to her chest. A water jug had been knocked over, soaking the white tablecloth, and the beautiful scone was now a crumbly splat of jam and cream on the floor. The entire room went still and silent, and for a moment everything seemed frozen like a picture. Then chairs scraped back and people began to move.

'She's choking,' Fliss whispered.

'She's been poisoned,' Betty gasped.

But Lady Fortuna wasn't choking, and she hadn't been poisoned either. She was staring with horror into her teacup, her pink lips parted in a perfect circle, the eyes of everyone in the entire room upon her.

'She must have found something yucky in her tea,' Charlie said rather gleefully. 'Maybe a fly, or a bug ...'

'Or mouse droppings,' said Fliss, looking queasy. 'Granny

once found a rat's tail baked into a loaf of bread, and that was after we'd eaten most of it. Urgh!'

'Nothing wrong with rats,' Charlie said indignantly, reaching up to her collar to pet an invisible Hoppit. 'Don't listen to her,' she whispered.

Betty, however, watched in silence. She was starting to get an idea of what the mysterious woman might be looking at. A moment later she was proved right as Mr Sneed appeared and rushed to her side.

'The tea leaves,' Lady Fortuna moaned in a feeble voice which, thanks to the silence in the room, everyone could hear. 'Oh, it's the tea leaves – something dreadful is going to happen. It's a warning!'

'Eh?' said Charlie, puzzled. 'What's she on about?'

'It's a way of telling fortunes,' Betty explained. 'Granny used to do it sometimes. After you've finished drinking your tea you look at the shapes of the tea leaves left in the cup and they're supposed to predict your fortune.' Fortune ... Lady Fortuna. Now the strange name made sense. 'She must be a fortune teller!'

'What do you see, Lady Fortuna?' asked Mr Sneed.

'Scales,' the lady answered, her voice gaining a little more strength now. 'A wrong is about to be put right ... but there, you see?' She pointed into the teacup. 'A crow! An omen of death!'

A flurry of whispers swept around the room. Some guests looked anxious while others appeared thrilled. Betty felt a mixture of both, along with a healthy dash of disbelief. *Death? Could that – or anything else – really be predicted by the shapes in tea leaves?* It was true that she was far more open to magical possibilities than she used to be – she had experienced more than enough magic to be a firm believer in it – but she also knew that putting too much trust in superstitions wasn't always a good thing.

'A crow?' Fliss said, giving Betty a meaningful, but worried, look. The girls had grown up with plenty of superstitions and links to crows, magpies and ravens – all symbols of bad luck that seemed to have a way of following them wherever they went. Now it seemed Wilderness was no exception.

Just then, Betty spotted a movement at the back of the room and realised someone was moving through it, unseen. It was the coppery-haired lad she had seen being turned away earlier. With everyone's attention on the commotion, the boy slipped through to the food tables virtually unnoticed and began filling his pockets with bread rolls, cold meats and other goodies. Then, just as stealthily as he had arrived, he left. Again Betty briefly wondered who he was, but she turned her attention back to Lady Fortuna. She was being led away from the dining room unsteadily by Mr Sneed, who was telling her in a soothing voice that she needed to lie down and rest.

With the spectacle over, the rest of the guests resumed their eating, but the air of excitement remained. Unable to contain her curiosity, Betty got up under the pretence of getting another jug of custard, passing by the table Lady Fortuna had vacated. Stepping round the scone on the floor she peered into the teacup in search of the worrying symbols the lady had described. Disappointingly she wasn't able to make out anything like a pair of scales, although there was a blurry shape that might have resembled a bird. Too quickly the serving staff hurried over and snatched the teacup away, clearing the table and sweeping the floor.

'Good thing Granny didn't see that,' Betty said with a yawn as they climbed the stairs to their room a short while later. 'She'd have been clutching her horseshoe all night.'

'Hmm,' said Fliss, eyeing the stags' heads on the walls around them. 'I might do the same if I had a horse-shoe with me.'

'Oh, look,' said Charlie, pointing. 'That's our trunk, isn't it?'

Sure enough, the Widdershins' shabby old wooden trunk had been left in the corridor a few doors along.

'Wonder why they didn't bring it all the way to the door?' Betty panted as they heaved it the short distance to room number six. Once inside, they unlocked the trunk and got ready for bed.

'Come on, Fliss,' Betty said sleepily from under the blankets, watching as her sister fussed around unpacking things and folding them neatly into the set of drawers. 'Let's unpack tomorrow. Come to bed. Tomorrow's market day.' She thought of all the people who had travelled to Wilderness especially for it, and hugged herself under the covers.

'Market day!' Charlie repeated, burrowing down next to Betty. Seconds later she was snoring softly.

'I will in a minute,' said Fliss, absentmindedly chewing her thumbnail as she pushed the drawers closed.

'Are you all right?' Betty asked, recognising the signs of anxiety in her older sister. 'Has what happened with Lady Fortuna scared you?'

Fliss smiled in spite of herself. 'Yes, a little,' she admitted. 'The stories about the haunting had already spooked me, even before Lady Fortuna's talk of crows and death!'

'It's probably all nonsense,' said Betty. 'I couldn't see much when I looked in that teacup. I bet she'll be reading fortunes tomorrow at the winter market, you wait and see. After all those people saw her in the dining room, well – let's just say, she'll have a very long queue.'

'Mmm,' Fliss conceded, brightening up suddenly. 'I wonder how much it costs to have your fortune told?'

'Too much,' said Betty with a snort. 'I hope you're not thinking of it. You know Granny will get the hump if you do.'

'Granny doesn't have to know,' said Fliss, looking uncharacteristically defiant. 'I'd like to find out what my future holds.'

'You mean whether you'll be kissing anyone in Wilderness?' Betty teased. 'Well, I wouldn't. Where's the fun in that? I like every day to be a surprise, and to never know what adventures might be around the corner.'

A peaceful lull settled over the room, interrupted only by Charlie's soft snores and the occasional creaks and footsteps of more guests passing by the room as they arrived late into the night. Betty listened for a while, then drifted into sleep with thoughts of the ghostly tale of Elora and the highwayman – and the mysterious crystal ball – swirling in her head.

Chapter Six
The Highway Robber and the Fortune Teller

Part One: Elora

I T WAS THE HARSHEST OF WINTERS, BUT WILDERNESS was used to that. Its trees were accustomed to snow on their branches, dressing them like thick white coats. The buildings had come to expect the weight of the icicles which dangled, gleaming, from their rooftops like heavy crystals on chandeliers. The lake had iced over, as always spending more time solid than it did liquid. Yet this was the winter that would change everything and give Wilderness the story that would stay with it for ever, as though frozen in time.

It began with a winter market, a fortune teller and a girl with a secret . . .

*

Elora had lived in Wilderness all her life. She had no brothers or sisters, just a quiet, hardworking mother and a surly father who had little time for either of them. Together they worked in Wilderness's Echo Hall: Elora's father as a stablehand and her mother a cook in the vast and busy kitchen.

From a young age, Elora had been expected to help too, chopping vegetables with her mother or helping her father with the horses. In return the family were provided with regular meals and servants' rooms at the hall, along with a wage. When Elora wasn't helping she had the run of the place with the other servants' children. They were left to do as they liked as long as they stayed out of trouble and away from the paying guests. For most of her childhood this suited Elora well enough. After all, she didn't know any different.

Days were spent playing chase in the large corridors and hide and seek in the empty rooms of the hall; quietly listening to the cooks gossiping and telling ghost stories which were then retold and exaggerated; scrounging the odd carrot or apple from the kitchen to give to a favourite horse. Nights were spent listening to her parents argue. As the years went on, her chores increased and so did her parents' discontent with each other. And Elora found herself beginning to wish for a way out of Wilderness.

Winters came and passed, each one colder than the last. And with winter came the market. Every year, bigger and better than before. For three whole days, Wilderness was filled with noise and bustle and people who came from far and wide. Echo Hall was swept out and decorated with ivy and berries, and every available room was booked. Three glorious days in which the cold didn't seem quite so noticeable, and when the normally grey and white landscape was suddenly full of colour. Afterwards, when the market had packed up and gone, Wilderness seemed even bleaker than before, to Elora, at least.

In the spring of Elora's fifteenth year something happened that would change her life. Something dangerous, and unexpected and thrilling. A highway robber on horseback began to lie in wait on the lonely roads in and out of Wilderness to ambush the carriages of the rich. The attacks came swiftly and without warning, sometimes with weeks or months in between and at other times two nights in a row. Each time it happened it was on a night when there was enormous wealth in Wilderness; nights when there were weddings or balls in the great chamber of Echo Hall.

Fear spread throughout the hall. Everywhere Elora went it was all people spoke of, from the kitchen cooks to the stablehands to the guests having breakfast in their rooms. Elora listened at doors, gathering snippets of information like firewood.

'He only targets the rich,' one of the servants said in a hushed voice one morning. 'But how does he know when they're here?'

Elora held her breath and peered through a tiny gap in the door. Two women were at work in one of the guest rooms, one sweeping out the fireplace and the other stripping the bedclothes. Their voices were full of excitement at having something new to gossip about.

'Some say he works at the hall,' the other servant replied. 'Or knows someone who does. How else would he find out about the rich guests?'

By the end of the summer, wardens were sent out to patrol the lonely roads and the ambushes stopped abruptly. Some said the robber had been captured and was being held in secret, or that he had been chased to his death. Others suggested he was simply being clever and had moved on to another place to avoid being caught.

Within the hall, Elora heard all of this. She found herself secretly thrilled by it and hoping he *hadn't* been caught. If nothing else, the stories were a bit of excitement that livened up her dull, servant life – but she didn't dare tell anyone. When other servants asked for her thoughts on the matter she simply shrugged and replied, 'What would I know?'

There was only one person she told the things she heard to: her best friend, Robin. Quiet, dark-eyed and quick-witted, Robin was two years older than Elora – and someone she couldn't imagine, or remember, life without. They had grown up together but, unlike Elora, Robin had no one. No parents or other family to speak of, only Elora, who wasn't close to her own family. Elora had no real love for her father, who treated her like she was a stray cat to be fed and shooed away, and while she cared for her mother, she found her weak when it came to standing up to Elora's father. The bond between Elora and Robin grew, forging into something deeper and stronger. Both dreamed of escaping Wilderness, and before long their dreams became talk. Talk became a plan. And the plan became a secret.

'We'll go when you're sixteen,' Robin said one day, when summer had long passed and autumn had come. 'Run away, far away to new lives where no one knows us and no one will come looking. And even if we're found, well . . . you'll be sixteen and no one can force you to come back.'

The two of them were by the stables alone, speaking in low voices. Elora stood in the doorway of a stable while Robin brushed the coat of a grey mare until it gleamed. Specks of dust and horsehair floated around their heads in the shaft of pale light streaming in through the door. Outside the sun was setting and a few red-brown leaves drifted into the stable on a light, cold breeze. Elora shivered and pulled her shawl more tightly around herself.

'But how . . . how would we afford it?' she asked. 'We earn so little here.'

A strange look crossed Robin's face, one Elora couldn't quite read. 'We'll manage. I've got it all worked out.'

Elora wasn't able to believe it. Without enough money they'd be forced to return and beg for their jobs back, and she didn't see Master Greave, the hall's owner, taking kindly to that – not to mention her parents.

'You really think we can?' she asked miserably.

'I know we can.' Robin patted the horse on the rump, then hung the brush up on a hook. 'Can you keep a secret?'

'I thought I already do,' Elora replied, feeling a twinge of excitement as she was led from the stable to a dusty corner of the nearby barn. Here, next to the tack corner, junk had piled up: wood to be burned, broken furniture from the hall and old horseshoes and tools. Robin clambered over it and rummaged in a cracked water trough which was filled with hay and sacking. From under it, Robin removed a scratched tobacco tin and, after checking no one else had entered the barn, eased the lid off.

Elora leaned closer, expecting a pile of money saved over months or even years. What she saw shocked her.

There were several gold coins. A paperweight of solid silver. A delicate necklace with a diamond pendant, and a pocket watch with a mother-of-pearl face.

'Where ... where did you get these?' Elora gasped, her eyes wide. Thoughts of the hall's guests flashed through her mind. There had been only one theft reported recently: a pair of silver candlesticks, and those had been found hidden among the belongings of a servant who had since been sacked. According to Elora's mother they were lucky to have been let off so lightly. Most people caught thieving lost their fingers, or worse. Could her dear Robin really be *stealing* from guests? She could hardly believe it, but the proof was right in front of her.

'What if you're caught?' she whispered, horrified. 'They'll

throw you in jail, that's if you didn't hang! I can't lose you – you're the only thing that's good about this place.'

'I won't get caught.' Robin's dark eyes flashed like the stash of gold and jewels. There was an arrogance there Elora hadn't seen before. An odd kind of pride. 'Even if I did, it's worth the risk to get out of this place. I thought that's what you wanted, too.'

'Of course,' Elora stuttered. 'I do! But I thought . . .'

She didn't know what she had thought. Perhaps that the talk of leaving would only ever be talk. Or, if it did happen that it'd be in years to come, once they'd both saved up enough money. Not like this though. This was real, and dangerous, and suddenly very, very possible.

Elora's gaze lingered on the diamond pendant again. 'What if Greaves, or a guest, catches you . . . ? They come back to their rooms all the time!'

To Elora's surprise, Robin laughed. A deep, throaty chuckle.

'I don't steal from rooms. That *would* get me caught.'

'Then what?' Elora stared back, bewildered.

'You're still not getting it?' Eyes flashing in amusement, Robin turned to grab an old cocked hat that had been left on a wooden post, and pulled it on.

'Now imagine I have a black mask over my eyes,' Robin said softly, gesturing around. 'And that I'm on a horse. Any horse that I know is here for the next night or two. And I point my pistol, and hold up a carriage and say, "Stand and deliver! Your money or your life." *Now* do you understand?'

Finally, Elora did. '*You?*' she breathed, staring at her friend. 'All this time it was you? You're the highway robber?' *Her* Robin? *Robin the robber?*

'The one and only.' The arrogant smirk was back. 'And who'd suspect it? Not a seasoned criminal, master horseman like everyone's saying. Just me, a poor servant who doesn't even own a horse. Well, I'm sick of being poor, being looked down upon. And you know something? These things, these trinkets? They're nothing to the folk who owned them. *Nothing.* It's just a little scare, a little inconvenience. They go back to the rest of their wealth unharmed. But to us it's different. It's a chance – *our* chance – for a new life. Don't you see?'

Elora did see, and as Robin took her hand and pulled her into a gleeful dance about the barn, it finally felt real. They were going to escape Wilderness for good.

'We've almost got enough,' Robin whispered, brushing a stray golden curl from Elora's face once they'd finished dancing. 'I just need a few more lucky rolls of the dice. And that's it. We'll be off, away.'

'When?' Elora asked, dizzy with the possibility of it all. 'How much more do we need?'

'Just one more night,' Robin promised. 'The winter market's coming up. I'll do it then. One night's worth of rich pickings and we'll go.'

And that was the moment Elora entered into something that couldn't be undone. The biggest, and last mistake of her life.

Chapter Seven
Wolf

WHEN BETTY AWOKE THE NEXT MORNING it was to a strange grey light filtering through the window. She saw that Charlie was already up, but only just, judging by her little sister's sleepy eyes and hair that was even untidier than usual.

'Betty, look!' Charlie said, in a croaky whisper. She pointed to the window excitedly.

Betty shivered out of bed, pulling her stockings on. The little fire in the grate had burned out overnight and now the room was freezing. She tiptoed towards Charlie, already guessing what she was about to see.

'It's snowing,' Charlie said delightedly, looking fully awake now.

'So it is,' said Betty, gazing out on to the square where tiny white flakes drifted through the air outside the window. It was still early, for there were only one or two people in the marketplace setting up their stalls. Their footprints looked like stitching through white fabric, but the snow wasn't heavy. And judging by the light dusting on the window frames it couldn't have been falling for long. Even so, it was enough to transform the landscape in that magical way that only snow can, with the lake like spilled iced milk in the distance and the land lighter than the sky.

'Hurry up, let's get dressed and go outside! I want to play in it,' said Charlie. 'Come on, Fliss, you too!'

'Mmph,' said Fliss sleepily as she stirred. She opened her eyes and stretched a pale, delicate foot out from under the covers before snatching it back. 'It's freezing!'

'Charlie,' said Betty, suddenly noticing something. 'You've made a mess over here – why have you pulled all those clothes out of the drawers?'

Charlie shrugged, her nose still glued to the window. 'Wasn't me.'

'Well, it wasn't like this last night,' Betty said. 'Fliss put all those things away before we went to bed.' She strode to the wooden chest and began picking up a handful of garments that had been carelessly dropped on the floor. She shook them out and folded them, placing them back in the top drawer which lay open. She checked the wooden nesting dolls were there, safely tucked into the jumpers and bobble hats, before closing it. It was then she saw that the flowers in the vase on top of the drawers were either wilting or dead. *That's strange*, thought Betty. *They were fresh yesterday.*

Quickly, they took turns to wash in the little basin in the

corner, teeth chattering all the while. As usual it was Fliss who complained the loudest about the cold, while Betty scoffed and told her to put on another jumper. But soon they were dressed, excited and eager to get breakfast, and then get out. As Fliss locked the door to room six behind them, Betty felt a swell of exhilaration. However much she loved Granny and Father, it was fun to be doing this, just the three of them!

Once in the corridor, the pleasing smells of cooking bacon and tomatoes wafted through the air to greet them.

'I wonder if we're allowed *two* breakfasts?' Charlie said greedily.

'I wonder what the fortune teller will say,' murmured Fliss.

'I wonder if there'll be any maps of Wilderness or Echo Hall for sale,' said Betty, who was always on the lookout for maps of places she had visited.

But as they rounded the corner towards the stairs, all thoughts of breakfast, fortune tellers and maps were wiped from their minds. For between the sisters and the stairs, an enormous grey and white wolf barred the way. The three girls froze, and Betty somehow found that she and Fliss were slightly in front of Charlie, shielding her from the huge creature.

'Betty?' Fliss whispered. 'What do we do?'

Betty didn't know. All she knew was that the animal's eyes looked like slivers of pale blue ice – and they were firmly fixed on the three girls. Its paws were the size of saucers, and as for its jaws ... Betty really didn't want to think about its jaws but she couldn't help it. They were easily big enough to snap an arm in two. Her knees went weak with fear. What was it doing here? How on earth could it have got into Echo Hall – had it attacked people downstairs on a rampage? *Surely we would have heard screaming*, a tiny part of her whispered. But there had been nothing, no warning. Even now she could hear the scraping of cutlery across plates, as though everything were normal and there wasn't a giant wolf about to gobble up the three sisters.

And then a low whistle sounded nearby, breaking the wolf's unblinking gaze.

'Bonbon,' came a voice, and Betty was startled to see a figure emerge from a nearby doorway. At once the tension left the wolf and it turned and began wagging its tail ridiculously, a thick pink tongue lolling from its open mouth. Betty was so shocked that it took her a moment to recognise the figure as the copper-haired boy who'd helped himself to the dining-room food last night.

'Bonbon,' the boy repeated, slipping a hand in his pocket. 'You know we mustn't scare guests like that. Sit!'

Bonbon sat, bushy tail continuing to swish from side to side over the wooden floor.

'Oh,' Charlie breathed, completely entranced. 'You have a tame *wolf*?'

'Yep.' The boy kneeled down and the wolf rolled on its back, feet in the air, as he rubbed its grey tummy.

Looking half-dazed, Charlie took a few slow steps in the wolf's direction. 'Can I touch?'

'Careful, Charlie,' Fliss warned, eyeing the animal warily. 'It's still wild, however tame it looks.'

'Wait a minute,' said Betty, remembering something. Charlie had once begged, cried and pleaded to keep an injured fox cub that they'd nursed back to health, but Granny had stoutly refused. 'You're not allowed to keep wild animals as pets, it's against the law. So that can't be a wolf.'

'Yes,' said Charlie. 'Betty's right.'

'Oh,' said the boy, looking cross. 'All right, then. He's half wolf. The other half is dog, though I don't know what kind.'

Charlie muttered *fibber* under her breath but managed to keep her manners, as she clearly wanted to stroke the wolf-dog. 'Why's he called Bonbon? Is it like the sweet?'

The boy nodded. 'He was pure white when I found him two winters ago,' he replied, his expression softening. 'Just a little ball of fluff, half dead from the cold and covered in snow. I had a paper bag of white sugar bonbons, and the snow on his coat looked like sugar dust, same as the sweets. I think his mother was killed by hunters. He wouldn't have survived if I'd left him so I brought him back here.'

'So you must live here,' Fliss said. 'Does your family own this place?'

The boy snorted. 'My mother works here,' he said. 'She's the one on the front desk – Mrs Chambers. So, yes, Echo Hall is our home. Or prison, depending on how you look at things.'

'You want to leave?' Betty asked. She was curious now,

not just about the beautiful wolf-dog but about the boy, too. She knew how it felt to be trapped in a place and long to be able to leave it.

'I'd like to, someday,' the boy said, still rubbing Bonbon's tummy vigorously. The wolf-dog was giving little grunts of appreciation now. 'But my mother doesn't want to, as much as I've tried to persuade her.' He shrugged. 'Looks like we're stuck here.'

'I like it,' said Charlie. 'I bet there's lots to do at the winter market.'

'There is,' said the boy. 'But it only comes once a year. The rest of the time the hall's almost empty.'

'Sounds lonely,' said Betty. 'Do you have any brothers or sisters?'

He shook his head. 'It's just the two of us. I never knew my father. Mother said he worked here for a while, then left when she and him didn't work out. I was a surprise, she always says.' He smiled faintly. 'She didn't think she would have any children, and then I came along late.'

The words poured out of him like they'd been bottled up and suddenly uncorked. Betty guessed he didn't get many opportunities to speak to children his own age.

'I'm Sonny, by the way,' he said, looking awkward, as though he had shared too much.

'I'm Betty,' said Betty, smiling to put him at ease. 'And these are my sisters, Fliss and Charlie. We're just visiting Wilderness with our granny for a few days.'

Sonny nodded, then ruffled Bonbon's silky, pointed ears and glanced at Charlie, whose fingers were twitching. 'Go on, you can stroke him.'

Charlie bent down and sank her hands into the thick grey fur. 'Ooh,' she said. 'He's so soft!'

Bonbon gave a little *wuff* and licked her hand, and Betty marvelled at how different the dog seemed from a few moments ago when she had been convinced it was about to attack.

'He likes you,' said Sonny, as Bonbon rolled on to all fours and began sniffing at Charlie's collar with interest.

'He can probably smell my rat,' Charlie explained, patting the wolf-dog's snout. 'He's called Hoppit and he's invisible.'

'That's lucky,' said Sonny, smiling again, wider this time. He had a nice smile, Betty thought. Friendly, with gappy white teeth. 'We've never had an invisible rat at Echo Hall before.' He pulled a rather squashed cube of cheese from his pocket and broke it in half, giving some to Bonbon who swallowed it without even chewing. 'Would Hoppit like some cheese?'

'He would love some,' said Charlie, solemnly accepting the cheese and tucking it into her collar, much to Sonny's amusement. 'He *is* real, you know.'

'Right.' Sonny peered at her collar, uncertain now. 'Well, he's probably best staying invisible while you're here. Which reminds me, if anyone asks you, you haven't seen me – and you especially haven't seen Bonbon, right? I'm not really supposed to bring him near the guest rooms.'

Charlie mimed locking her lips and tucking a key in her pocket. Sonny smiled again and gave a low whistle, starting to walk away.

'Bonbon, come on, boy.'

Bonbon gave another attentive *wuff* and followed Sonny as he went off round the corner. Charlie stared longingly after them. It suddenly struck Betty that perhaps Sonny might like to accompany them around the market. Even if he'd seen it all before he might be able to tell them more about Wilderness, and at the very least it would give Charlie a chance to spend more time with the enchanting dog. Betty stepped back and looked into the corridor they had just left, ready to call out.

But there was no sign of anyone, human or hound.

'Weird,' she muttered, thinking of the maid who'd disappeared, too. 'Why does everyone in this place keep vanishing?'

After a breakfast of hot, honey-drizzled pancakes the girls dressed in their warmest clothes and left a message for Granny at the front desk to explain where they were going.

'Poor Granny,' said Fliss. 'I do feel bad that we're swanning off to the market when she's been stuck with Clarissa all night.'

'We'll go and help her this afternoon,' said Betty, who was also feeling slightly guilty, but not enough to deter her from the market that she was so eager to explore. She watched Mrs Chambers taking down the message, noticing her coppery-coloured hair was the exact same shade as Sonny's.

'Wonder why she stays here?' Betty said in a low voice, as they left Echo Hall by the huge stone steps. 'She never seems happy, does she?'

'No,' Fliss agreed. 'But we saw for ourselves on the journey here that there's nothing else for miles. It must be hard to find work around here.'

Once outside, they got their first look at Echo Hall in the daylight. It looked every bit as grand with its weathered stone façade set against the snow-topped mountains behind it, and after a few minutes the girls were delighted to spot Fliss's red hair ribbon streaming out like a flag from the window of their room.

'Told you we were high up,' said Betty, shielding her eyes from the dazzling white mountains beyond. For a moment she thought she saw a shadowy movement behind the glass, but she blinked and it was gone.

The winter market was already busy. The log cabins' shutters had opened, people bustled around and warm breath misted the cold air. Betty marvelled at the different kinds of folk, both sellers and visitors, who seemed to have travelled from all corners of the earth to be there. Unfamiliar sounds and smells enveloped her. There were exotic foods from faraway places and a kaleidoscope of faces and languages that all mingled into one glorious, giant patchwork blanket of a crowd. The soft snowflakes had stopped falling but the sky was still white and everything was dusted with a layer of snow so fine it looked like sugar on a cake. Within minutes, the tip of Charlie's nose had turned pink with cold.

'Let's go over there,' she begged, pointing to a stall selling puppets of all colours and sizes. She tugged Fliss's hand but her older sister was scanning along the rows, looking for something.

'We'll start here,' said Betty, herding them to the edge of the market. 'Look, it goes in rows. We can walk along each one, and that way we won't miss anything.'

They began moving along the first row, drawn to the different stalls by colours and objects and sights and smells. They *ooh*ed and *ahh*ed over tiny decorations of delicate silver or spun glass: miniature ice skates, stags, icicles and frosted orbs that looked like snowballs, each one perfect and unique and wintry.

'I want this one,' said Charlie, choosing a tiny silver wolf. 'It looks like Bonbon, and it will make me think of Wilderness.' She handed over some of the precious spending money given to each of them by Father, and hugged the tiny decoration.

Fliss bought a pretty glass snowflake and Betty, always the most adventurous of the three, chose a silver sled threaded on a pale blue ribbon. By the time the three decorations had been wrapped up in gold paper, Charlie had already darted ahead. When Betty and Fliss caught up to her they found her staring open-mouthed at an array of snow globes, some large, some small, but all expensive and each one as beautiful as the next. Some had fairy-tale ice castles, gingerbread men and white snow bears inside them. Fliss reached out and carefully lifted up one with a tiny white cottage inside. She gave it a light shake and a flurry of white snowflakes settled softly over the little house.

'Beautiful,' she whispered, putting the globe back in its place.

The morning passed in a swirl of excitement and they looked at so many stalls that soon everything became a blur: thick woollen coats embroidered with silver thread; knitted scarves and hats; music boxes with swans on mirror 'lakes'. Betty didn't know where to look first and wanted to buy everything. She only realised it was lunchtime when they reached the middle of the market to find the food stalls selling candied chestnuts, hot chocolate spiced with nutmeg and sugary mints that looked like shards of ice. Many stalls were offering free samples to try, so Betty and her sisters tasted them all.

The best things they tasted, however, were the snow dome iced drinks. Each came in a glass ball with a paper straw through a hole in the top, and they had names like Berry Blizzard and Frosty Fortune.

'Won't these make us even colder?' asked Fliss, though she still couldn't resist buying one called Winter's Kiss.

'Worth it,' said Charlie, crunching up crushed ice

with chattering teeth and reluctantly handing back the domed glass.

They turned into the next row of stalls and here the market changed once more. A handsome sculptor was carving something from a huge block of ice; his cap was on the floor to collect money from passers-by. Fliss threw a coin and an admiring glance his way, and the sculptor flashed a dazzling smile which made her blush. Already Betty could see the ice block taking shape as a figure on horseback, the horse's mane flying in the air. Next there were artists drawing portraits, and people painting faces.

'I want my face painted,' Charlie said at once, and without waiting for a reply she hopped into the line of people queuing up.

'I'll wait with Charlie if you want to have a wander,' Betty told Fliss.

'I know exactly where I'm going,' said Fliss, standing up a little straighter and pointing ahead. 'In *there*.'

The crowd parted to reveal a tent draped in velvet of a deep midnight blue. There was a sign next to it which read LADY FORTUNA PREDICTS in squirly writing. It showed a teacup and the same silvery orb Betty had noticed on the black case at Echo Hall. Not a moon, she realised now. A crystal ball!

Her mind flashed back to the tale Clarissa had told them, about the highwayman and the fortune teller ... and the magical crystal ball. According to the tale, the lost crystal was still out there somewhere – probably at the bottom of the lake if the story were true. She remembered the fortune teller's strange outburst in the dining room last night and felt a flicker of apprehension.

'Are you sure you want your fortune read?' asked Betty. Fliss, like Granny, was very superstitious and Betty didn't want to see her older sister frightened. But she had to admit she too was curious. Did Lady Fortuna really have the power to see into the future?

'Yes, I want to,' said Fliss, firmly.

'Because if you're wondering if there's anyone in Wilderness to fall in love with, I'm sure you can take your pick,' Betty joked, gesturing to the crowded marketplace. Wherever they went Fliss was never short of admirers. She had, however, had her heart broken a few times – and broken a few herself.

Fliss went red. 'Not exactly. Not in Wilderness, I mean. But falling in love one day would be nice. It just seems –' she sighed, staring into the distance – '. . . like a bit of luck is needed with it, that's all. And not just for me.'

Betty frowned, trying to read the hazy look in her sister's eyes. 'What do you mean?'

'I'm talking about Elora and the highwayman,' Fliss explained, her eyes taking on a dreamy look. 'It's such a terribly sad story. To love someone so much that you'd be willing to search out in the cold for them even though Elora knew there must have been so little chance he would survive.

That's romance. That's real love. That's what *I* want, just not the dying in the snow part. Maybe Lady Fortuna will see something in my future.'

'You'd better hurry up then,' said Betty, nodding at the tent. 'Because I can see a very long queue in your future at the moment.'

'Do you think the fortune teller would perdict *my* future?' Charlie asked, as Fliss hurried off and the face-painting queue shuffled along.

'*Predict*,' Betty corrected. 'Hmm, even I could do that. Let's see,' she teased, closing her eyes and pretending to concentrate. 'In your future, Charlie Widdershins, I see animals. Lots and lots of animals! Big ones, small ones, feathered ones, furry ones, smelly ones ...'

'Lots and lots,' Charlie agreed, looking pleased. 'What else?'

'Sweets,' said Betty, lowering her voice to sound spooky and mysterious. 'So many sweets you could build a castle from them! There would be candied roses and violets growing up the walls, and a moat of raspberry sauce all around it—'

'And sugar mice living in the walls,' Charlie added, excited now. She bent her head and whispered into her collar: 'But you'll always be my favourite, Hoppit.'

It got very chilly waiting in the queue and soon they were having to blow into their hands and stamp their feet for warmth. Betty was glad when it was finally Charlie's turn. She had spent the past few minutes looking at the different designs and couldn't seem to make up her mind about what she wanted. When she emerged a few minutes later Betty was amused to see she had chosen to be a snowman, complete with a glittery white face, large black coal 'eyes' and a very realistic-looking carrot painted on her nose.

'Look at you!' Betty exclaimed, rearranging Charlie's scarf. 'You're a proper little snowman.'

Charlie grinned happily. For a long time she had had a large gap where her front teeth had fallen out, but now her new teeth were growing and filling the space. Betty felt strangely sad about this. Her little sister was getting bigger all the time.

'Can't wait to show Granny,' said Charlie. 'Perhaps if I stand very still she might think I'm a real snowman.'

'Perhaps,' said Betty, rubbing her hands together. 'Look, Fliss is next to go into the fortune teller's tent!'

Charlie's eyes glinted mischievously, looking greener than ever now they were rimmed in black paint. 'Let's sneak round the back and listen.'

'Good idea,' said Betty, knowing full well how annoyed Fliss would be if she discovered she was about to be spied upon. 'Then maybe we can have some fun with Fliss ourselves! Let's get a hot chocolate first though. My hands are freezing.'

They bought two large mugs of frothy hot chocolate, smothered with whipped cream and vanilla marshmallows. Then, checking the coast was clear, they slunk round the back of the midnight blue tent, finding a space in between it and the log cabin in the next row where they could both crouch.

'Good thing I'm not a real snowman,' said Charlie, blowing on her drink. 'This cup would melt my hands!'

'Mmm,' Betty agreed, then she pointed to the tent, holding a finger to her lips. 'Shh.'

'Greetings,' a deep voice boomed out from nearby. Betty almost slopped her hot chocolate down herself. It was so close and loud that for a moment she was convinced she and Charlie had been discovered, but she quickly realised that Lady Fortuna must be right on the other side of the velvety fabric ... and was addressing her next customer.

'I've been expecting you, Felicity Widdershins.'

Chapter Eight
The Fortune Teller and Fliss

ETTY AND CHARLIE STARED AT EACH OTHER, wide-eyed and frozen in astonishment. From the other side of the curtain they heard their sister's voice and she sounded every bit as puzzled as they were – and more than a little spooked.

'H-how do you know my name?'

'How *does* she know her name?' Charlie mouthed, leaning so close to the starry fabric that her hot chocolate was almost running over the rim of her mug.

'Careful,' Betty said in a low whisper, straightening Charlie's hand. The last thing either of them needed was to spill their drink and burn themselves – any loud noise would instantly give them away. And now Betty wanted to listen more than ever to what Lady Fortuna had to say.

Charlie took a long slurp of her drink and carefully placed the mug down. There was a blob of cream on her carrot-painted nose and a very determined look on her face.

'Charlie!' Betty whispered as her sister began poking at the folds of the tent. 'What are you—?'

'Look,' Charlie mouthed, pointing.

She had found a small gap, only about the width of a coin but it was enough for them to both peer through. Betty put her eye to it, her chin resting on Charlie's head below.

If the outside of the tent was intriguing, the inside could only be described as mesmerising. The beautiful dark velvet was reversed on the inside and fell in soft folds of silver, with tiny dark-blue crescent moons. Tea-light candles in glass jars glowed round the edges of the tent, bathing everything in a warm golden light.

There was a strange smell in the air, something like the cloves and spices in Granny's pipe smoke, only sweeter. Betty guessed it was coming from a small silver urn which stood nearby on a little table, for a thin trail of smoke drifted out of it and spiralled through the air to turn the inside of the tent misty.

Like the Crowstone Marshes, thought Betty, remembering the place she had grown up where dense fogs would appear without warning, and even those who knew the place like the back of their hand could get dreadfully lost.

At the centre of it all was a round table draped in shimmering cloth. On one side was Fliss, sitting upright and nervous in a spindly chair. Opposite her was Lady Fortuna who seemed quite recovered from her outburst the evening before. She wore a dress that looked as red and soft as a rose petal, and her lips were painted the same colour. A black silk veil covered her face and hair, falling loosely down her back and, within its black waves, Betty could swear she saw little flecks of light like shimmering stars, too.

In the middle of the table was a clear orb on a tiny golden stand.

Betty felt Charlie go very still and knew she had spotted it, too. Fliss seemed equally enchanted by it. Her brown eyes were flitting all over the tent; from Lady Fortuna to the flickering candles to the teacup in the fortune teller's hand ... but always back to the crystal ball.

A crystal ball. Even without the story of the highwayman fresh in her mind, Betty would have found herself mesmerised by it. Perhaps it was the flickering of the candles within the dim tent, but the glass orb seemed to glow. It cast reflections of dotted and dashed light on to the tablecloth, which looked like spilled coins.

'I know many things, Felicity Widdershins,' Lady Fortuna said at last. She was sitting very still and, from under her veil, her dark, penetrating gaze was trained on Fliss. 'There is always more to know than what the eye can see.' She paused, placing a hand on her chest. 'Sometimes our hearts can tell us things, too, if we listen closely enough. That's what we call *intuition*. But –' another dramatic pause – '... sometimes we must look in the most unlikely places to find the answers we seek. Places others would not think – or dare – to look. The fact that you are here, Felicity, tells me that you have the courage to ask questions. You are curious and you are brave.'

At this Charlie let out a barely concealed snort. 'Ain't brave,' she muttered. 'She's even scared of spiders.'

Betty nudged her to be quiet. There were different ways to be brave, and she suspected that even Charlie knew this deep down. All the same, she thought it was a strange thing for the fortune teller to say.

'Before we begin, there are three things we must do.'

Fliss nibbled her lip nervously. 'Three things? You still haven't told me how you know my name ...'

Lady Fortuna waved a hand which somehow had a silencing effect on Fliss.

'The first thing is that you must cross my palm with silver.'

Fliss frowned. 'Cross your palm with ... ? Oh, you mean *pay* you!'

Lady Fortuna made a delicate coughing noise, but held out her hand as Fliss rummaged in her purse.

'I don't have a silver coin,' she said, sounding worried as she looked through a handful of loose money.

'The gold one will do.'

'Oh.' Fliss blinked and placed the gold coin in Lady Fortuna's outstretched palm. She hesitated. 'Will I get change?'

''Tis bad luck to ask questions,' Lady Fortuna replied in a hushed voice.

'The charlatan!' Betty whispered, struggling to keep her voice down as she bristled with anger.

'A Charlotte-on?' asked Charlie, puzzled. 'But that's *my* name.'

'No, it's a different word,' Betty explained. 'A charlatan means a crook, a swindler. She's just robbed Fliss silly and she hasn't even told her a thing yet!'

'The second request,' Lady Fortuna went on, 'is that you must share a secret with me.'

'A . . . a secret?' Fliss looked alarmed. 'Wh-why do I need to do that? I thought you were the one who was supposed to tell *me* things?'

Good, Betty thought, glad to see Fliss sticking up for herself a bit.

'My dear,' said Lady Fortuna, in a silky voice. 'You are quite right. But fate favours those who give something back. It's an exchange. If you open up then fate will look upon you more kindly and reveal more secrets of its own.'

'I see,' said Fliss, not looking very happy about this. 'Well, let me think.' She chewed her lip, and suddenly her face changed, flushing a deep red as she remembered something. 'I once . . . oh, this is dreadful.'

Lady Fortuna leaned forward eagerly. 'Go on, my dear.'

Betty found she was holding her breath. She felt a strange mixture of shame and excitement as she wondered what Fliss was about to reveal.

'We really shouldn't be listening to this,' she whispered guiltily.

Charlie shushed her. 'Quiet, I'm trying to hear!'

96

'I once . . .' Fliss continued, taking a shaky breath. 'When I was six years old I found some scissors that Granny had forgotten to put away. She'd left me watching my younger sister, Betty, for a couple of minutes while she pegged some washing out to dry. And while Granny was gone I . . . I gave Betty a haircut.' Fliss was almost whispering now and her cheeks were red as berries. 'I had this doll, you see. It was called Molly-dolly, and she had this sweet little hair style that was bobbed around her shoulders. And Betty's hair was – well, *is* – so unruly, that I thought it might help if there were less of it. So I gave it a snip here and there, and before I knew it, it was up to her ears and frizzier than ever. Poor Betty – she looked like a little brown dandelion!'

Betty listened to all this in silent astonishment. She had heard this story before – Granny had repeated it many times over the years. Only, when Granny had told it, it had been a bit different . . .

'Then I trimmed the cat's whiskers,' Fliss confessed. 'It had one white one, you see. I was aiming for that but I took the whole lot off by accident. But that still wasn't the worst of it.'

No, thought Betty. *It wasn't.*

'When I heard Granny coming back I panicked,' Fliss went on. 'So I put the scissors next to Betty. I knew Betty wouldn't get into trouble as she was too little, but Granny still told me off for not watching her properly. So I got into trouble anyway, even though Betty took the blame for it!

And I've never been able to tell them that I fibbed about it, even though I felt dreadful.'

Betty stifled a giggle. All those years she'd believed she was the one who'd cut off her own hair and the cat's whiskers, and all this time it had been Fliss, too prim and proper to admit she had lied.

'Thank you for your honesty, Felicity,' Lady Fortuna said, bowing her head. 'Your secret is safe here.'

Fliss rubbed her nose and nodded. 'What's the third thing?' she asked warily. 'You said there were three things I had to do.'

'The third thing is that you must trust,' Lady Fortuna said, in a voice like a cat's purr. 'Now, place your hand in mine.'

Fliss did as she was told. Lady Fortuna's long fingers wrapped around Fliss's hand like an octopus's tentacles, drawing it closer to her. She leaned over it, her long veil swishing over Fliss's upturned palm.

'Hmm,' she said after a moment. 'Interesting.'

'Interesting good or interesting bad?' Fliss asked anxiously, squirming as the fortune teller traced her palm with a long, pointed fingernail. 'Ooh. Ha ha! That tickles.'

'Your life line is good and strong,' Lady Fortuna said. 'And so is your heart line. You have a long, healthy life ahead of you. But the love line . . .' She paused, shaking her head. 'This is where it gets *complicated.*' She peered closer, pointing. 'This line here, see it? If it were a piece of string, yours, my dear, would be one of the knottiest pieces of string I've ever seen.'

'That's about right,' Betty whispered. She and Charlie were forever teasing Fliss for falling in and out of love all the time. Perhaps there was some truth in Lady Fortuna's abilities after all.

'You have had many loves,' Lady Fortuna continued, turning Fliss's hand this way and that. 'And there will be more before you find your one true love. But when you do, it will be for ever.'

'Oh,' said Fliss, looking relieved. Then she frowned. 'But how will I know which one is for ever? Will there be a sign?' A dreamy look came into her dark eyes. 'Will he have a musical voice, or a crooked but charming smile? Or . . . or a black horse?'

Charlie nudged Betty and mimed being sick. Betty rolled her eyes. *A black horse?* Could it be that the story of the highwayman wasn't far from her romantic sister's mind?

'Featherhead,' Charlie whispered.

'My dear, you will know,' said Lady Fortuna. 'True love will always find a way.'

'Yes, but . . .'

'It will be sooner than expected,' Lady Fortuna said. 'And . . . *oh!* Your destiny shows me a broken arm!'

'Jumping jackdaws,' said Fliss, looking pleased. 'That's good news! Well, not about the broken arm, but at least I know what to look for.'

'*However*,' the fortune teller said, 'you must beware. Beware of those who are not what they seem, who not only mask their faces but their true intentions.' She released Fliss's hand. 'Now we must look *closer.*'

A light flared within the crystal ball on the table, making it glow.

Magic? Betty wondered, her breath catching in her throat, before she saw that Lady Fortuna had moved a small candle closer to it. The flickering flame danced playfully within the reflective glass orb like something alive and mischievous. The fortune teller leaned in, gazing into the crystal ball, and Betty was reminded of a witch leaning over a cauldron.

'I see three girls,' Lady Fortuna said, her voice like softest velvet. 'Three sisters.'

'Yes,' Fliss whispered.

'Three sisters who have shared many secrets and adventures . . .'

'And haircuts,' whispered Charlie, pretending to snip with her fingers.

'. . . and heartache,' Lady Fortuna went on, frowning. She moved her hands over the crystal ball, not touching its surface, but stirring the air and causing more flickers of light from the candle. 'Your mother . . . she is gone.'

Fliss nodded, her lips in a tight line. 'She . . . she died when we were young.'

'She will always be with you,' the fortune teller whispered. 'Those we love never leave us.'

An icy blast of air whooshed through the tent, making every one of the candle flames flicker. A tiny noise rang out from above and immediately Betty's eyes – as well as everyone else's – were drawn to a small silver bell which dangled over the table from a purple ribbon.

'We are not alone,' Lady Fortuna whispered, her voice full of excitement. She pointed at the bell. 'There is an unseen presence which wishes to make contact ... to bring you a message.'

'There is?' Fliss squeaked.

Lady Fortuna wiggled her fingers over the crystal ball again and, even from her position at the edge of the tent, Betty could see something about the glassy orb had changed. There was a shape within it: misty white and almost fog-like. It hadn't been there before, Betty was certain of it. Her skin rippled with goosepimples. She could only imagine how Fliss must feel, sitting so close and seeing the shape appear seemingly out of nowhere. It was thrilling, but spooky.

The image in the crystal ball was simple and clear.

'A key,' Fliss murmured.

Charlie clutched Betty's hand tightly. Betty squeezed back. Strange ... it looked very much like the old key left for them by the maid at Echo Hall.

'A secret will be unlocked,' Lady Fortuna said. 'And you will have an important part in it.'

'What kind of secret?' Fliss asked, her eyes darting all over the tent as the candles flickered and the air grew icier still. 'How did that appear in the crystal ball?'

Before the fortune teller could respond, another rush of

101

cold air swept around them. It ruffled Lady Fortuna's veil and hair, and took every flame of every candle with it. The tent was plunged into eerie darkness. Betty felt Charlie's fingers grip hers even harder, and the smell of candle smoke filled her nose.

'*Betty!*' Charlie wailed fearfully, forgetting to keep quiet.

Betty heard Fliss gasp and knew she had heard Charlie's voice, too. She clamped a hand over her little sister's mouth. At the same time a match was struck and Lady Fortuna re-lit the candle on the table. Betty felt another chill as she noticed that the image of the key in the crystal ball had vanished. She searched her sister's face and saw that Fliss was unsettled, too. But had she recognised the voice as Charlie's?

'All is well,' said Lady Fortuna, lightly touching Fliss's hand. She looked unruffled, as though she were used to strange voices coming out of the dark all the time. 'The extinguishing of the candles signals that the ghostly presence has departed ... the crystal ball is clear once more and we are left with a name: Betty. Your sister's name.'

'Yes, my sister's name,' Fliss repeated, eyes narrowing. She stared at the glassy ball on the table, looking more upset by the minute. 'But ... but it's also my granny's name! Only, no one really calls her Betty, everyone calls her Bunny.' She paused, more anxious than ever. 'Why would a ... a ghostly voice call out my sister's name? Or my granny's?'

'It may be a sign that one of them needs your help,' Lady Fortuna replied. 'But the peaceful feeling I'm getting assures me that you will be there at the right moment.' She carefully draped a dark cloth over the crystal ball, and with that it was clear that Fliss's time was up. Rising from the table, Lady Fortuna swished elegantly to Fliss's side and escorted her to leave. The fringed curtain swept closed, leaving the tent empty.

'Come on,' Betty said to Charlie, feeling more than a little guilty now. 'Let's get out of here.'

They sat back, allowing the chink in the fabric to fall closed. After the dimly lit tent everything seemed brighter and more dazzling than ever as they slunk back to the crowded market.

'Oh, no,' Charlie wailed, patting her pockets. 'I've lost Hoppit! He must have crawled out when we were by the fortune teller's tent.'

'Charlie!' Betty snapped, exasperated. 'You and that blasted rat! Wait over there by the candyfloss stand and keep an eye out for Fliss. I'll go back and look – although how I'm supposed to find him I don't know, seeing as he's bleedin' invisible!'

'Please, Betty,' Charlie urged, suddenly upset. 'I couldn't bear for him to be lost!'

Betty hurried back to the edge of the tent where she and Charlie had hidden. She found the gap and carefully eased it open a crack to look inside. The tent was still empty, with no sign of Lady Fortuna. The air was hazy with candle smoke and everything was dim after the brightness outside.

The crystal ball was on the table, still covered up. Betty's heart sank. How on earth would she spot an invisible rat? Then she noticed a movement from the long, fringed fabric draped over the fortune-telling table. It rippled as something scurried along its edges on the floor. *Hoppit!* Betty slipped into the tent and pounced.

'Oh, no, you don't!' she scolded, crouching down to scoop up the naughty rat. 'That's enough of your mischief.'

Her elbow knocked into something hard that was under the table, hidden behind the cloth. Betty winced as a sharp pain shot up her funny bone, then stared as the object rolled out from under the fabric, stopping by her feet.

It was a crystal ball, almost identical to the one sitting on the table above. Only this one wasn't clear. Inside it was a little house, and as Betty watched, tiny white flecks settled around it.

'It's not a crystal ball,' she whispered to herself, understanding in a flash. 'It's a snow globe!' She lifted the tablecloth to peer beneath, and gasped. Under the table was a cleverly built revolving shelf with rows of rounded indents. Each one contained a heavy glass globe, just like the ones Betty and her sisters had seen earlier in the market. They were exactly the same size as the crystal ball on the table, but all of them had something different inside. Betty's face burned as she looked through them. In one there was a tiny clock. In another, two figures dancing together. And then Betty found it – the key.

She must have switched the crystals, Betty realised, feeling furious. She recalled how their attention had been grabbed by the tinkling of the bell. And then, when the candles had gone out, Lady Fortuna must have switched the globe with the key back to the plain one.

'What *exactly* do you think you're doing?' hissed a cold voice, startling her.

Betty froze and slowly turned round, expecting to find Lady Fortuna looming over her. But the fortune teller was not looking at Betty, who was half hidden behind the table. Her icy words had been directed somewhere near the entrance, where the velvet curtain was rippling softly.

Who is she talking to? Betty wondered, shrinking further behind the table.

A figure moved into the tent, so darkly clothed that at first Betty could only see his head, but it was enough to recognise him: the ginger-moustached man from Echo Hall. *Mr Sneed.* He was holding something that looked a little like a pointed frying pan. Betty had seen something similar before, but she couldn't think what it was.

'I don't like surprises,' Lady Fortuna snapped, throwing the veil off her face and glaring at him. Her pretty face was twisted into something unpleasant and menacing. 'You have one simple job. No calling out, no funny voices.'

'I didn't,' Mr Sneed protested, in a far meeker tone than the one Betty had heard him use at Echo Hall. 'I did as you asked, same as always: snuff out the candles and blast icy air at the right moments. That's it.'

Snuff out the candles? Blast icy air . . . ? Betty's anger deepened into disgust and disappointment. Now she remembered what the object Mr Sneed held was for. It was a bellows: a tool for pumping out air which was used to help light fires. A well-aimed puff could easily snuff out a candle. *It was a trick,* she thought. *All of it.* The vision in the crystal ball, all those candles going out and the well-timed blasts of cold air had been nothing, just an eerie illusion to get her sister's money.

'Then who called out?' Lady Fortuna demanded. 'I heard it, clear as anything. It sounded like a child.'

'It must have been someone outside,' Mr Sneed answered. 'Either that, or you really *are* starting to make contact with ghostly presences.'

And at this, the pair of them threw their heads back and laughed.

Chapter Nine
The Frozen Lake

BETTY CREPT AWAY FROM LADY FORTUNA'S tent. Poor Fliss had just been told a pack of lies – and paid for it, too. It seemed Granny had been right to warn them away from fortune tellers, and not just because she claimed it was unlucky to 'poke your nose into your future business'.

Charlie was hopping anxiously from foot to foot by the time Betty returned.

'Did you find Hoppit?' she asked. 'You were gone *ages!*'

Betty nodded and handed over the squirming rat.

'Naughty,' Charlie scolded, tucking him safely in her pocket. She glanced up at Betty. 'What's the matter? You look all cross.'

'Nothing,' Betty lied, spotting Fliss by a stall selling toasted marshmallows on sticks. 'I'm just getting cold now.' She didn't want to tell Charlie what she had overheard. It would only add to the secret of the pair of them listening in. 'Come on, I can see Fliss.'

They weaved their way through to her.

'There you are,' she said, sounding breathless and looking more, as Granny would say, like she had her 'head in the clouds' than ever. 'Oh, Charlie – your face! I thought you were a *real* snowman for a minute.'

'Did you?' Charlie asked, not sounding convinced but enjoying the pretence all the same.

'Betty, you should have heard her,' Fliss went on, patting Charlie's head distractedly. 'Lady Fortuna, I mean. She's wonderful!'

Charlie smirked, nudging Betty with her elbow. Fortunately Fliss was too caught up in relating her story to notice.

'Is she?' Betty said flatly. Should she tell Fliss what she had overheard – or at least the last part of it? She suddenly felt very, very sneaky and didn't like it one bit. It had only meant to be a bit of mischief to listen in but instead she felt icky, like she had read Fliss's diary ... and seeing her sister so excited about it all only made it worse. If she told Fliss the truth it wouldn't only burst her bubble of happiness, it might also destroy her trust in her sisters. Either way she knew she would feel wretched.

'She just ... knew things,' Fliss said in a low, dramatic voice. 'Things she couldn't possibly have known!'

'What kind of things?' Charlie asked innocently.

'Just ... things,' Fliss said. 'Secrets. And she knew about Mother dying when we were young. And the strangest thing is, I think Mother was there because there was a little bell that tinkled and a whoosh of freezing air, and Lady Fortuna said there was an unseen presence—'

'Fliss,' Betty began uncomfortably, 'you know these things are just a bit of fun, don't you? They shouldn't really be taken too seriously.'

'Oh, it *was* fun,' Fliss said excitedly. 'Well, sort of. The parts where she told me about how I'm going to meet my true love, and how I'll help to unlock a secret. It was so strange – there was a crystal ball on the table and all of a sudden a key appeared in it! You should have seen it, Betty! I wouldn't have believed it either, if I hadn't seen it with my own eyes!'

'Strange,' Betty repeated. 'Like I said, though, best not to read too much into it. Sometimes these fortune-telling people can have ... tricks up their sleeves.'

'It wasn't a trick,' said Fliss, a little huffily. 'You weren't there, so *you* don't know.'

At this Charlie giggled and Betty nudged her to be quiet.

'Anyway,' Fliss went on, lowering her voice, 'I don't see why you're so reluctant to believe it. The three of us know better than anyone that magic exists. Perhaps fortune telling is just a different kind of magic.'

Betty went silent, thinking of their nesting dolls tucked away safely in the drawer at Echo Hall. Magic existed all right, but not as far as Lady Fortuna was concerned.

'It was very spooky,' Charlie agreed. Betty frowned at her. 'I mean, it *sounds* very spooky,' she corrected hurriedly.

'Mmm,' said Fliss, who hadn't picked up on Charlie's mistake and was scanning the marketplace with a reluctant look on her face. 'Well, I suppose we ought to be getting back to help Clarissa soon. She's probably driving poor Granny to despair.'

'Just a little longer,' Charlie begged, pulling her sisters along. 'Let's go a bit further.'

Betty and Fliss followed, easily persuaded, and eventually they found themselves at the edge of the frozen lake. There, set back from the stalls, was a wooden shack with a painted sign that read: *Ice Skating*. Inside the little shack an old man with a crooked back was handing out ice skates in return for copper coins.

'Can we go skating?' Charlie pleaded, her green eyes wide. 'Please, please, *please?*'

Fliss gazed doubtfully out over the ice. 'I don't think so, Charlie.'

'Why not?' Charlie whined. She flung her arm out towards the lake, where dozens of skaters were gliding over the ice. 'It looks such fun!'

'You know why,' Fliss said quietly.

'Because of Mother,' Charlie said, sulking. 'That was an accident! Look at all those people out there. It's safe.'

'Granny wouldn't like it,' said Fliss. 'And I'm not sure I would, either.'

'Then Betty can take me,' Charlie persisted.

'Come on, Fliss,' Betty added. She glanced across the lake and the haunting tale of the highwayman and Elora

110

sprang into her thoughts. Could the magical crystal ball still be under the ice after all this time? She stared at its glassy surface, wondering what dark secrets lay hidden beneath. Plus, she reasoned, Charlie was right. It *did* look fun. 'When do we ever get the chance to do something like this? The ice is thick enough, or people wouldn't be allowed on it.'

'Accidents can still happen,' Fliss said primly, but there was a softening in her voice now. Her gaze levelled suddenly and she squinted across the lake with a determined look that hadn't been there a few moments ago. 'Well, I suppose if we were very careful and stayed near the edges where it's shallower ...'

Betty stared into the distance, trying to work out what could have changed Fliss's mind. It was no surprise when she spotted two figures in the distance, one of whom had an arm bound up in a sling.

'Destiny shows me a broken arm,' Fliss muttered under her breath, then without another word she turned and stalked towards the ice-skating log cabin like a wolf going after a rabbit.

'Uh-oh,' said Betty, rolling her eyes. Charlie looked delighted, and the two of them followed Fliss to the counter, where she had already handed over her money and boots in exchange for a pair of black leather ice skates. Betty paid for herself and Charlie, and collected their skates.

'You get them for an hour,' the old man told them, tucking away the sisters' shoes into a little cubby hole at the back of the cabin.

'Is ice skating hard?' Charlie asked as they sat on a bench and slipped their feet into the skates.

'Don't know,' said Betty. 'I've never tried it.' She nodded to people out on the frozen lake who were gliding around gracefully. 'It looks easy enough.'

'What about those people over there?' Charlie pointed to someone who was wobbling badly and being held up by the person next to them.

'Erm,' said Betty doubtfully, 'well, there's only one way to find out.' She laced up her skates, then checked Charlie's were done up properly.

'Ready?' asked Fliss, appearing in front of them, already on her feet. 'Let's go.'

Betty stood up and immediately wobbled before managing to get her balance.

'Meddling magpies!' said Charlie, clinging to Betty's arm. 'I don't like it! Take them off, I don't want to do it any more!'

'We're not even on the ice yet,' Betty pointed out. 'It might get easier.'

They hobbled to the edge of the lake. It felt strange to be balanced on such thin blades, and the boots were tight and stiff around Betty's ankles. It didn't feel at all the way she had imagined it would and, stepping on to the ice, it wasn't much easier – especially with Charlie hanging off her arm.

'Come on!' Fliss chirped, stepping past them impatiently. 'It can't be that hard, can ... eeeh!' she wailed, throwing her arms out for balance before landing hard on her bottom. 'Ouch!'

Charlie giggled, and together she and Betty half walked, half skidded towards Fliss and helped her up.

'It's not as easy as it looks,' Fliss muttered, her cheeks burning as she brushed flecks of ice from her clothes.

Little by little they picked their way across the ice, watching others who were doing it more successfully. After a few minutes of practice, their steps turned into slides and soon they were skating. Not very gracefully, but skating nonetheless – even Charlie, who looked a lot like a newborn calf unsteady on its feet. Fliss, with her arms flapping for balance, complained that she must look like a dizzy pigeon, but after a few minutes they began to gather speed and confidence.

'Look! I'm doing it!' yelled Charlie, before tumbling to the ice with a bump. She had barely hit the surface before she was up again with a grin and setting off once more.

They continued round the lake, staying close to the edges as Fliss had instructed them to. Betty didn't mind. However much she admired the beauty of the frozen water under their feet, she couldn't help but think of their mother and the terrible accident that had taken her from their family. Frozen lakes and ponds might be beautiful, but they could be deadly, too.

However, even thoughts of the tragedy were pushed from Betty's mind as she approached the far side of the lake. There were fewer people here, just one or two lone skaters who were practising their jumps and twirls in the open space. But it wasn't the skaters who caught Betty's attention. A startling formation of ice ran between the edge of the lake and what appeared to be a thin road that was higher and set back. It looked like a set of breathtakingly beautiful caves, and Betty skated nearer, curious to get a closer look. The noise from the market faded the further she got.

'They're *trees*,' she whispered in wonder, at last making sense of criss-crossing branches in the tightly knitted copse. They were so encrusted in ice and snow that they were barely recognisable. Huge, jagged icicles as large as Charlie sliced between the branches like blades. Her eyes travelled over the little gaps and hollows in between, imagining the icicles were towers, turrets and chandeliers in a snow queen's palace.

'What *is* that?' Charlie breathed, skidding to a stop by bumping into Betty.

'Charlie!' Betty gasped, jolted from the strange sight. 'You almost knocked me over!'

'Sorry!' Charlie protested. 'I ain't got the hang of stopping yet.' She peered up at the frozen trees. 'Bats and broomsticks! It looks like one of those thingies Father used to tell us about in his stories, you know ...' She looked at Betty excitedly. 'You know. A what's-it-called ... a grotty!'

'*Grotto*,' Betty corrected, remembering their father's tales of smugglers and treasure hidden in labyrinths of caves and grottos. She had quite clearly imagined those ones, echoing and watery and filled with the stink of seaweed and the glitter of treasure, but she had never known that similar things could exist from trees and ice, too. It was beautiful and eerie to behold, with the iced-up trees so tightly packed together that it was almost impossible to see where one tree ended and the next began.

'We could get in there,' Charlie said, skating a bit closer. 'Look, if we just squeezed through there, it could be a little den.'

'I wouldn't do that if I were you,' a voice said from nearby.

Betty turned swiftly in surprise. Sonny had arrived silently behind them, in a fleece-lined sled pulled by the beautiful wolf-dog which was now in a leather harness. Betty wondered if perhaps Sonny *had* wanted to come with them earlier. Had he followed them, or simply spotted them by chance?

'Dangerous,' he said, pointing to the trees. 'They might look pretty, but it's bigger than you think when you're inside. Once you're in, it's not so easy to get out. Some parts are frozen so solid they're stronger than a castle wall.'

'Have you ever been in it?' Charlie asked curiously, edging closer to Bonbon and ruffling his fur. Bonbon nudged her fingers with his black nose and then sniffed the icy air. He looked even wilder out here, Betty thought, with the frozen lake beneath them and the ice-capped mountains in the distance.

'No, but I know people who have. My mother – she went

in there one winter and almost never made it out.' His grey eyes skimmed the edge of the lake. 'There should be signs warning about the dangers, but they go missing.'

'How?' Betty asked, feeling a shiver spread over her skin.

He shrugged. 'Sometimes they rot, or slip under the surface when the lake thaws. It's got a name, you know, this place. It's because of the way the icicles are formed; the water drips down from the branches and freezes. It looks as though the trees are crying. Also, this is where it happened.'

'Where what happened?' Fliss swooped up to them, her breath puffing in the air.

'The highwayman?' asked Betty, feeling a tingle of anticipation. 'This is where he and Elora died?'

Sonny nodded, pointing past the trees to the road. 'This is where they think the robber must have fallen from. Elora spent the night searching and calling for him, until the cold got the better of her. When they found her the next morning she was within those trees. Her face was frozen with tears, and the icicles on the trees seemed to be weeping with her. So this place is called Elora's Tears.'

'How terribly sad,' said Fliss. 'And they never found the highwayman?'

Sonny stared at her for a long moment before answering. Betty wondered if he hadn't heard the question properly, but then a muscle in his cheek twitched and he replied.

'They never found a body. Only his black hat out in the water, frozen in the ice.'

'So he died in the lake?' Betty asked, transfixed by the gruesome tale.

'That's the way the story goes.' Sonny blew into his hands to warm them, staring down at the frozen lake's surface. 'But I came to tell you that people stay away from this area, so you should, too. It's unlucky. Some say it's cursed.'

Unlucky. It was a word the Widdershins could never seem to get away from, Betty thought. Like a bad smell that followed them around.

'Thanks for the warning,' she began, but Sonny had made a clicking sound to Bonbon and the sled was already gliding back across the lake.

'Well, that was spooky,' said Fliss, frowning after him. She gazed at the frozen trees and shuddered. 'And so is this place. Let's move closer to the market. It's too quiet and lonely over here.'

'All right,' said Betty, but despite the ghoulish details they had just learned she found she was rooted to the spot, as though the tangle of iced trees had ensnared her deeper into the old legend. The few lone skaters nearby had moved on, leaving the three sisters by themselves on the deserted stretch of ice by the grotto of trees.

'Come on,' Fliss called, noticing that her sister was lingering behind. But Betty wasn't the only one.

'Wait,' Charlie said, staring at something. 'Betty, Fliss – look. I can see something moving under there.'

'Under where?' Betty's eyes moved over the frozen trees,

so strange and haunting and beautiful. She searched for a sign of movement between the icy branches. They were so dense that things could well be hidden in there. A mouse, perhaps – or even a fox? 'I can't see anything.'

'No.' Charlie pointed down, beneath her feet. 'There. Under the ice.'

Betty and Fliss drew closer to the spot where Charlie was. She had crouched down and was peering at the ice like a cat watching a spider.

'I thought I saw a shadow,' she said. Her voice suddenly sounded too loud and Betty became aware that the freezing air was very still. *Unnaturally* still ... as though time had stopped.

'I don't see anything,' she murmured, her gaze darting over the ice. All she could make out on the frozen surface were the lines carved into the ice by the blades of their skates, but at the same time her heart began to beat a warning. *Stop it,* she told herself. *You're being silly. There's nothing to be afraid of – it's just the story of what happened here and Sonny's warning. It's an eerie place, that's all ...*

A thud came from beneath them. Betty felt it more than she heard it; a bump from somewhere under the ice. Somewhere close.

'What the heck ... ?' Fliss whispered.

'Look!' Charlie gasped. 'Told you!'

A dark patch was appearing in the milky white ice. It was small, around the size of a plate, but it seemed to be spreading

118

and bleeding out at the edges. Within it there was a shadowy movement. Charlie had been right.

'I think I see bubbles,' Fliss exclaimed. 'Perhaps there's an underwater spring that feeds water into the lake ...'

'Then what was that bump?' Charlie asked.

'Maybe a bit of floating wood hitting the surface?' Fliss suggested doubtfully.

She had barely finished speaking when a second thud came, followed by another stream of bubbles. The darker patch of ice continued to grow and spread like a bruise.

'I don't like this,' said Betty, her eyes glued to the spot. 'It looks like the ice is thinning, it might be thawing out.'

'So why does it feel even colder?' Fliss asked with a shiver.

Something white hit the ice from underneath. They all saw it: a pale hand pushing at the frozen surface. Charlie screamed; Fliss reeled back. Only Betty stayed motionless, but it was with fear.

'Someone's under the ice!' Fliss gasped. 'We have to help them!'

Betty turned this way and that, frantic. She could see no cracks anywhere. Every part of the surface – except for the thinning dark patch – was frozen solid. So how could someone have fallen in? There would surely be screams, cries for help ... unless no one had witnessed it. Whatever the truth, Betty knew they had to act, and fast.

'Quickly, grab something to break the ice!' she yelled, urging Fliss in the direction of the frozen trees. 'There must be a broken branch or a rock we can use . . .' Glancing desperately at the trees, she saw it was hopeless. Whatever branches might have broken off had been covered in layers of snow and ice, and now Betty realised something else.

'We can't break it without putting ourselves in danger. If we crack it, the whole area could shatter!'

'Maybe it wasn't a hand,' Charlie whispered, staring at the dark space, maybe it was a really strange fish . . .'

The hand appeared again, slapping at the ice from beneath. This time all three of them shrieked. There was no mistaking it.

'Someone *is* under there!' Betty cried. 'We have to go for help!'

The edge of the lake where the market was seemed a long way off, but she knew it was their only hope. There would be someone there who could help, some way of breaking the ice. 'Fliss, Charlie – go,' she croaked. 'Get help. I'll stay – if we all leave we could lose the spot and then they'll be done for.'

Fliss nodded, and without a moment's hesitation she took off in the direction of the skate hut, flapping her arms like a ridiculous dizzy pigeon again with Charlie trailing behind her, slipping and sliding on the ice. Only now it wasn't funny any more. Now, a life depended on it.

Betty skidded to her knees, resting by the ever-darkening spot on the ice. She shouldn't be out of breath and yet hers was ragged, catching in her throat. Her heart pounded like an angry fist at a door.

'Hold on!' she shouted, searching the dark water for any sign of life. 'We're getting help! We'll get you out!'

Only silence and emptiness answered her. She willed the hand to appear again, or for any sign the person had heard. But what appeared from the darkness this time wasn't a hand.

A cloud of long yellow hair was floating like weeds under the surface. Betty scrambled back in shock, banging her knee on the cold ice.

She scanned the lake, seeing cheerful skaters in the distance, even people laughing and joking. Fliss had reached the middle now, with Charlie just behind. Soon they would reach the market and raise the alarm.

'It'll be all right, it'll be all right,' Betty repeated, the words hollow in her head. She looked back for the hair in the water . . . but it was gone.

Instead, Betty heard a deep groaning as the surface creaked underneath her. Before it even happened she knew what was coming.

The ice cracked.

Chapter Ten
The Highway Robber and the Fortune Teller

Part Two: Robin

I HATE THEM ALL.

The thought followed me everywhere, through every mindless task. I felt the words with each sweep of a broom, every throw of a hay bale. *I. HATE. THEM. ALL.*

I hated the servants, with their hopeless eyes. Always following orders, ready to obey their master's and mistress's every command. Most of them didn't know how to dream of a different life, and those who did usually gave up. Oh, some of them hated it as much as I did, but it was a different kind of hate. One that made them bitter and miserable and took them to their graves early. My hate was different, because I used it. I *needed* it.

I hated Master Greaves and his wife, too, of course, and

the guests at the hall. Hated them more than the servants. Most of them were lazy and piggish. You'd think that being so rich would afford them some manners or kindness, but it turns out that even the wealthy don't have everything. To them we were invisible, only called for when something was wrong. When a breakfast was late or a boot left unpolished, that's when we were wanted.

The only one I didn't hate was Elora.

I'd known she was special from the start. Even though I was two years older, she took me under her wing from the moment I arrived at Echo Hall, and we'd been inseparable ever since. Even if I'd had anyone, a family of my own, I would have always loved Elora Goode. She was kind, sweet and beautiful. Everyone adored her, except that father of hers who didn't know how to love anyone.

Even so, it had taken me some time to trust her with my secret. We'd always shared everything, right down to the last slice of bread. Whether it was gossip, a ghost story or a whisper overheard at a door, Elora and I shared it all. But secrets are different when telling them could get you killed. And my biggest secret was a deadly one for sure.

The law doesn't look kindly upon thieves. To be caught stealing runs the risk of losing a finger or a hand – if you're lucky. That's for petty thieves – ones caught pickpocketing or stealing a chicken to feed their family. But for violent robbers, who use weapons, the consequences are serious and final. It had been that way for my own father.

I told Elora I'd never known my parents, but that had been a lie. It was easier to say I'd grown up in the care of a servant who'd abandoned me at Echo Hall. If I'd told the truth I'd always have been looked at with suspicion – that's if they'd let me stay at all. My father had been robbing highways since he was fifteen, as part of a notorious gang feared and spoken of for miles. They were called the Bloodhounds, for their seeming ability to sniff out money and wealth. He had learned everything about robbing from them and had a very successful few years plundering highways and taking what, he said, 'the rich didn't deserve'.

I clung to every story of his, making him tell me them over and over again. I memorised every detail. Where to hide, what to look for, what to say. And most importantly, when to run. I heard those stories so many times that soon they felt like memories of my own, and I saw them so clearly in my mind it was hard to believe that I hadn't been there when the action unfolded.

'Always strike at night,' my father told me one evening. 'That's the first rule. Darkness is a highway robber's best friend. It hides us like a cloak; its shadows confuse and play tricks. The second rule is to know your targets.' He tapped his ear and grinned. 'You watch, and listen for the wealth. People who have money will often let you know, whether it's the things they say, or do, or wear. Don't take the risk of robbing five carriages when only one will do. Understand?'

I nodded, excited. *Only target the very rich.* It made perfect sense.

'And the third rule?' I asked, sensing there was more. These things always seemed to come in threes.

My father took a swig of ale and stared thoughtfully into the firelight. He paused for so long that I wondered if perhaps there wasn't a third rule, or if he was going to say something obvious like *Don't get caught.*

'Know when to stop,' he said finally. 'In other words, don't get greedy. No loot is worth your life.'

I felt myself shudder as he said that, and the old superstition about someone 'walking over your grave' popped into my mind. *I'd know when to stop,* I thought. *I wouldn't get greedy.*

My father followed all the rules and we lived well, for a while. He'd been sensible, or so we thought, stashing enough stolen goods to live off for the rest of our lives. By the time he was caught, he hadn't stolen a thing for years. But this, and following his rules, wasn't enough. In the end, he was betrayed by one of his own men who'd drunkenly bragged to the wrong people, and thought giving my father up would save his own neck. It didn't. Both of them were taken to the gallows at High Point Cemetery on a sunny October morning. A pretty, golden, perfect autumn day, the kind where you wouldn't expect horrible things like that to happen. The other two Bloodhounds lived the rest of their days in hiding, with a price on their heads. What became of them I never knew. Perhaps they got away.

What happened to my father could have changed my mind about following in his footsteps. It *should* have changed my mind, but deep down I knew it never would. I was biding my time until I was big enough and strong enough. No one would be afraid of a child, after all. I was happy to wait. It gave me time to plan. Time to add my own rule. Because while my father's rules were good ones, he had overlooked one thing: the thing that got him caught. So rule number four, *my* rule was: *Trust no one.*

I didn't need a gang. I'd be just fine on my own, I decided. A lone wolf, with only my own skin and my own secrets to worry about. And one day when I'd stolen enough, I'd leave and live a comfortable life with servants of my own. I had it all planned.

The first time was the hardest. It was past nine o'clock, and supper was finishing up in the hall with guests either retiring to their rooms or the smoking lounge. I'd told Elora, in front of some kitchen staff, that I was feeling tired and would be early to bed. Once in my room, I'd locked the door and squeezed out of the tiny window above the bed, leaving it on the latch so I could get back in. I was trembling like a cobweb in the wind as I sneaked out in the dark and headed for the stables. I knew when the stablehands were changing over, when there was a gap of ten minutes which allowed me to steal away Master Greaves' horse, Bess, a beautiful black mare with a diamond white flash that, for this night, I blackened with coal dust. I'd befriended her long ago and she liked and trusted me.

My heart was thumping as I took her round the back of the stables and led her away through the woods behind Echo Hall. I saw no one. The woods were quiet and dark, and her hooves and my footsteps made little sound on the mulched leaves underfoot. From a hollow tree trunk I pulled out my father's old tricorn hat, a black mask to hide my eyes . . . and a gleaming silver pistol, also my father's. It was cold and heavy in my hand, the weight of it somehow reassuring me that it would keep me safe.

I'd practised shooting the gun many times, even as a child. But I'd never, ever hit a living target, let alone killed anything. Greaves employed a couple of servants to shoot at rabbits and foxes that came into the kitchen gardens, but what he didn't know was that I was a better shot than both of them put together. One day, thanks to the retirement of the hall's longest serving cook, the servants were given a rare afternoon off. Glenda, the cook, had requested a garden tea and games for the hall's staff, including hide and seek, blind man's buff, musical chairs and so on. But there was also an archery stand.

'Go on, Robin,' Elora had giggled, nudging me. 'Have a turn. You can't be any more terrible than me!'

Oh, I wasn't terrible. Far from it. I could have hit the target ten times over, but I forced myself to miss every time. It hurt my pride, I'll admit. To have to smile politely, pretend to be embarrassed at my dreadful aim and then watch as the other stablehand, Duggan Trent, tutted sympathetically as he collected the arrows and took aim, hoping to impress Elora. He fared only a little better than my deliberately failed attempt, and I had to turn away to hide my smirk.

So to see me now, gliding through the dark on horseback, masked and armed, none of them would have ever believed it was me. And that was just the way I wanted it.

I took the quiet road over Chill Hill and looped around through the thin lanes that bordered Shivershock Lake. Above it, the moon glowed softly behind a thin ribbon of cloud. The lake was still and quiet that night, with hardly a breath of wind to ripple its mirror-like surface. On the other side of it, Echo Hall stood watching me, its lit windows like the yellow eyes of an animal on the hunt.

I remember pausing then, hit by a moment of doubt. If I did this it would change me for ever. True, if I got away with it, I wouldn't have to do it again if I didn't want to, but it would always be there – a secret part of me, a bad thing. If I went through with it I'd be a criminal. If I got caught I could end up dead.

I'd got this far though. I knew if I turned back now I'd regret it. I'd feel like I'd failed my father. I'd still be poor. And more than anything I wanted the excitement.

So I carried on. Past the snow-capped mountains towering in the distance and towards Dead Man's Curve. Bess trotted on, ears twitching every now and then even though the only sounds were the clip-clop of her own hooves and quiet murmurs from me to her.

The road curved sharply and steeply. I already knew the exact spot where I was going to hide. I steered Bess off the road and through a narrow gap in the trees. There, just a stone's throw from the roadside, I turned her around and waited. From my position I could see the road clearly, and when the time was right a quick 'Hup!' would get Bess on to the road in seconds.

In darkness, I waited. Everything was silent, and there was not even a breath of wind. A couple of times Bess let out an impatient snort as if to say, *What are we waiting for?* but I scratched her ears and she settled down.

Very soon there came the rumbling of a carriage and the clip-clop of hooves. My heart began to drum in time to the hoofbeats, eventually overtaking them as they became louder and closer. Through the low branches I saw the carriage, and the white horse that was leading it. Another moment of doubt gripped me. *I could let it go,* I thought. *It could just continue on its journey and I could head back to Echo Hall. Nothing will have changed . . .*

But I wanted things to change, however scary it was. Before I could hesitate again, I dug my heels into Bess, urging her on to the road. We arrived in a clatter of hoofbeats that caused the other horse to rear up in fright. I caught a cry of surprise and fear from the carriage's driver, who fought to get the white horse back under control. I remained still, blocking the road.

'Fool!' the driver yelled, not yet realising what was about to happen. 'We could have crashed!' His voice was high-pitched and scared. He was young, I realised. Twenty or so, only a few years older than me.

From my waistband I whipped out the pistol and pointed it. Its silver barrel gleamed perfectly in the moonlight, glinting as sharply as a knife. I heard the driver gasp, and everything went deathly silent. I had been practising my lowest, manliest growl, but I didn't need it. I didn't need to raise my voice at all.

'Stand and deliver,' I hissed. 'Your money or your life!'

The driver gave a tiny squeak but made no attempt to move. *Good,* I thought. *This would be easy.*

'Stay there,' I commanded, remembering to keep my voice gruff. 'You're surrounded. Right now six men have weapons pointed straight at you from within the trees. Make any move and I promise it will be your last.'

Slowly, and still clutching the horse's reins, the driver raised his hands in surrender. I nudged Bess onwards to the side of the carriage and approached the door. Little did the driver know that he could take off at this instant, but the threat of my imaginary men kept him in place like a piece of washing pegged to a line. I couldn't help feeling smug at the thought – knowing I had all the security of a gang but none of the risks.

The carriage door gleamed, all polished wood and silver handles. A dark curtain covered the window from inside, hiding the passengers from sight. I lifted my gloved hand to knock on the glass, but before I could, the curtain was drawn sharply back and the window lowered in one swift movement.

'I demand to know *why*—?' a shrill voice began, then cut off abruptly. The shocked face of a woman came into view. She gave a little gasp as her eyes settled on me. Her face was white with powder and she wore the kind of sneer that, even as a young servant, I was already weary of. Her body dripped with jewels: diamond droplets dangling from her ears, a ruby at her throat, rings on almost every finger. Her dress alone was probably worth more than what ten servants earned in a year. My resolve deepened.

I held myself still in the saddle, allowing her eyes to roam over me before I spoke. I knew I must look frightening, with my masked face and highwayman's hat, not to mention the long black coat and leather boots which went right up to my thighs. I was tall and slim, and though I wasn't at all muscly, hard work had made me strong. Even so, I'd made sure my coat was two sizes too big and I'd sewn extra layers of padding into it to make my silhouette as burly and menacing as possible. And it seemed to be working.

Of course, the pistol helped. I raised it now, using it to cock my hat a little. The lady's hand flew to her mouth, the sneer dissolving like ice melting into water.

'Please,' she whimpered. 'Don't hurt ...'

'Your money,' I hissed again. 'Or your life!'

'B-but I don't carry any money,' she began. 'My husband ...'

Oh, yes. Her husband. He'd arrived at Echo Hall a few days ago and quickly made himself unpopular with the guests and servants alike. When I'd heard him telling people in the lounge that his wife would be joining him in a few days I'd immediately noted the date and arrival time in my head. I knew where the money would be and when – that was all I needed to know. Or so I thought.

'Mama?'

The little voice almost made me drop the pistol. I lowered it a little, trying to disguise that my hand was now shaking. A small face with wide eyes and a mop of black hair stared back at me. A *child?* I'd had no idea a youngster would be travelling in the carriage. If I'd known, I wouldn't have targeted it. Now it was too late. I couldn't back out. Even if I truly wanted to, the damage was done. The boy was terrified, the gun was in my hand and wealth was almost at my fingertips. All I had to do was take it.

'So you see, I don't have any money,' the woman babbled.

I almost laughed. Did she think I couldn't see the dazzling jewels on display? Did she think darkness was enough to hide them?

'Your rings,' I said calmly. 'Give them to me. The necklace, too.'

'My . . . ? Oh,' said the lady, staring down at her hands as though she had only just noticed them.

Typical, I thought, watching as she removed the jewellery. She was so rich she didn't even have to think about it.

By next week, everything I'd stolen would probably have been replaced.

'What's he doing, Mama?' the boy said slowly, his eyes never leaving my face.

'He's stealing our precious things,' the lady whispered, shoving the rings and necklace at me with trembling fingers.

The child sniffled and fidgeted in his seat. 'Won't Papa be cross?'

'Yes,' his mother whispered. 'He will. Very cross indeed.'

I felt a wicked glow of satisfaction at this, but just as quickly it was snuffed out as the child pushed something towards me with a sob. It was a small raggedy bear, a favourite toy. *A precious thing.*

I almost handed everything back at that moment. What was I doing? The poor boy would probably have nightmares about this for years to come. I hesitated. Then I forced myself to remember why I was doing this. For a different life, a *better* life. The kind of life this child had been born into. I hardened. Suddenly, I didn't feel bad, not even for the child. I mean, yes – it was a horrible thing I was doing, but I'd seen enough spoiled, rich children at Echo Hall to know that most of them grew into spoiled, rich adults. Adults with power over people like me, and Elora.

But not tonight. Tonight, *I* was the one with the power, and I hadn't been prepared for how good it felt. How *addictive*. I didn't want it to end.

'Keep it,' I said, remembering to keep my voice gruff. With

a final warning wave of my pistol, I dug my heels into Bess and galloped away into the trees. When I was far enough in I stashed the jewels, mask and pistol. There was no way I could risk returning to the hall with the stolen goods or my disguise just yet. They could wait in my hiding place until it was safe to move them. And until next time ... because I already knew there would be a next time.

Arriving back at the hall, I returned Bess to the stables with no one any the wiser that she had been gone. I crawled back through my window, realising as I did that someone was thumping on my door.

'Robin!' Elora called from the other side. 'Open up, quick!'

Alarmed, I glanced round the room, remembering to ruffle my sheets and hair, as though I'd just woken from a deep sleep. *Had someone seen me? Were my robbing days over before they'd even begun?* Slowly I opened the door, doing my best to look and sound groggy even though my heart was racing. But no, it was simply Elora with the news of the robbery, which had, of course, spread around the hall as soon as the esteemed lady had arrived.

'You'll never guess what's happened!' Elora whispered. 'A highwayman, right here in Wilderness!'

I almost laughed out loud right then, but it wasn't until a few days, then a few weeks had passed that I let myself relax. After that, it got easier every time and I looked forward to the buzz that the robberies created, humming through the hall like a swarm of bees for days on end.

Time and again I got away with it. I'd fooled them all, and it was only the start. I was giddy with it all, the growing wealth and the thought that almost anything I wanted was there for the taking.

And then I heard about a prize like no other. A crystal ball belonging to a fortune teller, and not just a silly trinket. A real piece of magic that I could use to see into the future . . . future targets, future enemies and dangers. I had never laid eyes on it, and yet the mere thought of it had bewitched me.

I knew I had to have that crystal ball, no matter what.

Chapter Eleven
The Drowning Girl

FREEZING WATER GUSHED OVER BETTY'S KNEES and soaked her skirt and hands. A thick sheet of ice shifted underneath her and separated from the rest, and she felt herself losing her balance as her weight tilted it dangerously to one side. There was another crack as a smaller piece of ice under her foot splintered and broke off. Her skating boot was suddenly under water so cold that Betty felt as though her blood would freeze.

She yelled, clutching for something to hold on to. But on the frozen lake there was nothing, only smooth ice.

Don't panic.

The voice in Betty's head was Granny's. It was calm but slightly cross, as if to say, *'What have you got yourself into this time, Betty Widdershins?'* But while Betty might have been imagining the huffiness of it, she wasn't imagining the words. She was remembering them. After their mother's death Granny had, at least once every winter, told Betty and her sisters what to do if they ever found themselves on thin ice.

'You don't panic,' she'd said, pipe smoke puffing around her. 'You try to stay calm. Thrash about and you'll only break the ice quicker. And the most important thing to remember is to lie flat if you can.'

If you can. Betty understood now why Granny had said that, because it was a very big 'if'. The last thing she wanted to do was lie down on the ice that was threatening to give way beneath her and plunge her into the freezing lake. However, as Granny had explained, by lying down she would spread her weight more evenly and lessen the risk of the ice breaking further. Gritting her chattering teeth, Betty forced herself to do it. She shook uncontrollably as more water flooded on to the frozen surface and soaked into her clothes, making her heavier.

She glanced across the lake. She couldn't see Charlie or Fliss now, but in the distance she noticed that other skaters had stopped. Some were motionless, staring across the lake in Betty's direction. Others were hurrying off the ice. The alarm had been raised – but how long before help arrived?

There. A sled pulled by dogs was speeding towards her. It would soon arrive, she just needed to stay still and hold on ... but her thoughts switched to the hair she had seen under the ice. It had been a girl, she was sure of it. She felt sick and scared, not just for herself. Where was the girl now? Was it already too late? Was she sinking to the bottom of the lake, unable to fight any more?

137

Lying on her tummy, Betty tore her gaze away from the sled and scanned the ice around her. She could feel the large piece she was on softly bobbing on the water. The dark patch, through which she had seen the hand, was an arm's length away. She peered at it, seeing no movement.

'Come on, come on,' she whispered, urging the sled on faster.

Icy fingers slid over Betty's ankle. She cried out, and in that moment of shock and panic all Granny's warnings were forgotten. Betty jerked, trying to sit up . . . and with that the sheet of ice holding her tipped, leaving her with nowhere to go except headlong into the water.

The cold sting of it felt like a cut, then burning. The shock of it took her breath away, made her thrash and scream all at once. Water filled her mouth, then her nose, and white dots of pain danced before her closed eyes like tiny snowflakes.

Don't panic, said Granny again in her head.

Betty forced her eyes open, holding on to what little breath was left in her lungs. The lake around her was dark and murky. Above her the ice was misty, grey and blurry. She tried to kick her legs but they felt too heavy. She couldn't feel the bottom, only the weight of her clothes and the sensation of other things tangling around her legs . . . weeds?

A shadow passed over the ice from above. Muffled voices sounded, but Betty couldn't understand the words. She looked up again, her eyes stinging with the cold lake water. She didn't think she had moved far from the spot she had fallen in, but it was impossible to tell. This was why falling through ice was so dangerous, as Granny had often explained. It wasn't just the cold, although that would be enough to kill you within a short time. But when a person fell in, they didn't always come up in the same spot. They'd often surface somewhere else where the ice was still solid, trapping them underneath it.

Her sisters' faces flashed before Betty's eyes: Fliss and Charlie, followed by Granny and Father. Would she ever see them again, or was this it? Her lungs strained with the need for air and the faces in her mind faded to black. Something tugged at her foot again and she felt herself bob higher in the water. Her hand cut the surface, sliding between chunks of ice to find air. She tried to find something to grip but her fingers wouldn't seem to do what she wanted them to. And now she was tired, and the water didn't feel quite so cold any more. In fact, Betty thought, she could easily just go to sleep.

Her eyelids fluttered, almost closing. Long hair floated past her face, but it wasn't hers. Betty's eyes snapped open. Someone was in the water with her, a figure sinking into the lake's black depths . . .

Strong hands closed round her wrists, hauling her out of the water.

'Easy now,' a deep voice said. 'You're safe.'

Betty coughed. Water, and water, and water. She couldn't feel her body, only the brightness of the winter sky. A sturdy wooden ladder had been placed flat on the ice nearby.

She heard panting, saw dogs clustered near a sled. She focused on them, trying to stay conscious. One had four white legs, another had black ears ... but the edges of her vision were going black now and closing in.

'There's ... someone else,' she managed to croak.

'What? Who?' the voice demanded. 'Steady now, stay still.'

'A girl,' Betty mumbled, losing consciousness. 'She's under the ice ...'

'Jumping jackdaws, Betty!'

Her eyes opened to meet Fliss's red, puffy ones anxiously peering into hers.

'Let *me* see her!' Charlie demanded, elbowing Fliss aside.

She was warm and covered in blankets, inside somewhere with a wooden roof. She remembered the ladder, the dogs, a deep voice. She was safe.

'How long have I been asleep?' asked Betty. 'Where's Granny?'

'We've sent for her,' Fliss replied. She was pale with shock, and her voice was croaky, still on the verge of tears. 'Someone from Echo Hall has gone up Chill Hill to Clarissa's house. You've only been here for about ten minutes.'

'We thought you'd snuffed it,' Charlie said seriously. Her snowman face paint was ruined, streaked with tears.

'The lake marshal got you out,' Fliss added. 'You should have seen it! The sled arrived so quickly, and then the ladder was across the ice—'

'It didn't feel quick,' Betty muttered, her voice sounding thick in her ears. She probably had water in them. 'It felt like for ever. It felt like ... the end.' She shuddered.

'They closed the whole lake,' said Charlie. 'Everyone had to come off the ice.'

'Good,' Betty whispered, unable to shake off the feeling of fear. 'It's not safe.'

'It should have been.' The voice came from behind her sisters, the same deep voice of the person who had pulled Betty out of the lake. She eased herself up and peered over the blankets. A handsome man with black skin and a thick grey beard and hair stared back at her.

'You're the lake marshal?' Betty asked.

He nodded, holding out a hand for her to shake. 'Finn Sharkey's the name.'

Betty gripped his fingers limply. His hand was strong and warm, a bit like Father's. She felt a fleeting pang, a longing for home. 'Thank you for getting me out of the water.'

'You shouldn't have been in there.' His voice was gruff and troubled.

'Ain't her fault!' Charlie blurted out indignantly. 'She didn't want to end up in there!'

'Of course she didn't,' Finn replied. 'That's not what I meant.' He rubbed his beard thoughtfully. 'The ice is tested carefully before people are allowed on to it. It should never have broken the way it did.'

'Then, *how*?' Fliss asked. 'Because it wasn't just Betty under there. We saw someone else! There was a hand under the ice . . .'

A vision of floating blonde hair flashed into Betty's mind. *The girl.*

She sat up straighter. Water leaked from one of her ears, trickling warmly down her neck. She shook her head, but everything was still muffled.

'Yes,' she said. 'The girl! Did you find her?'

'A girl?'

She nodded. 'I saw her. After my sisters went for help. I saw her blonde hair. She was banging against the ice from underneath, she was trapped. That's why I stayed out there.'

A strange look crossed the marshal's face. Betty didn't like it.

'I kept telling them someone else was under there,' Fliss insisted, her eyes wide in horror. 'A *girl?* You saw her, Betty?'

'Yes.' Betty shivered. 'She grabbed me – grabbed my foot!' She remembered the sensation of those cold fingers around her ankle. Had that been the girl, reaching for help? If so, Betty had failed her.

'There are still people out there searching,' the marshal said slowly, not meeting Betty's eyes. 'But when we got you out we found no sign of anyone else.'

Betty went silent as she tried to make sense of this. Suddenly her insides were churning, even though her thoughts were slow and muddied. 'No . . . no one else?' she croaked.

'No. And no reports of anyone missing. All the skaters were accounted for. If anyone had had an accident or fallen in, well – we'd know about it.'

'But that doesn't make sense!' Charlie interrupted. 'We saw it! We saw the hand. That must have been what broke the ice and made Betty fall!'

A cold feeling of dread was spreading through Betty, like it had seeped into her bones. She thought of the hand appearing under the thinning ice, and those icy fingers clutching at her ankle again. If there had been no one else in the lake, then there could only be one explanation for what she and her sisters had seen.

'Has there . . . has there ever been an accident in the lake?' she asked quietly. 'Has anyone ever drowned in it?'

Fliss gave a frightened gasp. 'Betty! Are you suggesting that what we saw was a . . . a *ghost*?'

Betty bit her lip, thinking of the blonde hair swirling under the water like pondweed. The desperate hand, reaching out to them.

'Well, we've seen 'em before,' said Charlie, matter-of-factly.

There was a brief silence as the three girls considered their past adventures.

Betty turned to the marshal expectantly. 'You haven't answered my question. Has anyone ever died in Shivershock Lake?'

Finn hesitated. 'Well, there's the story of the highwayman, which I'm sure you'll have heard about. His sweetheart,

Elora, also froze to death within the trees beside the lake. And a father and son drowned, but that was some years after, in a fishing accident.'

'Not a girl, then?' Betty asked, feeling the chill on her skin grow icier still.

'No, but . . .' He paused, rubbing his chin.

'Go on,' Betty urged, sensing something big was coming.

'There've been sightings before, a few times,' he said reluctantly. 'People skating have seen things under thawing patches of ice, a face or a hand, just like you saw. Locals call her the Drowning Girl, but no one knows who she is.'

His voice had lowered to a whisper. Betty found herself leaning closer, trying to catch every word. The water in her ears made his words sound muffled, as though they were also coming from underwater.

'But there must be some explanation,' she pressed, grabbing on to this new mystery. 'Surely someone would have missed her, or been searching for her?'

The marshal reached up and touched a small silver pendant hanging from a leather strap round his neck, and the way he did it reminded Betty of Granny and how she touched her horseshoes and charms when she was trying to ward off bad luck. The sight of it unsettled her. Surely this big, burly man wasn't scared?

Finn, looking increasingly uncomfortable, didn't answer. Instead he got up. 'I'll leave you to rest a little longer.' He left the girls alone in the small wooden hut, closing the door behind him to an unsettled atmosphere.

The moment he was gone Betty threw back the blankets, feeling a cold draught as the air hit her still-damp clothes.

'Come on,' she said. She attempted to stand up but was strangely off-balance, and ended up plonking down again.

'Come on *where?*' Fliss demanded. 'You're going nowhere, Betty Widdershins. You nearly drowned, for crow's sake!'

'We need to start asking questions,' Betty argued feebly, annoyed with herself. 'I have to find out who that girl in the lake was.'

'You do *not* have to find out,' said Fliss at once. 'In fact, that's the very opposite of what you should do, which is stay away from that deadly lake and whatever ghosts and ghouls might be lurking in it!'

'You sound just like Granny,' Betty said, rolling her eyes.

'I don't care,' said Fliss. 'All I know is that that lake gives me the heebie-jeebies, and . . . and . . .' She sniffed suddenly. 'And I nearly lost my sister today.'

'But that's just it,' said Betty. 'I could have died because of what we saw on the lake. The next person might not be so lucky! What if the Drowning Girl is trying to tell us something? We could help solve the mystery of who she is and what she wants! And then she won't haunt anyone else.'

'Maybe she wanted to drown you,' Fliss said darkly. 'You said she grabbed your ankle – did she pull you under the water?'

'I . . .' Betty paused, unsure. 'I don't think so. It didn't feel

145

that way. It seemed more like she was grabbing for anything or anyone who could help.' As she said this she wondered if it were true. Could the icy fingers have been trying to pull Betty to her death? It had all happened so quickly, it was hard to know. 'Wait,' she said, suddenly noticing something. 'Where's my other ice skate?'

'At the bottom of Shivershock Lake, probably,' said Fliss, her voice softer now. 'You weren't wearing it when they pulled you out. It must have come off when you went in.' She nibbled her lower lip, looking concerned. 'I do hope the man gives you both your boots back.'

'He will,' Charlie said. 'If he doesn't, we'll set Granny on him.'

'Set Granny on who?' a voice boomed. The door flew open, startling them all, and then Granny was stomping into the log cabin, breathing heavily and reeking of pipe smoke. 'Oh, Betty Widdershins, what have you gone and done now?' she thundered, pulling Betty into a fierce hug which almost crushed her.

'I didn't do anything, Granny,' Betty protested. 'I just fell through the ice!'

'"*Just fell through the ice!*"' Granny squeezed even harder, and Betty could feel that under the anger her grandmother was trembling with shock and fright. 'You silly, silly girl! And *you*!' She rounded on Fliss, her eyes wild. 'You're supposed to be the sensible one. What on earth were you thinking, allowing your sisters on to a frozen lake? How many times have I told you *what happened to your mother?*'

There was a dreadful silence which was broken only by a sob from Fliss.

'I'm s-sorry, Granny,' she whispered, wiping away tears. 'You're right – I knew you'd be cross. It's all my fault.'

'Ain't,' Charlie said in a small voice. 'We pestered Fliss to let us go ice skating.'

'It was an accident,' Betty added, feeling wretched. *Poor Granny.* Betty didn't think she'd ever seen her so frightened. 'Please don't blame Fliss – it wasn't her fault and it won't happen again. We'll keep off the lake, I promise.'

'You're darned right you'll keep off the lake,' Granny growled, still fuming. 'Because we're leaving!'

Chapter Twelve
A Little Bit of Magic

'PLEASE, GRANNY,' BETTY BEGGED AGAIN. 'Don't make us go home. It really wasn't anyone's fault, and there's so much we'd still like to do here. The winter market is wonderful – we can take you there! Please?'

'*Please!*' Charlie echoed.

'And the masked ball is coming up, too,' Fliss added, starting to sniffle now at the thought of missing out on this.

But Granny was having none of it. 'You know, they couldn't find me at first,' she said. 'They knocked at Clarissa's but I'd popped out to get groceries. By the time they caught up with me I'd already seen that something was going on down at the lake, that a girl had fallen through the ice.' She held a wrinkled hand over her heart. 'And somehow, *somehow*, I just knew, in here, that it was one of you. Because no matter where you go, the three of you always manage to find trouble. I don't know how, but you do.'

'That's not fair,' Betty said quietly. 'I'd say that trouble usually finds us.'

'What if the worst had happened?' Granny went on, her voice cracking with emotion. 'If I'd had to go back to your father, with only two of you? What would I tell him?'

'But it didn't. I'm fine, really I am!'

Granny didn't answer. Her lips snapped shut and remained that way as she marched them all the way back to Echo Hall, stopping only at the ice-skate hut to retrieve Betty's boots.

'Anyway,' Betty panted, as they climbed the stairs at the hall, 'what about Clarissa? If we leave now, how will she manage?'

'Clarissa can come back to Pendlewick with us,' Granny said tartly. 'It's not ideal, but then neither is what's just happened to you. And do stop sniffling, Felicity,' she added, tutting at Fliss. 'Go and give your nose a good blow.'

Fliss nodded mournfully and tried to sniff more quietly as she unlocked the door to their room. They went in and Granny wrinkled her nose, glancing around.

'Smells a bit damp in here. And those flowers need throwing out.' She moved to the window and looked out over the square, her eyes narrowing at the lake in the distance. 'Right. Into bed, Betty. You've had a nasty shock and probably swallowed all kinds of germs in that water. You need to rest. I'll bring you something to eat in an hour or two.'

'I'm not hungry,' Betty said glumly, changing into her nightdress and sinking into the cold bedsheets. She wasn't tired either. Her thoughts were whirling, and the last thing she wanted to do was sit in bed, especially if this was to be her last day in Wilderness. But they had made Granny angry enough for one day, so she decided it was best to do as she was told. 'Granny, please say you'll at least *think* about staying a bit longer?'

Granny snorted, but when she spoke next some of the temper had left her, and she seemed calmer now Betty was safely in bed. 'I'll think about it,' she said finally, tucking the sheets around Betty and kissing her hard on the forehead. 'We won't be going anywhere tonight, that's for sure. I want you rested and properly warmed up before we travel. Charlie and Fliss, you come with me. I'm making soup for Clarissa, so you can help me chop the vegetables. That should keep you out of mischief.'

'Yes, Granny,' Fliss said meekly.

Charlie said nothing, but stuck out her bottom lip. Food was for eating, not cooking!

'Good,' said Granny briskly. 'Fliss, wash your face. You, too, Charlie – get that muck off. I'll see you both downstairs in five minutes.'

She left them alone, her stomping footsteps fading away down the corridor.

Betty woke to find Fliss leaning over her. For a moment she was utterly confused and couldn't remember where she was. Then as the unfamiliar room came into focus everything

150

flooded back to her in a rush: Echo Hall, the frozen lake, the ghostly girl . . .

'Well, good afternoon, sleepyhead,' Fliss said, opening the curtains a little to allow some thin light in. 'Although there's not much of the afternoon left.'

'I feel like I've been sleeping for hours,' Betty croaked. Her mouth had never felt so dry and her whole body ached like she were coming down with the flu.

'You have, silly,' said Charlie, plonking herself next to Betty on the bed. She offered Betty a glass of water, which she gulped down gratefully.

'Then how can it still be the afternoon?' Betty groaned, pulling herself up into a sitting position.

Fliss and Charlie glanced at each other.

'Betty,' Fliss said gently. 'You slept all through yesterday afternoon and this morning. It's the next day.'

'The next . . . ?' Betty stared at them, noticing for the first time that her sisters were dressed differently to how they had been before. 'But I didn't wake up once! You really mean I've lost a day?'

Charlie nodded. 'Granny's been backwards and forwards all day. She said you stayed fast asleep the whole time, and that you were muttering about ice and sinking to the bottom of the lake.'

'I *was*?' Betty felt unsettled at hearing this. She didn't remember a thing, not stirring, dreaming, nothing. Her sleep had felt like being in a black void, and the thought of losing a whole day without knowing it was the worst part of all. 'What have you two been doing all day?'

'We had another poke round the winter market,' said Charlie. 'But it wasn't much fun without you,' she added loyally. 'Granny's been with us all day, even though we promised to behave—'

'And they've closed off the lake, obviously,' Fliss interrupted. 'So no one can go skating on it.'

'Is Granny still saying we have to go home?' asked Betty. She was foggy with sleep but she knew she didn't want to return to Pendlewick. Not yet, when there were so many unanswered questions about Wilderness.

'Yes,' Fliss replied. 'She's not budging. The only reason we're still here is because you were resting and she didn't want to disturb you. She's trying to arrange a carriage back first thing tomorrow. Anyway, perhaps it's a good thing we're leaving. Whatever happened down at the lake, we shouldn't get mixed up in it.'

'It feels as though we already *are* mixed up in it,' Betty argued, sitting up. 'I could have drowned there, right next to where Elora died. Wouldn't you at least like to know what went on? And who that girl in the water was?'

'Not really,' Fliss muttered.

'Maybe Granny will change her mind?' Charlie said, chewing one of her pigtails.

Betty wasn't convinced. She had only seen her grandmother rattled like that a handful of times, and Granny always said exactly what she thought. But the idea of going home and leaving behind the unsolved mysteries of Wilderness was starting to feel rather unbearable to Betty. She felt as though she were at the centre of it all, with the mystery deepening around her. She simply had to find out more if she could. 'Well, don't say anything else to Granny until she's had a couple of whiskeys. She'll be in a better mood after that.'

'Granny's right to be worried,' Fliss said. 'There's something creepy about this place, and I should have known something bad was going to happen. I had a . . . a warning.'

'What kind of warning?' asked Betty, before suddenly realising what her sister meant. 'Hang on – you're not talking about that fortune teller, are you?'

'That's exactly what I'm talking about,' Fliss replied unhappily. 'A ghostly voice called out "Betty". I wasn't sure if it meant you or Granny, but obviously I know now. Lady Fortuna said you might need my help and she was right!'

'I helped, too,' said Charlie. 'Didn't I, Fliss?'

'Yes, poppet,' Fliss said.

Betty clenched her fists under the covers. Blast Lady Fortuna and her lies! She needed Fliss on her side – if anyone could persuade Granny to let them stay, it was Fliss with her charm. Betty so very badly wanted to tell the truth about what she had heard but right then she didn't think she could bear Fliss being cross and upset, as well as Granny. She would tell her later, she decided guiltily. Once everyone had had a chance to calm down.

'We'd better get back to Clarissa's,' said Fliss, with a heavy sigh. 'Back to being bossed about every five minutes. Can you believe she made me polish every pair of her boots? It's not even as if she can walk far at the moment!'

'And she keeps telling me not to say "ain't",' Charlie added, scowling. 'Well, I ain't going to!'

Betty couldn't help grinning.

'Granny'll be pleased to hear you're awake, anyway,' said Fliss, putting on her scarf.

'I'll come with you,' said Betty, keen to pester Granny to stay put in Wilderness a little longer. But as she threw back the covers a crafty idea came to her. It would be far easier to avoid travelling back if she simply stayed where she was – in bed. And she was still rather foggy-headed. Perhaps a longer nap would help to clear it.

'Actually, I'll stay here,' she said. 'My head still feels a bit woozy.'

Fliss gave her a suspicious look. 'You wouldn't just be saying that to avoid going home, would you, Betty?'

'Of course not,' Betty fibbed, although she did feel a little guilty.

'Hmm,' said Fliss. 'I'll leave you the key, then.' She rounded up Charlie to leave. 'Remember to lock the door after we're gone. Granny said she'd pop back at around half past five to bring you to Clarissa's for supper. She also asked for a tray to be sent up to you earlier, but it looks as though they forgot. The service in this place is getting shoddier and shoddier!'

Shortly after, her sisters left and Betty locked up, leaving the key in the door. She found a book she had packed in the trunk and snuggled under the bedcovers with it, supposing she should at least try to do as Granny had told her if they were to have any chance of staying. She read a couple of chapters and even managed to enjoy the rare silence. Quiet was not something the Widdershins were used to, having grown up in a pub. There were a few noises – footsteps of other guests passing the room and voices once or twice – but mainly Betty heard nothing except the words in her head. Eventually, with the wintry light from the window fading, she felt herself becoming drowsier. The shadows in the room stretched and deepened.

I'll just rest my eyes for a moment, she thought, placing the book face down on the bed. *Five minutes, that's all.*

The room was dim when she awoke, the window just a pale slash of dark grey. Light footsteps crossed the floor, and Betty felt the weight of something being placed at the foot of the bed. It was too light-footed to be Granny – her sisters must have come back.

'Fliss?' she muttered groggily. 'Charlie? Is that you?' She lifted her head off the pillow and shook it a little, wishing the water in her ears would clear. They felt more muffled than ever. *And why was it suddenly so cold in here?*

She thought she could hear a low voice muttering, but the water in her ears was making it hard to understand the words. It sounded like 'shouldn't have ... shouldn't ...'

A dark figure was by the window. Betty blinked and squinted through the gloom, recognising the uniform of Echo Hall's maids. One of them must have brought her something to eat, as Granny had requested.

'Thank you,' said Betty, as the figure moved soundlessly to the door. The person – a young woman – had her head bowed and didn't look up or answer. Instead, she headed for the closed door ...

... and walked straight through it.

The hairs on Betty's arms and the back of her neck stood up, and an icy shiver went from the tips of her toes right up to her scalp. She shrank into a tiny ball under the bedcovers, not daring to move.

'I was awake,' she whispered to herself. 'I *was*. I didn't dream it.'

Seconds turned into minutes, but nothing else happened. The room grew colder still until finally Betty forced herself to turn her head towards the window. It was wide open and moving slightly, not even on the catch. It was as though someone had thrown it wide in a hurry and not bothered to close it.

Slowly, heart racing, Betty eased herself out of bed and stood up. Her breath misted the icy air and, after spending so long in bed, she felt wobbly on her feet. She crossed to the window and closed it with a shaky hand, wincing at the loud bang it made and at the same moment noticing that the top drawer of the chest was open, its contents spilling on to the floor. Just like they had been yesterday morning.

Betty stared at it, her fear deepening. She was certain the window had been shut when her sisters had left earlier, and she *knew* the drawer had been closed. More bravely than she felt, Betty strode over to the door and tried the handle. It was locked, and the key was still in the hole where she had left it. So how could someone walk through a closed, locked door?

Elora. The name came into her head, unbidden.

Shivering, Betty lit the lamp. The warm glow of the light made her feel less afraid, and under the shock she couldn't help feeling a buzz of excitement. *A ghost!* A real ghost in their room. The mysteries of Echo Hall seemed to be deepening like shadows, and if there was one thing Betty refused to ignore it was a mystery. Yet if they returned to Pendlewick tomorrow her chance to solve it would be lost.

It was then she remembered feeling a weight at the end of the bed as she'd woken. She turned, for a moment thinking she had been mistaken. Then she saw it: dark leather between the rumpled blankets. She reached out and folded back the covers, already knowing what it was.

An ice skate, just like the one she had lost yesterday. Which, according to what Fliss had said, should have been at the bottom of Shivershock Lake. So how was it possible that it was now here, on her bed?

Betty touched her fingers to the leather. It was icy cold, the laces heavy and wet. Droplets of water rested on the blade and more had soaked into the blanket underneath. It was as though the skate had just been pulled out of the lake. More than that, it was proof Betty hadn't imagined the figure in the room. Someone, or rather some*thing*, had been there.

Betty knew she couldn't stay here a moment longer. And while she was prepared to admit that this was partly because she was more than a little spooked, it was also because she wanted a chance to snoop round the hall while Granny was safely out of the way. Something very strange was going on here in Wilderness, and particularly at Echo Hall.

'And I'm going to find out what it is,' Betty whispered to herself.

She also knew exactly how she was going to do it without raising any suspicion. From the drawers she took out the wooden nesting dolls, the Widdershins' magical family heirloom. Opening them up, she removed the smaller painted doll and separated its two halves. Then, as she'd done many times before, she pulled out one of her brown frizzy hairs and placed it inside the second doll before replacing the top half and hiding it away in the largest doll once more. Carefully, she twisted the two halves of the outer doll so that the painted edges were perfectly aligned, then checked the mirror inside the wardrobe.

Though Betty stood in front of it, the looking glass reflected an empty room back at her. She was now completely invisible.

Chapter Thirteen
Room Nine

THERE WERE QUITE A LOT OF THINGS YOU could do in a place where no one could see you. You could clap as hard as you wanted in an empty corridor, so that the sounds echoed back off the high ceilings like slaps. You could swing your leg over the curved wooden banisters of the grand staircase and slide all the way down them like you were riding a broomstick. You could watch people picking their noses and scratching in places that weren't polite because they thought they were alone. You could even help yourself to as many chocolate eclairs as you wanted from the dinner buffet without other guests thinking you were greedy.

Betty did all these things and a few more at that. With the weight of the iron key in one pocket and the nesting dolls in another, she headed through Echo Hall towards the dining room. The large clock on the stairs told her it was just coming up to four o'clock, and a few guests and sellers, including the handsome ice sculptor, were taking tea. After helping herself to her third eclair, Betty headed for the same table she and her sisters had been seated at on the first evening. It was the little one by the back wall, right next to several framed pictures and newspaper cut-outs about Jack Frost, the highwayman of Wilderness.

But the table wasn't empty. Two old ladies were sitting at it with plates piled high with scones, jam and cream, and an enormous pot of tea between them. There were still two seats free, so Betty decided to slide carefully into one of them while she peered at the pictures on the wall. After the drama at the lake and the excitement of whooshing down the stair banisters she felt a little dizzy, probably not helped by the water still in her ears. Fortunately the old ladies seemed none the wiser that there was an invisible guest at their table.

Searching the wall, Betty quickly found one of the things she was looking for: the old photograph of three people on the steps of Echo Hall. There was a mousy-looking woman, a surly dark-haired man and a pale teenage girl with an equally unhappy expression. Betty leaned in closer and squinted. The picture was in black-and-white and very old and grainy, so it was hard to see it clearly, but she could make out that the girl's frown mirrored the man's exactly.

She read the caption under the photograph: *Servant Elora Goode and her family at Echo Hall.*

Elora.

It was said that she haunted the hall, but how much of it?

Had it been Elora's ghost that had walked in and out through a locked door earlier?

She caught sight of a handwritten piece and remembered the letter Fliss had begun to describe, just before Lady Fortuna and her teacup had caused the commotion. It was a letter from another servant to the management at the hall, explaining why she no longer wanted to work there. It looked newer than the Jack Frost newspaper cutting but the date on it revealed it had been written more than twenty years ago. Betty read it silently, momentarily distracted by the old ladies' excited conversation.

'Better not have *too* many of these custard tarts or I'll never fit into my costume for the masked ball.'

'Oh, just one more – this pastry is so buttery!'

The letter was smudged in places, and the spelling was a bit 'iffy', as Granny would say, but Betty was able to understand it perfectly well.

Deer Sir,

Unforchunitlee I have had enuff. I carnt carry on workin in a place like this. It is dredfull for my nerves and I am too young to be gettin grey hares the way I am. I did ask you if I can be put on a diffrent job, in the kichin, praps, insted of cleanin the rooms – well, one room in perticular witch is room 9 as you know. If you ask me, that room shood not be used for gests no more. All it brings is complaynts about the window bein opened, wisperin voices and things bein moved abowt. It also goes freezin cold for no reason. And it ain't just that room, it's the hole bleedin corridor.

I am not the only one who's seen the ghost of Elora Goode along there. Sobbin and wailin, with eyes as black as the coal in her bucket, and walkin threw walls and doors. Its only a matter of time till somone else sees her threw that window and then you will have blood on your hands. Peeple have not foregot abowt the other times.

So I must thank you for the hopperchewnittee, but my sister has found me a new job on a farm.

Yours sinseerly,
Dorinda Hewitt

Betty read the letter twice, her eyes lingering on the middle section. *The window being opened, things being moved about, the temperature dropping to freezing . . .* These were all the things that had been happening in *their* room! But they were in room six, and the letter clearly said the ghostly goings-on were in room nine.

And as for the 'walking through walls and doors', Betty felt a jolt as she remembered the maid with the coal scuttle, who'd seemingly vanished through the wall next to the brass lamp. Now she felt certain that she hadn't been mistaken about what she'd seen. Had that been Elora, too?

'Meddling magpies,' Betty whispered to herself. She

stared at the old photograph once more, but it was too faded and grainy to make out properly. There was no way to tell whether the girl in the picture resembled the one she had seen on that first day, especially when she'd barely glimpsed the maid's face.

She scanned the rest of the wall, noticing a picture of Shivershock Lake and the frozen trees that bordered it. It reminded her of the girl she'd seen under the ice. *The Drowning Girl*, that's what Finn Sharkey had called her. It was odd, very odd, that it had happened so close to the spot where Elora had been found, and now she couldn't help wondering if there was a connection. Her mind wandered uneasily back to what Clarissa had said about the sighting of Elora's ghost at the window, and how it was believed to lead to a loved one dying. What if ... what if the Drowning Girl *was* Elora?

There was nothing else for Betty in the dining room, and now she wanted to make the most of the time she had before Granny and her sisters returned to get her. If Granny learned Betty was up and out of bed she'd have them all straight on the road back to Pendlewick – and Fliss wouldn't approve of Betty's investigations into the ghostly goings-on, either.

Unfortunately, it was just as she was about to get up that the old lady sitting next to her decided to push her chair back, blocking Betty's exit, as she picked up her bag from under the table.

Betty waited impatiently as the lady rummaged through

her bag to retrieve a toothpick. However, they both got an enormous shock when, instead of placing the bag back at her feet, the old girl plonked it straight on to the seat next to her – or rather, straight on to the invisible Betty's lap.

'They should really have these on the tables,' she was saying, waving the toothpick about. '*Oh!*'

Betty stared down speechlessly at the bag which was now balancing on her knees. The problem was that to everyone apart from Betty it didn't look as though it was balanced on anything. It looked like it was floating several inches above the seat.

'Crumbs!' the lady exclaimed, managing to spray crumbs from her mouth across the table at the same time. 'Would you look at that!'

Her friend peered across the table, and a butter knife clattered to her plate.

'I'm sure there was nothing on that chair,' the lady said, grabbing the bag from Betty's lap. 'I was right, see?' She pushed the bag down again, more firmly this time.

'Ouch!' said Betty, unable to help it. The word just popped out.

The lady gave a squeal and shrank back in her chair. Several diners looked over. Very carefully she reached out a long, knobbly finger and was about to poke Betty's leg with it – but Betty was faster. She lifted the bag up and batted the poking hand away, knowing very well that although the dolls kept her invisible, she could still be felt.

'OH!' screeched the lady. 'A ghost!'

Betty shot back in the chair, scraping it loudly across the floor, and ran.

'Follow that bag!' someone yelled. 'Stop! Ghost thief!'

Ghost thief? She still had the bag! Betty dumped it on to a nearby empty table, dodging a man who had been charging towards her with a silver soup ladle. He stopped abruptly and for some reason smacked the bag with the ladle, allowing Betty to move past him undetected.

For the second time since she had arrived, Betty left the dining room in a commotion. In the entrance hall, Sonny's mother was polishing the countertop half-heartedly and staring into space as Betty swept past her.

She was about to head back upstairs when she spotted a small door with a sign above it that said STAFF ONLY. The smells of food and laundry seemed to be coming from it, and the letter she had just read ran through her mind again. If anyone would know things about a place, who better than the people who worked there? Now Betty had accidentally stirred things up in the dining room, perhaps it would spark a conversation about Echo Hall's ghosts.

Her whirling thoughts returned to the letter she had read. If Elora's ghost was doing the same things, and had been for nearly forty years, then it made sense that she was carrying out those things in a certain order, starting with going into the guests' rooms and finishing by walking through the wall. Perhaps it would be worth Betty investigating that part of the corridor again, and trying to make sense of it all.

A short way into the servants' corridor, the age of the hall started to show. Paint peeled and bubbled, floor tiles were cracked and window catches were rusted. The walkway was narrower here, and twice Betty had to step quickly aside when staff members emerged from nearby doorways: first a maid with a pile of fresh towels and then a porter on his way somewhere in a hurry. She flattened herself against the cold brick wall as they passed, so close she felt the swish of the maid's skirts and smelled the oil on the porter's greased-back hair.

At the end of the corridor Betty found a huge kitchen, bustling with noise and activity. Cooks chopped, stirred and shouted to each other through clouds of steam and for a moment Betty thought better of lurking around any longer. It seemed too busy for any of them to have time to gossip and tell ghost stories. Then someone entered the kitchen from another door at the opposite end in a flurry of drama and excitement.

'Ghost in the dining room!' the young man announced, his face flushed and sweaty. He pushed his large spectacles up his nose and smoothed down his tufty hair. 'Lots of witnesses this time – a bag floating in mid-air!'

'Not Elora's usual style,' commented a stocky cook who was kneading a mound of pastry. 'And right after that teacup silliness yesterday, too!'

A couple of people laughed, but an older woman paused

from peeling potatoes and wagged a mud-speckled finger. Her hands were like knobbly brown twigs, bent up from years of hard work, and she had hair as white as snow and as puffy as candyfloss. 'Cold weather's a-comin',' she said. 'Mark my words. Always starts this way, ever since I been here. She starts makin' her presence felt, slowly at first. A sightin' in the corridors upstairs, things bein' moved round ... we're in for bad weather. A cold snap.' She flicked a bit of potato peel into the bin. 'When I were younger, just after it all happened, we had a sayin':

'"When Elora's ghost's about

Wrap up warm and don't go out."'

'Mildred's right,' someone else chimed in. 'Did you hear about what happened on the lake yesterday? Someone went through the ice. A young girl, a guest at the hall, apparently. Reckoned they saw someone under the frozen water – the Drowning Girl. Some people believe it's Elora, don't they?'

Mildred nodded. 'The description fits all right. Long blonde hair under the ice, that's what folk have witnessed. And everyone who saw Elora Goode said she had the most beautiful golden curls you've ever seen. No one else it could be, if you ask me.'

Betty found she was holding a breath. *Long blonde hair under the ice . . . the most beautiful golden curls you've ever seen.*

'Oh, people think it's romantic and all,' Mildred went on. 'Elora ridin' out into the night searchin' for her lost love by the lake and freezin' to death rather than return without him, but . . .' She trailed off thoughtfully. 'Perhaps she didn't freeze. Perhaps she fell into the lake too, and drowned. I always thought that friend of hers knew more than she was sayin'.'

'What friend?' the stocky cook asked. 'Someone who still works here?'

But Mildred's lips clamped up tightly. 'Not my place to say.'

'Ooh,' said a young girl, who was scrubbing dishes in the sink and not doing a very good job of it from what Betty could see. She guessed the girl was new, likely one of the extra staff brought in to help while the market was on. 'Have you ever seen her?' the girl asked. 'Elora, I mean?'

'Once or twice,' the old woman replied, slicing a potato into four before starting on another. 'Up near room nine, the usual spot. Both times she vanished, walkin' straight through that wall at the end of the hall. Plenty others seen it, too – usually only the ones who are brave or stupid enough to stick around a while.'

At this, Betty wished she could ask the question which was burning on her lips. Perhaps she *could* ask it: there were so many people in the kitchen getting on with their work, talking over each other, and so many pots hissing or clanging . . . Would any of them notice a new voice among them?

What the heck, thought Betty. *I might not get another chance.*

'What's on the other side of the wall, though?' she asked, making her voice sound slightly deeper and more grown-up.

'Oh, it was an old staircase,' Mildred replied without looking up. 'The servants used it years ago so they didn't get in the guests' way. After Elora died, there were stories about her ghost seen hurryin' down the stairs in the dead of night, so people started avoidin' it. And then one day, another young servant fell down them and badly injured himself. Apparently he'd seen Elora weepin' on the stairs and it gave him such a fright he'd slipped and fallen.'

The kitchen had gone much quieter now. Many of the staff had paused in their work to listen to Mildred, and Betty guessed that, like her, this was the first time they had heard this information.

'And then, of course,' Mildred went on, 'they built another part on to the back of the hall to make it bigger, more rooms.' She sniffed. 'Greedy, if you ask me. So, the old staircase was done away with and a wall was built in its place. And now, whatever path Elora follows, it's a ghostly one that exists only in her world, not in ours.'

Mildred's words sent a thrill though Betty that was half horror and half excitement. It was eerie to think of Elora following a ghostly route that was locked in the past, yet at the same time frustrating. How could she follow and see where the phantom went if there was no way through the wall?

Betty lingered a couple of minutes longer but the conversation soon shifted from ghostly girls to how many pies were needed for the masked ball the following evening, and whether the winter berry garlands could be stored outside in the kitchen gardens to keep them fresh. On the way back through the corridor she noticed a little door she hadn't seen on the way in. Above it were the words: HOLDING CELL.

A *cell?* Betty was immediately curious. What on earth was a cell doing here? She checked no one was coming and then tried the door. It swung open to reveal a dark, cobwebbed walkway with a low ceiling. At the end of it, sure enough, there was a tiny cell which held only an iron bed and a bucket for unmentionables. A barred window was set high above it, barely wide enough for a child to squeeze through.

Was it unusual for a hall like this to have a cell? Betty wondered. She supposed not, seeing as it was in such an isolated place. She remembered the Bootleg Beak lock-up back on Crowstone – she had played near there, growing up (and Granny had once spent a night inside). And she knew that ships often had cells for keeping lawbreaking or unruly passengers in until they reached land. All the same, the cell, and these old, twisting servant corridors were a little creepy.

Betty returned upstairs, passing Mrs Chambers on the front desk again. She had finished polishing it and was staring into space with the same sad expression she always wore. Betty wondered again why she stayed at the hall if she was so unhappy here.

It was coming up to five o'clock as she hurried up the grand staircase. Good, thought Betty. Still half an hour before Granny was due to collect her. She passed a few people on their way down for supper, including a family whose parents were so busy chatting that they didn't notice their older child pinching the younger one when they were not looking. Unable to help herself, Betty leaned close to the girl's ear and whispered, 'Be kind to your brother. The fairies are watching!' The girl stopped what she was doing and immediately patted her brother's curly head, looking around in wonder.

The upstairs was quiet and empty. Only Betty's invisible footsteps echoed off the wooden floor. She decided to have a quick look at the end of the corridor where she had seen the maid vanish. At least now, if Granny turned up earlier than expected, Betty would easily hear her stomping along and could return to the room first if she needed to. She felt a little nervous now, being up here by herself, especially after hearing about the servant who had been given a fright by the ghostly figure of Elora. Despite so many people being in the hall, this floor was strangely deserted and the ghostly stories and the distorted sounds of Betty's own footsteps echoing back to her didn't help matters.

She walked towards the spot where the brass lamp was. On the way she passed a tray with a covered plate that had been left near the same spot the Widdershins' trunk had been delivered to. Arriving at the wall, she reached out and touched the crack running from top to bottom, then gave it a tap with her knuckles. It sounded solid enough, but her fingers caught a light draught coming through. At the same time she thought she heard something: a faint, high-pitched sort of noise. Betty put her ear to the wall, listening. There it was again, from behind the wall – she was sure of it.

'Blast this water in my ears,' she muttered crossly, switching sides. Her left ear wasn't quite so bad. The sound was a little louder now, and with a shock she realised what it sounded like: someone crying softly. The old woman's words floated back to her:

Apparently he'd seen Elora weepin' on the stairs . . .

Betty backed away from the wall. Half of her wanted to run, the other half wanted to stay exactly where she was and find out more. This must be where the old staircase was, according to Mildred. And now Betty lingered over the other things the old cook had said. *Was* the Drowning Girl actually Elora? Mildred seemed to think so, but Finn Sharkey insisted she'd been found within the icicled grotto of trees. What was the truth?

The sound of footsteps snapped her out of her wonderings. Betty looked round. The corridor was still empty but someone was heading that way and would soon round the corner. Granny? No – two people. There was more than one set of footsteps and she could now hear low voices.

Lady Fortuna and Mr Sneed appeared at the opposite end of the corridor, sweeping along quickly beside each other. Normally Betty wouldn't have thought anything of it, but the way they were both whispering and looking about themselves made her immediately suspicious. What were they up to?

They seemed to be checking door numbers, and then

they stopped outside one about halfway down the corridor, not far from where Betty stood. With a jolt of surprise she realised it was the door to room six, where she and her sisters were staying!

What the heck are they playing at? she wondered, creeping closer. She drew level with the tray left on the floor and paused there. She was close enough to hear them and watch them. Any closer, and Echo Hall might live up to its name and give her away.

'Are you sure it's this one?' Lady Fortuna hissed, as Mr Sneed ferreted around in his pocket for something.

'Very sure,' he replied, checking over his shoulders once more.

She narrowed her eyes. 'But this is room six. All the stories of the haunting say it's number nine.'

From under the moustache a sly smile appeared, and Lady Fortuna's accomplice reached out for the brass '6' on Betty's door. In one quick movement he slid it up and changed its position on the door.

'Missing screw,' he explained, the smile broadening to a grin. 'This *is* room nine.'

Chapter Fourteen
Lady Fortuna's Secret

BETTY'S KNEES SUDDENLY FELT VERY WOBBLY indeed. *Room nine? They had been staying in room nine all this time and not realised?* But as she stared at the brass door number she knew it was true. Mr Sneed let it drop and it fell back in place, swinging round to hang upside down again as a number six.

Only now did Betty think to check the number of the door with the tray outside it. Number six – the real number six. The room they *should* have been in. She reached down and touched the covered plate, finding it stone cold. She remembered Granny promising to 'have a tray of something hot sent up' to her. The tray had been meant for Betty. Their trunk hadn't been left outside the wrong door at all. The key hadn't fitted the lock for a very good reason. The Widdershins had been in the wrong room all along.

But this was not the last shock Betty was about to receive. From his pocket, Mr Sneed produced a large black key which looked just like the one Betty and her sisters had found in the room.

'Master key,' he crooned, looking very pleased with himself. 'It's amazing what you can get hold of with a bit of flattery and distraction.'

'Hurry up and get inside, Sneed,' Lady Fortuna snapped, clearing not wanting to be seen lurking outside the haunted room.

'Your wish is my command,' Mr Sneed replied smarmily, slotting the key into the lock. He swung it open and the colour drained from his face. 'B-but ... but it's supposed to be empty. I don't understand!'

Instead of looking disappointed, Lady Fortuna appeared strangely excited. Her black-rimmed eyes widened and she wrapped her long fingers round Mr Sneed's arm. Once more, her grip reminded Betty of an octopus's tentacles. 'Haunted rooms are never really empty,' she breathed, taking a step inside. Mr Sneed followed her. 'Perhaps all this is a sign of ghostly activity.'

Betty crept nearer, until she was outside the door. The two intruders tiptoed round the room, examining everything.

'Someone is using this room,' Lady Fortuna declared, discarding a sock of Charlie's in disgust. 'Someone with children, by the looks of it.'

'It must be a mistake.' Sneed frowned. 'I was told this room is never used – hasn't been for years.' He suddenly looked deflated. 'All that banging we heard from above may not have been ghostly goings-on after all. More likely a load of beastly children jumping about!'

Betty remembered hearing him complaining of loud noises to Mrs Chambers at the front desk, and how she had reassured him the room above wasn't in use. It must have been Charlie jumping on the beds that he'd heard.

Broken ice, broken ice, falling through it isn't nice . . .

A sudden dread gripped hold of Betty. Charlie's silly game had been innocent, but had her words stirred something up in the haunted room? It was a horrid coincidence that one of the sisters had fallen through the frozen lake so soon afterwards.

'Whoever it is, they have dreadful taste in poetry,' Lady Fortuna sneered, flicking through a notebook of Fliss's. She tossed it carelessly aside and then sniffed a tiny bottle of rosewater scent that Fliss had sneaked into the trunk, making a face. 'And cheap perfume.' Her black eyebrows shot up suddenly in recognition. 'Just like that silly girl from yesterday, the one in the shabby clothes – smelled like she'd bathed in it.'

Betty's face burned with anger to hear her sister being talked about this way. She stared at the fortune teller's spiteful smile and showy gown, wondering how she could ever have thought she was pretty. Shabby clothes or not, Fliss was gentler, kinder and lovelier than Lady Fortuna could ever hope to be.

You want a haunting? Betty thought angrily. *I'll give you a haunting*. Whatever this sneaky pair was doing in their room, perhaps she could trick them into revealing it. More than anything, though, she wanted to give them a fright.

Betty walked into the room, treading deliberately heavily. Her footsteps rang out nicely, and she enjoyed the look of shock on their faces.

'Do you hear that?' Sneed whispered.

'A ghostly presence!' Lady Fortuna hissed back. She clasped her hands to her chest, frozen in shock. It seemed to Betty that the woman was not familiar with occurrences like this at all.

Betty stopped by the chest of drawers and slowly slid the top one open. She caught sight of the movement in the wardrobe mirror. Seeing the drawer move by itself was extremely spooky and judging from their expressions, Lady Fortuna and her companion agreed. Betty began roughly turning over the clothes in the drawer, rummaging through them as though she were looking for something.

'What is she searching for?' Mr Sneed whispered in fascination. 'Elora ... ?'

'Hush, Sneed!' Lady Fortuna whispered, increasingly alarmed. 'Don't disturb her!'

Betty left a couple of stockings draped over the sides of the open drawer and tossed Fliss's scarf to the floor. She was enjoying herself now.

Abandoning the chest of drawers, she leaned closer to the window and allowed her breath to steam up the cold glass.

Once it was misted enough, she undid the catch and pushed on the glass with her fingers. The effect of her handprint appearing on the glass was ghostlier than Betty could have hoped for. Lady Fortuna gave a little gasp and forgot her own advice to remain silent.

'She's looking for him!' she exclaimed. 'She's looking for her thieving ratbag lover!'

The window swung open and the mistiness cleared as cold air whooshed in, taking Betty's fingerprints with it. She held the catch for a few seconds and then let go, allowing the window to swing on its hinges. Then she turned and left the room as loudly as she'd arrived, her footsteps echoing in the hallway.

'Follow it!' Mr Sneed said, his hairy upper lip quivering in excitement. 'I mean, *her*!'

They emerged from the room, following Betty along the quiet corridor. She led them as far as the wall where the old brass lamp was, where she had seen the ghostly figure vanish. There, she stopped and crept away from the cracked wall to the other side, watching and listening.

'This must be the site of the old staircase,' Mr Sneed observed, running his fingers over the crack in the wall. 'The original floorplans of the hall show that the stairs had two exits: one at ground level which led towards the stables and a second in the cellar.' He tapped the wall, thoughtful but pale in the face. 'Elora was on her way to find him – it makes sense that she would have taken a horse from the stables and rode out in the direction of the lake, before meeting with her horrible fate.'

Lady Fortuna's eyes narrowed wickedly. 'Well, if she hadn't been planning to run away with a crook, then she might still be alive, mightn't she?' Her expression soured even further. 'And had he not decided to rob my mother of her most treasured possession, her livelihood wouldn't have been ruined, would it?'

Betty's breath caught in her throat. *Lady Fortuna's mother? Her most treasured possession?* Then that meant . . .

'Life was never the same for my mother after that,' Lady Fortuna continued, her eyes flashing. 'She went from being one of the most gifted, famous fortune tellers in the land to being a joke! Before, people would queue for hours to see her. Afterwards, the only people who came wanted to hear the story of the robbery.' Her lip curled into a sneer. 'The infamous Jack Frost! No one cared about Madam Divina's predictions any more. People laughed at her. "Well, you should have seen it coming!" they'd say.' Her face hardened and her fists clenched. 'And the worst thing is that one day that crystal was meant to be *mine*.'

'I know, my dear,' crooned Mr Sneed, placing his hand on Lady Fortuna's arm. 'Now, why don't we—?'

The fortune teller shook him off like he was an irksome beetle and continued her tirade.

'It was passed down my family.' Her voice softened, sounding almost dreamy. 'It came from my great, great-grandmother, who'd discovered it washed up from a lake, in a wooden box. She found she could use the crystal to conjure visions. And not just smoke and mirror visions. *Real* visions – of the future and the past. She could predict when a child would be born, a true love found, even when death would come. And so our great line of fortune tellers was born.' She smiled faintly. 'We were rich. Famous. Respected. And then it was all gone –' she snapped her fingers – 'like that!

'So you see, it wasn't just the crystal that was stolen. It was our family's history, and my mother's future. My future. We had to scrape a living. Selling her story of the highway robber to newspapers. When the interest died out she had to be smart and cunning. *Dishonest.* She took up fortune-telling again, changing her name and using other methods. Reading palms or tea leaves. But without that crystal ball her powers were gone, leaving her with nothing but fakery and pretence. And so that was all I had left to learn from her.'

'This really isn't the place for such a conversation, my dear,' Mr Sneed tried again. He looked around nervously. 'I know it seems empty, but with these echoing corridors anyone could be listening behind these doors!'

Or right next to you, thought Betty, unable to believe what she was hearing. *The daughter of the fortune teller, here in Echo Hall!* Her mind was bursting with questions, but there was no way to ask any of them. Why was Lady Fortuna here now, after all this time? Was she hoping for some way to find the stolen crystal ball, to use its power for herself?

180

'I'm past caring,' Lady Fortuna retorted coldly, but she lowered her voice a fraction. 'I've nothing to hide, not when it comes to my mother being robbed. And I'm sick of fakery, and faded velvet and costume jewellery. I want the *real* thing. I want the riches, the fame, and the visions. I want it all!' She grabbed the lapel of Sneed's smart jacket and looked him in the eye intensely.

'Someone here knows something, I'm sure of it. And if what my mother said was correct, if what the crystal ball showed her was true, then someone lied that night. We need to know who, and who might still hold the answers now.'

Betty's mind was whirling. What could Madam Divina have seen that might shed some light on the truth of that night? *Had* she predicted the robbery – or some part of it – after all?

Mr Sneed swallowed and gazed back at Lady Fortuna adoringly, like a rabbit that would happily let the hungry fox eat it. *He's in love with her*, Betty realised in disgust. And while Fliss was the one who knew all about love, not Betty, it looked very much as though Lady Fortuna did not return Sneed's feelings.

'I ... I have the list of employees,' he quavered. 'From back then. I'm just waiting for the current list to arrive, to compare the names. My source assures me I'll have it later this evening. From that we'll have proof of who worked here then and may still be here today.'

Lady Fortuna's eyes narrowed once more. 'Sometimes

names change, Sneed. When people marry, and so on.'

'Well, yes, there is that possibility . . .'

Lady Fortuna released Mr Sneed's lapel and ran a long, pointed fingernail down his cheek. 'I'm sure you'll figure it out, you clever thing, you.'

'Um . . .' Sneed gulped and went hopelessly red. 'I can certainly try.'

'I do hope so.' Lady Fortuna tapped him lightly on the nose with her finger. 'I kept my promise to my mother all those years – I never searched for the crystal ball while she was alive. She told me my obsession with it was bad news, that perhaps it was a good thing it was gone. But now I want it. I won't stop until it's mine.' Her eyes sparkled nastily. 'And woe betide any fool who tries to steal it from *me*.'

Chapter Fifteen
Snow

BETTY BARELY ATE A THING AT SUPPER. SHE did her best to force down Granny's lumpy stew but ended up pushing it around her plate. Normally, she might have got away with it but after her accident Granny was watching her like a child watching the clock at the end of the school day.

'What's up with you, Betty?' she asked for the third time, reaching out and putting a hand to Betty's forehead. 'You look peaky. Perhaps I *should* have a doctor check you over—'

'I'm fine, Granny,' Betty muttered, squirming away from Granny's hand and swallowing another spoonful of brown gloop that stuck in her throat. 'I think I'm still full from the tray you had sent up earlier.' The three eclairs she had eaten hadn't helped, but of course she couldn't admit this to Granny.

'Yes, stop mollycoddling her,' Clarissa said, evidently jealous that Betty was getting all the attention now.

'You're happy enough for me to mollycoddle you,' Granny muttered under her breath. She lit her pipe and puffed on it hard.

'Oh, Bunny,' Clarissa griped. 'Do you have to smoke that smelly thing?' She forced out a cough. 'I can't even get up and move away because of my poor ankle.'

'You'll get used to it,' Granny said shortly. 'And it helps calm me down when my nerves are frayed.' She gave Clarissa a mutinous look.

The conversation between Lady Fortuna and Mr Sneed had ended when a couple of guests had come up to their room nearby. The pair had skulked off in the direction of the stairs, leaving Betty dearly wishing she could follow them, but not daring to push her luck as Granny was due back at any moment. Instead, Betty had returned to room six – or rather, room nine – just in time, for Granny had arrived a minute later, fussing and flapping and asking whether she felt well enough to go over to Clarissa's for supper.

Now, sitting at Clarissa's cosy dining table with the log burner crackling merrily nearby, it should have been easy to forget about frozen lakes, drowning girls and highwaymen with stolen crystal balls. It wasn't, though. Not after everything she had just learned. The worst part was that Betty hadn't even had the chance to tell Fliss and Charlie what she had discovered about the room at Echo Hall and Lady Fortuna's link to the missing crystal ball, let alone the ghostly goings-on.

'Can we at least stay until tomorrow afternoon, Granny?' asked Charlie, her cheeks puffed up with bread like a hamster's. 'I'd love you to meet Bonbon the wolf-dog.'

'And it's the masked ball tomorrow evening,' said Fliss, looking hopeful. 'I wonder who'll be there?'

'And the winter market was so much fun—' Charlie began.

'Until your sister nearly drowned, you mean?' Granny asked drily.

It occurred to Betty then that Granny seemed worryingly alert. It was unlike her not to have had a whiskey or two by now.

'Um,' said Charlie. 'Well . . .'

'We're going home first thing tomorrow,' Granny repeated. 'Sorry, girls. I know you wanted to stay and I *have* thought about it, but the answer is no. I'd feel much safer with us all back in Pendlewick.'

'But—' Betty began.

'It's not just the lake,' Granny continued. 'Though I do think it's strange how any time something happens, it happens to us.' She glanced at her horseshoe, which she had perched on Clarissa's mantelpiece. 'Clarissa's been telling me more about Wilderness, and I just don't feel comfortable with you three girls over there and me over here. This weather's getting colder by the hour, and I've heard more snow's on the way. *Thick* snow. All the arrangements have been made – we leave tomorrow and Clarissa's coming with us until her bones have mended. She'll have to sleep in your room, Fliss.

185

She can't possibly manage those stairs.'

'*What?*' Fliss burst out, ungraciously. 'You know that cottage makes me seasick, especially the upstairs!'

Granny silenced her with an icy glare.

'Now, listen here, Bunny,' Clarissa interjected, looking uncomfortable all of a sudden. 'That's really not necessary because—'

'Nope,' said Granny. 'I won't hear of leaving you here. You're coming with us.'

Betty glanced helplessly at Fliss. She knew her sister hadn't been totally convinced about staying in Wilderness, but perhaps the thought of Clarissa in her Nest for an undetermined amount of time would sway her. *Say something!* she mouthed.

'Why don't I make some tea?' Fliss said, trying to smile though she looked more like she was baring her teeth. 'Would you like some whiskey in yours, Granny? Or perhaps just a whiskey on its own?'

'No, thank you,' Granny said. 'Just milk and two sugars. I'll be up early and the last thing I want is a stinking headache.' She gave them a shrewd look. 'Besides, I might change my mind after a couple of drinks, and we wouldn't want that, would we?'

Betty looked at her sister in dismay. Granny must mean business if she was keeping off the whiskey.

Fliss poured the tea sullenly. It looked even weaker than she usually made it, and Betty counted her adding three sugars to Granny's by mistake. Clarissa sipped hers and winced.

'About time you learned to make a decent brew, my girl. My dishwater tastes better than this.'

'Perhaps you can teach me when we're back in Pendlewick,' Fliss muttered. 'Instead of being waited on hand and foot.'

Granny frowned. 'Don't get lippy.'

'You drink dishwater?' Charlie asked, giving Clarissa a peculiar look. 'Weird.'

Betty felt oddly like she was a knot in the middle of a piece of string being pulled one way, then the other. On the one hand, she should be relieved to go home, for she couldn't deny that falling through the frozen lake had frightened her. On the other hand, she felt increasingly drawn into the mysteries of the place. First the mix-up with the room key, then icy fingers on her ankle ... the ghostly figure in the room with her. It felt deliberate, like Betty was becoming more entangled in it all. Why had the door been open, as though the room had been *inviting* them in? If they had returned the key to the front desk, perhaps the mistake would have been realised sooner ... but then Betty thought of the maid in the room, and the other, older key that they had found. Had Elora wanted them to use it?

'What else did Clarissa tell you about Wilderness, then?' she asked eventually.

'I just mentioned to Bunny how it's said that when things start to go bump in the night over at Echo Hall it usually means colder weather is on the way,' Clarissa replied. 'And of course, with Bunny being so superstitious . . .'

'No smoke without fire,' Granny put in darkly. 'And anyway, that's quite enough about it for one night. We can talk about it tomorrow when we're safely on the carriage home. The sooner we're out of here, the better. Now help me clear up.'

'We'll be fine, Granny. Honestly!' Fliss insisted once they'd washed and tidied up. 'We know our way back to Echo Hall perfectly well. We don't need you to walk us there. Besides, who's going to make sure *you* get back all right?'

'Don't worry about me,' Granny answered, gritting her teeth as she tied a scarf round her head with a sideways glance at Clarissa. 'A five-minute walk might just save my sanity. Right, then. Coats on, wrap up. Off we go!'

Outside, the temperature had dipped even lower and the sky was an odd purple bruise of a colour. Twiggy tree branches glittered with frost and they had to tread carefully around patches of ice as they came down Chill Hill.

'Snow's on the way,' Granny said, sniffing the air with certainty. 'And soon.'

Betty could smell it, too. A sharp, fresh smell that was so unique she would struggle to describe it.

'Great,' huffed Charlie. 'We could've played in that, and all.'

The winter market was deserted as they passed by; the stalls were covered over for the night. All was silent and dark, and then as they neared the steps to the hall the snowflakes began tumbling down. They were like nothing Betty had ever seen before. Back in Crowstone, snow had been rare, and when it had come the flakes were tiny as rice grains and turned to grey slush on the roadside before you could even taste one on your tongue. Here, they were as thick and fat as white feathers, and Betty imagined that if you caught one in your mouth it would melt slowly all the way down to your tummy.

'It's like a giant had a pillow fight!' Charlie said in wonder, slowing to a dawdle despite the freezing air. Snowflakes caught in her eyelashes and she laughed and blinked them away.

'It's like being in a snow globe,' Fliss whispered. She did a twirl, then looked sheepish as she skidded.

It's like the warnings about Elora and the weather are coming true, Betty thought, wrapping her scarf more tightly over her hair. The snow was certainly beautiful but as the landscape around them started vanishing under layers of white it felt dangerous and unfamiliar.

'Chop chop,' Granny said impatiently. 'Can we get indoors like all the sensible people, please?' She flapped her hand in the direction of the hall, and as she did, something flew out of the handbag on her wrist and clattered to the ground. 'Oh, no! I've dropped me horseshoe!'

'What did you bring that for?' Betty asked uneasily.

'Luck,' grunted Granny, stooping to hunt in the snow like

189

it was perfectly normal to carry a heavy chunk of iron round in your bag. '*Obviously.*'

Betty rolled her eyes in exasperation, but she bent down next to Granny. 'I'll help you find it.'

'Looks like we're not the only ones enjoying the snow,' Charlie said.

'What?' Fliss asked. 'I don't see anyone.'

'Up there.' Charlie pointed through the fluttering snowfall. 'Someone's leaning out of the window!'

Betty's hand paused, sinking into snow. Her head snapped up and she followed Charlie's finger through the flurry of snowflakes. 'Where?' Her voice trembled, eyes darting. Then she saw it; a shadowy blur at one of the windows on the first floor of the hall, but how Charlie had spotted it, she couldn't imagine. Only the faintest of lights was coming from the room, like the flickering of a candle, but it was enough for Betty to see long, pale hair streaming out of the window. And before Charlie spoke next, she *knew*. The cold seeping into her fingers matched the dread she now felt, for there was a streak of red in the candlelight.

'Hey,' Charlie said. 'Fliss, that's your ribbon. The one you tied to the window catch!'

'Then that's our room,' Fliss added, puzzled. 'Why would a maid be opening our window in this weather? And this late at night?'

'Because it's not a maid. It's *her*,' Betty whispered. 'It's . . . it's Elora.'

'Who?' Granny demanded, still scrabbling in the snow for her lucky charm. 'What?' She squinted up at the hall. 'Are you girls messing around, going on about that ghost? It's not funny, you know. Fliss told me about the window being left open and things being pulled out of the drawers. Whichever one of you is playing tricks, stop it.'

'It's not a trick,' Betty whispered, her eyes streaming with cold. She blinked, trying to keep the snowflakes out of them, and her vision blurred. 'She's there, don't you see her, Granny?'

'I couldn't see that far even if there wasn't a blizzard in my eyes,' Granny grumbled. 'Aha, here it is!' She seized her beloved horseshoe and, after tucking it safely back in her bag, she shielded her eyes and stared up at the windows. 'Can't see anything. Now, hurry up and get out of this cold!'

Betty remained frozen to the spot. 'She's right there . . .'

Except she wasn't. There was no one, only an open window which slowly swung back and forth in the night. The shadowy figure was gone.

Betty remembered the exact words Clarissa had spoken when they had first arrived in Wilderness.

A sighting of Elora's phantom at the window foretells death. The death of a loved one.

Now Betty, Fliss and Charlie had all seen her.

'There's nothing there,' Granny repeated impatiently. 'You girls aren't funny, playing tricks. Especially you, Fliss. You know I expect better.'

'But ... ?' Fliss began indignantly, until Granny flapped at her to go up the steps.

A cold terror was taking Betty in its grip. As Granny had said earlier, *there's no smoke without fire.* It meant that one thing could not exist without the other. That there was always a reason for something. So if people in Wilderness believed that seeing Elora Goode's ghost meant someone would die, then it hadn't come from nowhere. And the fact that Granny hadn't seen her ... Did that mean that Granny herself was at threat? Or Father, all alone back in Pendlewick?

And now they were heading back to the haunted room, which only Betty knew about. She had to tell Fliss and Charlie.

'Whatever is the matter, Betty?' Granny asked suddenly. She snapped her bag shut and peered at her. 'Do you really think you saw something at the window?' She glanced up, a little worried now.

'I ...' Betty hesitated. 'My eyes are just stinging from the cold.' Horrible thoughts whirled in her head like the snowstorm that was thickening around them by the minute. Thoughts she did not want in her head. *The death of a loved one* ...

They hurried up the steps of Echo Hall and through the huge old doors, finally out of the cold.

'Granny,' Betty croaked, as foreboding curled round her like a fist. 'Don't go back to Clarissa's. Stay here, with us.

Clarissa can manage without you for one night, can't she?'

'Well, probably,' Granny replied. 'But she's expecting me back now, and if I don't turn up she'll worry. I'd better leave now before this weather gets any worse. Now, off with you – straight upstairs and to your room.'

'But Granny,' Betty started.

'No buts. Pack your things and get an early night.' She gave a tired, crinkle-eyed smile. 'I know you had a horrible shock yesterday and it's probably catching up with you now. But this time tomorrow we'll be safely back home. Just be brave for tonight, I know you can.'

With a swish of Granny's skirts she was gone, back out into the cold, cold night.

'Betty,' Fliss said in a low voice the moment Granny was gone. 'That ribbon – my ribbon on the window . . .'

'Yes,' Betty finished. 'It's true. We're in the haunted room. And if those stories about seeing Elora at the window are real, then . . . then . . . one of our loved ones will die.'

Chapter Sixteen
Shivershock

THE SILVER KEY FITTED PERFECTLY INTO THE lock of room six. The *real* room six. The door opened to a very ordinary, welcoming room with one large bed and a smaller one. The walls were freshly painted, and neat towels were folded on the nicely made-up beds.

'See?' said Fliss at once. 'I told you it wasn't right that we had to make our own beds, or ask for clean towels.'

'Saying "I told you so" isn't helping,' Betty muttered uncomfortably. 'I need to think.' She sat down at the little dressing table and tilted her head on one side. Thinking would be so much easier if her ears were not full of Shivershock Lake water.

'Do you really think Granny's in danger?' Charlie asked in a small voice, chewing one of her pigtails worriedly. 'Or Father?'

'The story says a "loved one",' said Fliss, miserably. 'It could be either of them.'

'No!' Charlie whimpered. She began to cry softly, burying her face into Fliss. After a minute she looked up, sniffling. 'What about Clarissa?' she asked in a distinctly hopeful way. 'She's family. It might be her.'

'Charlie!' Fliss scolded, shocked. 'Don't be callous. I know she's a bossy old pain in the neck, but we wouldn't want anything bad to happen to her.'

'No,' said Charlie. 'But if it was a choice between the three of them I know who I'd pick.'

'*Charlie!*' Fliss said again.

Charlie spat out the pigtail and put the other one in her mouth. 'Just being honest.'

'Somehow I don't think it'll be Clarissa,' Betty said grimly. 'Like Charlie says, we're not close enough to her.'

Fliss looked jittery and upset now. 'Well, what ... what if it's one of *us*?'

It was an awful thought. 'No, it can't be,' Betty muttered. 'We all saw her and the legend says it happens to someone else.' Secretly, she wasn't convinced. None of them knew enough about the ghostly legend to be sure of anything, and that scared her even more. 'But there's more,' Betty rushed on, explaining what else she had discovered earlier; about the ghostly figure in the room as she woke and the way Lady Fortuna and Sneed had turned up to snoop in the room.

'Lady Fortuna is the daughter of the original fortune teller – Madam Divina. She's searching for the crystal ball belonging to her mother.' She shook her head again, wishing the muffled feeling in her ears would clear. 'She's a fraud, Fliss. Everything she told you was fake, and now she wants the crystal ball to bring her fame and fortune. That's why she and Sneed are investigating the haunting – and now that's what we have to do, too, only for different reasons. If there's a chance that the legend is true, then someone in our family could be in danger! There's no time to lose – we start tonight. Asking questions, snooping, ghost hunting and finding out everything we can.'

'G-ghost hunting?' Fliss stammered, pasty-faced. 'But we leave tomorrow. That only gives us tonight. What if that's not enough time for us to solve the mystery?'

Betty glanced through the window. There was no sign of a starry sky, only thick flurries of snow.

When Elora's ghost's about
Wrap up warm and don't go out.

'If the snow keeps coming down this fast then we won't be going anywhere,' Betty said, feeling suddenly certain as she said it. 'We'll be trapped in Wilderness. I don't think Elora is going to let us or anyone else leave.'

'Granny's right,' Fliss said. She sat down on the bed and distractedly twisted the sheets in her hands. 'We do always manage to get into trouble. I don't know how, but we do!'

'Yes, we do,' Betty agreed. 'But we've always managed to get out of it, too, haven't we? And if there's anyone who can prevent a death and undo a terrible curse, it's us!'

'It's us, that's who!' Charlie agreed. Then she gasped.

'Oh! What if it's Hoppit who dies? *Hoppit!*' She poked her collar. 'Wake up! Help – he's not breathing ... oh, wait, yes he is. He must be sleeping off that cheese I sneaked him earlier.'

'First things first,' said Betty, once the rat drama was over. 'We need to get our trunk out of the haunted room.'

Fliss made a face and shuddered. 'I really don't want to go back in there again.'

'Neither do I,' said Betty. 'But if we're going to solve this mystery then we have to.'

'I'll go,' said Charlie, bravely.

'We'll all go.' Betty got up from the dressing table. 'Come on. It'll be like pulling out a wobbly tooth. The quicker we do it, the better.'

Together they left the room and went along to room nine. Fliss reached out and touched the loose brass number, and it slid from side to side. Betty found her fingers were shaking as she unlocked the door with the old iron key and pushed it open. Even though she'd seen Elora's ghost already, she was still afraid of what they might come across.

'Brr,' said Fliss, rubbing her arms. She hung back by the door and peered into the dark room. 'It's freezing in there.'

'The window's still open,' said Charlie.

The window gave an eerie *cree-ee-eeak* as it swung slowly back and forth on its hinges. Soft snow was swirling through it and settling on the floor and the chest of drawers, as though the outside was trying to claw its way in.

'I opened it earlier,' said Betty. 'When I was trying to scare Lady Fortuna and Mr Sneed, but I'm sure I closed it again.'

'Hurry up and put the lamp on,' Fliss urged. 'It's even spookier in the dark.'

Quickly, Betty lit the little lamp on the shelf and a warm yellow glow filled the room – but it made none of them feel any better once they saw things properly.

'Jeepers creepers!' whispered Charlie.

Thick layers of dust lay upon almost everything: the chest, the picture frames, even the beds. Cobwebs flapped like ghostly birds in the cold air. At the same time Betty started to think she could hear something, a *shush-hush* whispery noise in her blocked-up ears.

'This is creepy,' Fliss muttered. 'It's like it hasn't been used for years.'

'Then let's hurry up and get out of here,' said Betty. 'Come on, help me with our trunk.'

Together, Betty and Fliss piled their belongings in higgledy-piggledy and began to carry it to the door. Charlie was gathering up other things that were strewn around the room but succeeded in dropping as many as she picked up.

'Notice how our stuff isn't dusty?' Betty remarked. 'But everything else is?'

The window slammed shut, with a bang so loud it was a miracle the glass didn't shatter. The three girls screamed, and Betty and Fliss dropped the trunk, narrowly missing their own toes.

'Stupid window!' Charlie gasped.

'I'll fasten it,' said Betty, crossing the room quickly and latching the window. She gave it a firm push to check it was done properly. 'There.' She and Fliss grabbed the trunk again. 'Charlie, get the door.'

But as the door opened there was another shock in store, for a figure stepped into the doorway, causing the three sisters to cry out again.

'GHOST!' Charlie yelled, before all three of them realised it was not, in fact, a phantom, but someone very much alive: Mrs Chambers. Only now, she didn't look weary or sad. Her face was twisted with anger, confusion and something that looked very much like fear.

'What ... are you ... *doing in here?*' Mrs Chambers' voice stuttered and stalled before rising to a shriek.

'W-we –' Betty began, her face suddenly hot and prickly. 'There was a mistake. We came to the wrong room ...'

'You're not allowed in here,' Mrs Chambers said, gazing around the room in horror. 'No one is allowed in here. EVER!'

'We're very sorry,' Fliss said in a meek voice. 'We were just—'

'How did you get in?' Mrs Chambers swished into the room, her eyes everywhere. 'It's always kept locked, *always*. I make sure of that.'

'Because of the ghost?' Charlie whispered. 'Is she ... dangerous?'

The woman didn't answer. She had spied the old key on

the wooden chest of drawers where Betty had left it. She snatched it up, her eyes blazing.

'Where did you get this?' she asked in a low voice that was brimming with anger. 'Tell me *right now!*'

'It was here in the room when we arrived,' said Betty. 'The door was already open but the key was over there on the chest—'

'I gave you the key to room six!' Mrs Chambers snapped. 'So why—?'

'You're not listening,' Betty said hotly, feeling her own temper rise. It wasn't their fault they'd come into the wrong room! At the same time she felt slightly afraid. Mrs Chambers had always looked so mild-mannered – she could never have imagined her to have such a temper. 'We thought this *was* room six – look at the door!'

Mrs Chambers whipped round to examine the door. Her mouth dropped open as she saw the brass number nine dangling upside down, masquerading as a number six.

'We only realised our mistake earlier,' Betty explained. 'That's why we're moving our things into the correct room.'

'The door was already open when you arrived?' Mrs Chambers asked. Her gaze was fixed on the window, her body tense like a cat about to spring out on a mouse.

'Yes,' Betty repeated. 'We thought it was meant to be that way.'

'But look at it,' Mrs Chambers whispered. 'How could you, with all this dust?'

'It didn't look like this when we got here,' Charlie put in. 'It was cosy. There was a fire burning and fresh flowers.'

'We found it a bit odd that the beds weren't made,' Fliss added. 'But we thought that maybe the staff had been too busy – the girl with the coal scuttle seemed in a rush when she left.'

A worried expression came over the woman's face. 'Please hurry up and leave this room,' she said quietly. She moved to the door and held it wide open for them.

Puffing and panting, Betty and Fliss lugged the trunk along the corridor and into room six. Then Betty returned to room nine and began helping Charlie collect the few odd things that were still dotted about. From within the folds of the bedclothes Betty spied the ice skate and grabbed it.

'Was it *you*?' Mrs Chambers asked suddenly, staring at the skate. 'Were you the one who fell through the ice yesterday?'

'Yes,' Betty admitted. 'And I saw someone in the water, a girl. The Drowning Girl. Other people have, too.'

An odd, closed expression came over the woman's face. The lines around her eyes suddenly appeared much deeper. 'Now, please come out.' She beckoned them to the corridor. 'This room really should be kept locked at all times.' Her fingers were curled tightly around the old iron key. Betty bundled the skate and a stray sock into Charlie's arms and gave her a gentle push.

'Go and help Fliss tidy things away,' she told her. 'She's probably feeling spooked all by herself.'

She waited until Charlie was gone and then turned to face Mrs Chambers.

'Please help us,' she said quickly. 'My sisters and I saw someone at the window in there earlier, when we were walking across the square. It was someone with long, fair hair. We've heard the stories about Elora, and what it means if she's seen . . . Is there any way to prevent it?'

Mrs Chambers stared back at her, her expression unreadable. 'You mean the death of a loved one?' she asked finally.

'Yes,' Betty whispered. Already, she had the feeling her question was a waste of time, but she had to ask if it meant there was even a chance of finding out what to do. The *shush-hush* whispery noise was back in her ears again. 'We're afraid. Afraid for our granny, and our father—'

'Listen to me,' Mrs Chambers cut in. 'Lots of things are said about this place, and yes, it's true that certain events did occur here at Echo Hall. Bad things. But sometimes the truth has a way of getting lost. All sorts of things get added on over the years – who knows why? People are bored, or want to scare others.' She gave a sudden, tired smile that made her stern edges melt away. 'The best thing you can do is leave this place. Go home. That way you'll all be safe.' She pulled the door closed and locked it.

'We'll be safe if we leave?' Betty repeated uncertainly. 'Are you sure?'

Before Mrs Chambers could answer, a loud bang came from inside the locked room.

Both she and Betty froze.

'Are you going to see what that was?' Betty asked.

'I know what it was.' Mrs Chambers unlocked the door and pushed it open to a swirl of snow so fierce that flakes of it settled on her coppery eyebrows. She marched into the room and slammed the window shut, latching it.

'I already closed that,' Betty said in a small voice as Mrs Chambers locked up once more. She waited, half expecting her to come out with some explanation, such as the latch being faulty, or a draught down the chimney, but none came.

'It'll open again before long,' was all Mrs Chambers said as she began to walk swiftly away. 'It always does. Just stay away from that room.'

Betty watched her pocket the key, and her footsteps became fainter as she moved along the corridor. All Betty could hear now was the growing *shush-hush* in her ears. And in the empty silence of the hall, it sounded more and more like a voice, and a familiar word.

Shivershock.

Chapter Seventeen
A Shocking Clue

BETTY RETURNED TO ROOM SIX, HER HEART pounding. Could she really be hearing a voice in her head? Or was it merely the effect of the water in her ears? *Perhaps I'm imagining it,* she thought. Or perhaps having water from a haunted lake in her ears was allowing her to hear the voices of those who had died there ...

Stop it!

'Now what do we do?' asked Fliss, nibbling her lower lip like a worried rabbit.

'Mrs Chambers seems to think that if we go home, then we should be safe,' Betty replied. 'But I'm not sure we can count on that being true. And even if it is, I don't think we'll be going home any time soon with the weather like this.' She glanced at the window. The snow was falling thick and fast and had begun collecting in little drifts against the glass panes. The feeling of danger was all around, building like the snow outside.

'We don't have time to waste,' she said, thinking quickly. 'There's an old lady who works downstairs in the kitchens – her name is Mildred. Fliss, I need you to go and speak to her. She's worked here a long time, I heard her talking about Elora and the Drowning Girl, but we need to find out what else she knows, and if there's a way to prevent a death after seeing Elora's ghost.'

'Why me?' Fliss asked. 'She might not talk to me.'

'Because you're good at charming people,' Betty replied. 'People open up to you. Take Charlie with you. Oh, and Charlie, if you see Sonny, ask him the same questions. He might know more about this place than we realise.'

'Where will you be, Betty?' asked Charlie.

'I'll be spying on Lady Fortuna and Sneed,' said Betty, feeling butterflies in her tummy at the thought of it. 'Sneed said he had two lists of names – people who worked at Echo Hall when Elora was here, and people who work here now. If I can get a look at those lists it might help us find someone else to question, someone who knows something they didn't tell before.'

'But Betty,' Fliss said, looking unsure, 'why would they speak up now if they didn't then?'

'All sorts of reasons,' said Betty determinedly. 'People keep secrets and lie to protect themselves – and others. But loyalties can change over time. And sometimes, big secrets are just too big to keep any more.' She removed the nesting dolls from her pocket. With her hair still inside, all she had to do was twist the outer doll until the two halves matched and *poof*, she was invisible.

'Let's meet back here in half an hour,' she said. 'Then we'll decide what to do next.' Together the three of them left the room, noting the time on the clock as they went down the stairs. Ten minutes past eight. It had been properly dark for hours now and felt so much later, but as they drew closer to the dining room the busy sounds of chatter and people eating reached them and made things feel the tiniest bit more normal. Servants were rushing about, no doubt preparing for tomorrow's masked ball. Guests were, too, some of them with fancy costumes draped in their arms which they seemed to be collecting from somewhere towards the back of the hall.

Betty watched them fleetingly, envying their carefree faces. Only hours ago she had wanted to go to the ball as much as anyone. Now, she just wanted to keep her family alive.

'Take that corridor there,' she whispered, before remembering Fliss and Charlie couldn't see where she was pointing to. 'Next to the front desk. That'll lead you to the kitchens. Good luck!'

'Thanks,' Fliss muttered, not looking very confident. 'We're sure to need it. You know luck's never on our side.'

Betty waited until her sisters had disappeared down the corridor, then turned towards the ground-floor guest quarters. She had taken two steps when she realised that she had no idea which rooms the fortune teller and Mr Sneed were staying in. However, from his complaint about the noise she knew Sneed was in the one directly below room nine.

With the front desk currently empty she wondered if she might be able to snoop behind it and find out which rooms the pair were in, but before she could do anything, Mrs Chambers appeared from the door behind the desk and took up her position at the counter. She looked more worried than ever, and Betty wondered if it were to do with finding the three sisters in room nine earlier. Guiltily she recalled the spooky, excited feeling she'd had when she'd first heard about the mystery and ghost story of Echo Hall. It must be quite different to have to work there all the time, knowing there was truth in the stories.

Mrs Chambers shuffled some papers on the desk, muttering something under her breath that Betty couldn't catch. She glanced towards the stairs then called out to a waiter who was carrying a silver tray:

'Have you seen Sonny, my boy?'

The waiter shook his head. 'Not since this afternoon.' He lowered his voice and said with a slight smirk: 'Caught him feeding Bonbon a cheese scone.'

'That doesn't surprise me.' Mrs Chambers rolled her eyes. 'That dog eats better than Sonny does. If you see him, tell him I want a word with him.'

Betty followed silently behind the waiter, who walked briskly along the lower corridor. She tried to remember how

207

many doors she and her sisters had passed on the way to room nine – was it six, or seven? It was hard to guess which room was directly beneath it, but she knew it must be on the right side.

The waiter stopped outside one of the doors and knocked smartly on it. Betty hung back, waiting to see who opened it, but it was a stern-faced lady complaining that her dinner was late. After snatching the tray the woman shut the door in the waiter's face, leaving him to stalk away down the corridor. Betty was now alone, standing in what she thought was roughly the right place. There were three possible doors that might be directly under room nine. She put her good ear to the first one and heard the sound of deep snoring.

From the second room she heard nothing. She gave the door a tentative knock, but no one answered. At the third door there were low voices. Sneed and Fortuna! From the sound of it Betty instantly knew that something important was being discussed. She pressed her ear harder against the door, but could only catch the words 'list' and 'time'. Everything else was too muffled. She needed to get into the room.

Betty raised her hand and knocked quickly, then darted to the side and pressed herself flat against the wall. At once the voices inside the room silenced and footsteps marched towards the door.

It was flung open and Sneed's moustache appeared just before the rest of him, twitching as he scented the corridor both ways like a nervous bloodhound. Clearly puzzled, he stepped out into the hall. Betty screwed up her courage and darted through the open doorway. Creeping into the furthest corner of the room near the top end of the bed, she wedged herself between a chair and the wardrobe. Her heart was drumming urgently at the thought of getting caught. The room was a mess, with beautiful glittering dresses carelessly draped over chairs, long black velvet gloves still inside-out from being peeled off, and sequinned shoes kicked into corners.

'No one there,' he said gruffly. 'Must have been a knock from another room nearby.'

Lady Fortuna was standing by the window, gazing out into the thickening snowstorm. She turned to face him, her expression sharp.

'You're sure? There was no one there, no one who could have found out—'

'Relax, my dear,' Sneed said oozily. 'I assure you, the only one who knows we have that key is the one who was paid to slip it to us.'

A bunch of papers was scattered on the chest of drawers as though it had been discarded in a hurry. Sneed crossed the room briskly and picked the sheets up, fanning through them.

The lists of names, Betty guessed. *It has to be!*

'At least this gives us a couple of leads,' Sneed said. 'And those will lead to more – they'll be able to advise us of others who were at the hall then, who might have changed their names.'

Lady Fortuna began to pace up and down. 'I want them questioned,' she said haughtily. 'Tonight! We'll pull them aside and take them by surprise.'

'My dear,' Sneed interjected, 'I know you're impatient, but we must stick to the plan. The success of everything rests upon the timing, and the masked ball is the biggest event of the year. The staff here will be on their knees! That's why we strike tomorrow evening and catch them off-guard.' He placed the papers down on the chest of drawers. Betty stared at them, desperate for a look. If only she could sneak closer ... but it was too chancy with Fortuna pacing so erratically, not to mention the risk of spearing herself on one of the fortune teller's many pointy-heeled shoes.

'It's only one more night,' Sneed purred. 'Tomorrow the masked ball will allow us to move around unseen.' His pale eyes gleamed. 'With everyone in disguise it'll be a perfect recipe for confusion, and our little costume switch will help enormously with our plan.'

Costume switch? Betty's ears pricked up immediately. Just what exactly did this pair have up their sleeves? She glanced around the room but despite the mess of dresses everywhere she couldn't see any evidence of masked costumes. Then she spotted the wardrobe door ajar. They must be in there, but Betty had no way of checking without being noticed. If the Widdershins did end up going to the masked ball then Betty wanted to know exactly what Sneed and Fortuna were dressing up as so she could look out for them.

210

'I wish we could just do it tonight,' Fortuna grumbled, pouting like a sulky child. 'Haven't I waited long enough?' She finally stopped pacing and flopped down on the bed dramatically, with one arm over her face and the other dangling off the side of the bed. 'Oh, Sneed, do you really think we're close, after all this time? Whenever I shut my eyes I can almost see it,' she murmured. 'That shimmering, smooth crystal.'

'Closer than ever, my angel.' Sneed swooped in like a moustached bat, kneeling by the side of the bed to take her hand. Betty's tummy gave a queasy lurch as he planted a furry kiss on her knuckles. Slowly and carefully she edged out of the corner and crept to the chest of drawers, where Sneed had left the papers. Betty leaned over the top sheet and read down the list of names. Three had been underlined in blue ink. First was *Master Randall Greaves (owner)*. Next, *Mildred M. Busby*, whom Betty guessed must be the same Mildred from the kitchens.

The last name was *Jacqueline R. Chambers*.

Mrs Chambers, the weary-faced woman at the front desk. With trembling fingers Betty went through the rest of the sheets. No other names had been underlined. She backed away, heart pounding. How old was Mrs Chambers? Not as old as Granny, that much was certain. Forty years ago she must have been very young – around the same age as Elora.

I always thought that friend of hers knew more than she was sayin' . . .

That's what Mildred had said down in the kitchens, Betty remembered. Could Mrs Chambers have been that friend of Elora's?

She recalled the look of panic and sadness on the woman's face when she had found Betty and her sisters in the room.

It's always kept locked, always. *I make sure of that . . .*

Yes, Betty thought, becoming more and more certain. *Because you were Elora's friend. You must know things. I bet you've heard things, too, or even seen them.* No wonder Mrs Chambers always looked so weary. Perhaps the burden of being at the hall was too much for her to bear after all this time.

'I don't think Greaves will give us anything useful,' Sneed muttered, still smooching Fortuna's hand. 'From what I've heard, he's as stubborn as a goat and has never spoken about Elora Goode's death or the highwayman. Understandable, I suppose, that he'd want to protect the reputation of the hall. So that means we concentrate on the other two.' Sneed finally lifted his moustache from Lady Fortuna's fingers. 'Anyway, my dear, let us go down to supper. It's getting late.'

Fortuna sighed and got up. Her beautiful dress fell perfectly around her without a single crease. She flounced to the door and flung it open.

'Come on, then.' She sniffed, pausing to check her hair in the looking glass.

Betty saw her chance and took it, zipping quickly past Fortuna and out into the corridor.

'Did you feel that?' said Lady Fortuna, rubbing her arms. 'Something rushed past me. Maybe there are other ghosts in this place!'

'Probably just a draught.' Sneed threw a feathery shrug around her shoulders and locked the door. 'One more night, that's all,' he said. 'And then . . .'

Lady Fortuna smoothed out her long velvet gloves and arranged her face in a smile.

'And then we find my mother's crystal ball.'

Betty watched the two of them swish along the corridor in the direction of the dining room. She found she was sagging against the wall, drained as the adrenaline rush left her body. It had been risky to rush past Fortuna like that, but if she hadn't darted out when she did, she would be locked inside the room with no way to escape. And she needed to get back to her sisters now that half an hour had surely passed.

As she neared the stairs Betty looked across to the front desk in the hope that Mrs Chambers might be there, but like Betty herself, the woman was nowhere to be seen. She passed the family with the two young children on the stairs once more, having to dodge round them, and then found herself alone on the first-floor corridor. Betty hurried along it, averting her gaze from the glassy-eyed stuffed animals on the walls. She'd unlocked the door to room six and was just about to turn the handle when she heard a door close quietly up ahead. She glanced up – and froze.

A maid was moving quickly along the corridor, away from

Betty. In her hand was a black coal scuttle ... and from under her cap a strand of long, blonde hair had escaped.

Elora.

Betty went cold all over. Very slowly she released the door handle and watched the figure walking along the hall. And then something clicked in her mind, a startling realisation: why would the ghostly girl have closed a door quietly, when she had simply walked through walls and doors before? Unless ...

'Hey!' she said sharply, before remembering she was still using the magical nesting dolls. The figure visibly jumped but did not look round. Instead, her pace quickened.

'Yes, you!' Betty called, more loudly this time. She set off in pursuit of the girl, who sped up again.

'*Oi!*' Betty yelled. Her footsteps pounded on the floor, and she caught the figure glancing back, face half-hidden behind a tangle of blonde hair. She began to run, the coal scuttle swinging wildly, and Betty broke into a run, too.

The maid raced to the end of the corridor, past the brass lamp where Betty had first seen her disappear on the first day. This time she sped past it and vanished around the corner into the next corridor. Betty ran harder, determined to catch up, but just before she rounded the corner she heard a dull *thunk*. She skidded into the corridor. There was no sign of the maid but the coal scuttle lay in the middle of the floor, still rolling from side to side where it had been dropped.

Betty stopped, panting hard. She listened, desperately

trying to hear where the maid might be but there was only the sound of her own ragged breathing. Slowly, she picked up the coal scuttle and made another shocking discovery.

'The handle is still warm,' she whispered. Which proved that whoever she had seen just now had been very much alive – and that someone was pretending to be the ghost of Elora Goode.

Chapter Eighteen
The Pirate, the Peacock and the Scarecrow

THE NEXT MORNING THE WIDDERSHINS WOKE to the news that they were snowed in. It hadn't entirely been a surprise, for the three sisters had talked deep into the night after Betty's discoveries the previous evening. All the while, chunky white snowflakes had flurried past the windows and settled into drifts on the ledges. They came down so thick and fast that Betty could barely make out sky from snowflake and Charlie swore she had seen one as big as her hand.

There was a strange, restless atmosphere at breakfast that day. Betty's mind was swirling like the weather outside. Who had it been last night, the person pretending to be Elora? There were so many questions she needed answers to. She had looked again for Mrs Chambers as they'd passed the front desk, but there was no sign of the woman and today the desk was staffed by someone else. Keen as she was to question her, Betty knew the chances of Mrs Chambers giving much information were slim. The way she had clammed up in room nine suggested that whatever she knew about Elora and the haunting, she wasn't willing to share.

Fliss hadn't been able to find Mildred the night before, either. By the time she and Charlie had reached the kitchens the old cook had finished work for the day, and this morning when they had politely asked one of the serving staff about her they'd been told she was far too busy with food preparations for the ball to be disturbed.

The girls huddled over steaming cups of tea and buttered toast, watching as other guests milled around in a state of panic or excitement. Betty was restless and not hungry at all. She was jittery, wanting to know exactly what Sneed and Fortuna had got planned for later on. All morning the sisters had been looking out for the pair over breakfast, but neither had appeared. A handful of guests who had been due to leave sat by the front desk with anxious expressions, and fed-up looking staff continued to repeat the same information they had been giving out all morning: no one was going anywhere. The roads in and out of Wilderness were blocked. Many of the winter market's stalls were half buried under piles of snow, and there was no hope of them opening today.

'So we really are stuck,' Fliss muttered. She smothered a crumpet with honey and sank her teeth into it. 'I want to go home. I'll feel safer there. And if what Mrs Chambers said is true, then we *will* be safe, and nothing bad will happen.'

'Get your head out of the snow clouds, Fliss,' Betty said,

more grumpily than she intended. 'We're not going home yet. The way things look outside it'll be lucky if anyone even gets to leave the hall today.' From their window that morning, they'd spotted the lake marshal, Finn Sharkey, and his dogs outside, having been called upon to help someone stranded in the snow. On their way down to breakfast the sisters had seen porters with shovels and heard talk of digging out and clearing the walkways around the hall. The domed glass ceiling was entirely white, filling the hall below with dull grey light. The breakfast room was busier than usual, on account, Betty supposed, that there was nowhere else to go.

'What about her?' Charlie said, staring hard at someone across the room.

Betty followed her gaze to a fair-headed young woman who was helping herself to a gooey-looking pastry. 'I don't think so, but I'm not sure. I didn't get a proper look at her, but she seemed . . . I don't know. Younger.' She thought back to the maid she had seen when they had only just arrived. She had only had the quickest glimpse of her, barely enough to see her scowling face.

All morning the girls had been watching the guests and staff, trying to work out if any of them could have been the person Betty had seen last night. No one seemed to match, and Betty couldn't think of anyone they had noticed at the hall in the days before who would fit the description.

'Are you absolutely sure it was a real person you saw?' Fliss asked yet again, suppressing a yawn which Charlie then caught. The three of them had barely slept, puzzling over Betty's unsettling discovery.

'Of course I'm sure,' Betty said, rubbing her gritty eyes. Her mind was turning over all the strange happenings at Echo Hall. 'I've told you a hundred times. Ghosts don't drop things, and they don't have warm hands. And there was something sort of ... *clumsy* about her. And oh – she didn't walk through any walls,' she finished sarcastically.

'Fair enough,' Fliss snapped. 'But if it wasn't a ghost you saw, then what's to say it wasn't that same person who was looking out of the window, pretending to be Elora?'

'That's what I'm hoping,' Betty admitted. 'Because it would mean the part about a loved one dying won't come true. But we can't know that for sure.' She felt a squeeze of fear somewhere deep in her tummy. *Please don't let it be true.*

'Why would someone pretend to be Elora, though?' Charlie asked. 'To play a trick? Like being scary on Halloween?'

'Maybe,' said Fliss. 'Only, Halloween scary is fun, and this *isn't*.'

'Could be lots of reasons,' Betty said. 'Maybe they want to frighten people. Or it could be someone just messing around – a visitor.'

'Bet you gave them a good scare, Betty,' said Charlie, grinning. 'Shouting "Oi!" at them like that, all invisible.' Her smile faded and a worried look came over her little face. 'I hope it *wasn't* the ghost looking out of that window.'

'Me too,' whispered Fliss.

'Me three,' Betty added, wishing she didn't feel quite so helpless. 'And I wish there was a way we could get to Granny and Clarissa to check they're all right. Even if they're not snowed in, Chill Hill will be treacherous.'

'Well, somehow they've managed it,' Fliss exclaimed. 'Look!'

At the same moment, Betty heard a distinctive, 'Yoo-hoo!' and there, across the sea of people eating breakfast, were Granny and Clarissa at the dining-room door.

'Granny!' Charlie leapt up and scampered across the room, flinging herself into Granny's arms.

'Jumping jackdaws!' Betty said, rushing after her sister with Fliss right behind. 'Granny, how on earth did you both get here? Weren't you snowed in?' She waited until Charlie had released Granny and then felt herself pulled into one of Bunny's ferocious hugs. Her big woolly coat was cold and flecked with snowflakes, and she smelled of pine needles and ice. Betty breathed in the scent of her clove-scented pipe smoke and a faint whiff of whiskey and her anxiety eased a tiny bit. Granny was safe, for now at least.

'Not completely,' Granny explained. 'Clarissa's back door is sheltered and escaped the worst of it. Can't say the same for the front – it looks like an avalanche hit it. I popped out the back first thing for some milk I'd left outside and saw a boy on a sled being pulled by a dog – enormous thing, it was – like a wolf.'

'Bonbon!' Charlie guessed. 'And the boy is Sonny.'

'Right,' said Granny. 'Anyway, he'd been sledding and said

he was from the hall. He knew a back way through the woods that hadn't been so badly hit by the snow, and kindly brought us over.' She fanned her face and unbuttoned her coat.

'That could have been dangerous,' Fliss scolded, taking Granny's coat and draping it over a chair. 'What if you'd fallen off, or had an accident? No one would've known where you were!'

'Meddling magpies, what a fusspot you are.' Clarissa had already flopped on to a seat nearby and was leaning a wooden crutch against an umbrella stand. 'We're perfectly fine.'

'We thought we'd be better off here,' said Granny, releasing Betty and sinking into the chair with an, 'Ooo, that's nice.'

'Well, I never,' a creaky voice exclaimed. 'Clarissa Widdershins! What brings *you* here?'

Betty spun round to find an elderly man standing nearby, the crotchety fellow who she recognised from the girls' first night in the dining room. Only now, he didn't seem crotchety, he was jubilant. He looked as creaky as he sounded, and was bending over his stick which he held with fingers as knobbly as twigs. Up close, his spiky white beard and eyebrows were like frost on thistles.

'Old Master Greaves,' Clarissa said. Her tone was civil, but her eyes were narrowed. 'The cold weather's still preserving you, then?'

Greaves. It had been one of the names on Sneed's list, Betty recalled. The master of the hall, who, according to Sneed, was stubborn as a goat and refused to talk about Elora Goode.

'Now, now,' said Master Greaves, with a toothless grin. He turned to Granny and winked. 'I'm Randall Greaves, master of Echo Hall. At your service, madam. And you must be Clarissa's younger sister, surely?'

'Ooh, cheeky,' said Granny, looking secretly pleased.

Clarissa scowled. 'What can we do for you, Greaves?'

'You've already done it,' the old man crowed. 'What was it you said ter me all those years ago? "I'll never set foot in your rotten hall again." And here you are! Ho, ho!'

'You can *ho, ho* all you like,' Clarissa said, her eyes gleaming. 'Because I remember what *you* said to *me*—'

'Which was that if ever someone as insufferable as yourself should have visitors, I'll gladly put them up, free o' charge,' Greaves finished. 'So's they can get away from you.' His smile froze on his face as his eyes rested on Granny, and then the girls who were all watching him curiously. 'I . . . oh.'

Clarissa beamed. 'Greaves, meet my family. They've been staying here for the last few days, completely free of charge. So the joke's on you. Ho, ho indeed!'

Greaves' eyes bulged. He made a strange choking sound and loosened his collar. Then, to Betty's surprise he began to laugh, in great rattles that shook his twisty old body. He wagged a knobbly finger, then extended a hand to Clarissa.

'You win, you old battle-axe. Now, then. What d'you say we let go of our past differences?'

'Oh, if we must.' Clarissa gave his hand a quick shake, and then Greaves departed, still chuckling and shaking his head.

'That's why we got to stay here for *nothing*?' Betty said in amazement. 'Because of some years' old squabble with the owner?'

Clarissa nodded smugly. 'Knew I'd prove him wrong one day.' She gave a contented sigh, then clicked her fingers. 'They say revenge is a dish best served cold, but I like mine with a nice steaming cup of tea. Two sugars, please, Felicity. And a couple of those buns over there. And stop scowling like that or you'll turn the milk sour.'

'Righty-ho,' said Fliss, through gritted teeth.

'You look a bit more cheerful this morning, Granny,' said Betty. She'd expected her grandmother to be raging that they couldn't leave Wilderness as planned, but she seemed surprisingly relaxed.

'I was rather cross at first,' Granny replied. 'But then I decided it was pointless. Besides, with everyone being confined to the hall – and with me here to keep an eye on you – you won't be getting up to any mischief, will you?'

'No,' Betty agreed quietly. 'I suppose not.' She was glad Granny was safe, but having her around would make it much harder for her and her sisters to solve the mysteries of the hall.

'Now we're here, we may as well go to this masked ball,' Granny went on. Her eyes shifted craftily from side to side before she produced her flask from her bag and poured a nip of whiskey into her own teacup and Clarissa's. 'What do you say we make a night of it?'

223

Clarissa clinked her cup against Granny's. 'I say we make a day of it, too.'

Betty stared at their flushed faces. It appeared as though they'd started making a day of it from the minute they'd got up.

'What are your plans?' Granny enquired. 'Now you're stuck in the hall?'

'Well,' said Betty, thinking quickly. 'We'll need costumes for this evening, but after that we thought we might play hide and seek to pass the time before we get ready.'

'Hmm,' Granny said. 'You won't get much of that, seeing as Fliss spends three hours in the bathtub. Just stay out of people's way and don't cause any trouble, do you hear me? Clarissa and I will be here and keeping our eyes on you.'

'You'd better go and choose your costumes,' said Clarissa. 'Or there'll only be the ugly ones left!'

'Ugly ones?' Fliss said in alarm. 'But I don't want an ugly one!'

'Chop chop, then,' said Granny.

The costumes were in a cloakroom towards the back of Echo Hall. When the three sisters arrived they were dismayed to see that the rails had very little left on them. Many of the wooden hangers were bare and there were items of clothing strewn across the floor where people had dropped them. A man with a kind face was gathering them up when the Widdershins arrived.

'Oh, no,' Fliss muttered, surveying the mess. 'We're too late, aren't we?'

'We'll find something,' said Betty determinedly. 'Anyway, it doesn't matter what we look like.' She lowered her voice and started searching through the hangers. 'The important thing is our faces are covered. We're not going for a good time; we're going to find out what Sneed and Fortuna are up to and to solve this mystery once and for all.'

'Fine,' Fliss grumbled. 'But we could at least do it in style.'

Betty snorted and pulled out a hanger. 'Here, what about this? Looks like it'd fit you.'

'I am *not* going as a chimney sweep!' Fliss said hotly, brushing Betty's hand aside. 'I've already got Clarissa treating me like a tea maid. She'd be sending me up the chimneys next! And I really don't understand why there would be things like chimney sweeps and –' she curled her lip '– *donkeys* at a masked ball. I thought it was all flowing gowns and sequins?' She gave the man a questioning glance and, sensing Fliss had directed the question at him, he paused from hanging something up.

'Well, you see, it was a masked ball when it began,' he explained. 'That was more than fifty years ago, but over time things have changed. The hall sometimes hosted travelling theatre companies to perform plays and such, and the staff even put on shows themselves during the year. Many of the costumes were left over from those shows, and the ball evolved into something new, between a dance and a fancy-dress party.'

'I see,' said Fliss, looking mildly disappointed by this.

'Got mine,' Charlie announced, leaping out from a curtained changing room at the back. She had pulled herself into a pirate outfit, complete with a skull and crossbones kerchief which she had used to cover the lower half of her face, and a pirate's hat and eyepatch.

'Nice,' said Betty. 'But where's the parrot?'

'Dunno,' said Charlie, looking around. 'Must've got lost. Oh, wait – maybe it's in here.' She began rummaging through a large box that was labelled 'odds' and was full of all sorts of mismatched hats, gloves and masks, and emerged with a feathery magpie. 'This'll do,' she muttered, fixing the bird on one shoulder, and then, for good measure, adding a knitted squirrel to the other.

'A squirrel?' Fliss asked doubtfully.

'I'm a land pirate,' Charlie insisted. 'It's a thing.'

'I'm surprised you don't just have Hoppit on your shoulder,' said Betty.

'He's in my collar,' said Charlie. 'But it's not much good if no one can see him.' She glanced at the man, who had gone back to folding clothes. 'That's my imaginary rat, by the way.'

'Of course,' said the man, as though he heard this sort of thing every day.

Betty found a jester outfit she rather liked, but the hat was nowhere to be found. Minutes ticked by and everything she picked up was either torn, dirty, too small or too large.

'Haven't you got anything else?' she asked desperately. 'Like a knight, or ... or a lion, or something?' She wanted something brave, something adventurous. But the man simply shook his head.

'There is one thing that would fit,' he said suddenly, darting to a little door at the back. 'It was returned to us yesterday morning, as someone had to leave unexpectedly.' He emerged with something glittering and iridescent blue draped over his arms. A trail of long, beautiful feathers skimmed the floor.

'Oh,' Fliss breathed, her eyes wide with longing. 'How beautiful. A peacock!'

'Absolutely not,' said Betty at once. She was as unpeacocky as a person could be! But after several more minutes of rummaging around and finding nothing, she realised there was no other option.

'It fits you perfectly,' Fliss said enviously, once Betty had given up and put the dress on in the changing room. 'I'd wear it if only it fitted me.'

'Well, it doesn't, worst luck,' Betty grumbled. She readjusted the mask and stared at herself in a long mirror. The mask had a gold, pointed beak and a spray of peacock feathers at the top that looked like a little crown. On Fliss, it would've been stunning, but on herself Betty hated it. The only good thing about it was that there were two large pockets cunningly hidden within the sequinned folds, which Betty had to admit were practical. The nesting dolls would fit nicely in them – and Betty planned to make use of them this evening.

'Stop wriggling,' said Fliss, lacing Betty into the corset. 'There, it looks lovely.'

'I don't *want* to look lovely,' Betty growled.

'Betty Widdershins, where's your sense of fun?'

Betty stuck her tongue out in reply.

Fliss wasn't having much luck either. She attempted, yet again, to squeeze herself into a fairy outfit two sizes too small.

'That ain't going on now, is it?' said Charlie, stroking the bottom of her face kerchief like it was a beard.

'It *will*.' Fliss gritted her teeth and pulled.

'Give it up,' said Betty.

'Never.' Fliss yanked harder. There was a telling crackle, the sound of a seam splitting. 'Oops.'

A stern cough sounded from outside the changing room. Meekly, Fliss peeled off the fairy outfit and handed it back through the curtain. The man took it, then passed her something that looked like a lumpy bit of sacking, with bits of straw sticking out all over it. It was a scarecrow, with a floppy brown hat, a sack mask with cut-out eyes and bright red cheeks.

Fliss stared at it in horror. 'You've *got* to be joking.' She sniffed it dubiously. 'It smells dreadful.'

'Come on, Fliss,' said Betty, with a smirk. 'Where's your sense of *fun?*'

'Oh, ha HA,' Fliss huffed. She signed the hire slips for the costumes and stuffed the scarecrow outfit into her arms. 'I suppose we'd better go and start getting ready, although it hardly seems worth having a bath when I'm going to smell like old potatoes.'

'We've bigger problems than what you smell like,' said Betty, as they left the costume room. 'There's a fake ghost to catch, a real one to lay to rest and a crystal ball to find.'

'Sounds like a busy night,' Fliss said, attempting a smile.

Betty tried to smile back. For a few minutes, when they had been picking out costumes, she had almost been able to forget everything else and feel like a child again, one that was dressing up for Halloween or a birthday party. But already that feeling was ebbing away, replaced by the memory of the face at the window of Echo Hall. If the stories were true then time was running out. She thought of Father alone at home in Pendlewick. Was he safe? Would anyone know if he wasn't? What if he'd had an accident indoors, or ... or ...

Stop! she told herself. She mustn't think that way. They had to stay focused.

On the way back to their room Betty looked for Fortuna and Sneed again. Still no sign. At least the weather meant that they were as stuck as everyone else. Mrs Chambers was also missing from her usual spot at the front desk. Betty felt a flicker of worry. Could Sneed and Fortuna be questioning her right now? Apart from Master Greaves and Mildred the cook, Sonny's mother was their only real clue to the past, someone who might be able to tell them what had actually happened and not just rumours – and Fortuna and Sneed might have got to her first. Betty wondered what else they knew. What could the fortune teller's mother, Madam Divina, have seen in her crystal ball? And just what was their plan, that they needed a costume switch during a busy masked dance to carry it out?

Betty was certain of one thing: it could be nothing good. But she wasn't prepared for just how bad it really was.

Chapter Nineteen
Bad Luck

THE BALL STARTED AT SEVEN O'CLOCK SHARP
but the Widdershins were ready long before then.
So were most of the other guests at Echo Hall. On
a day in which most had not left the building, what else was
there to do except get ready?

The sisters had gone over and over their plan for the
evening, as well as what they knew while they'd been getting
ready. Despite Fliss grumbling that 'with a costume like hers'
she 'didn't see the point' of having a bath, she still managed
to spend almost an hour in the tub. Charlie, always happy
to swerve baths wherever possible, made the most of Granny
not being around to force her.

'Anyway,' she said cheerily, 'I reckon real pirates are soap
dodgers, ain't they?'

Their only preparations were for Betty's frizzy brown hair
to be wrangled into a plait, and to ensure each of them
had something small belonging to them inside the magical

nesting dolls. The dolls were safely tucked away in Betty's pocket, ready for later. Betty and Fliss had both used a single hair from their heads, while Charlie's item was a milk tooth that she had named Peg and had been carrying around ever since it had fallen out in the hopes of catching the tooth fairy.

Their plan was simple. The peacock and the pirate were to attend the ball as soon as the grand doors opened. There, they'd make sure they were seen by Granny and Clarissa – telling them that Fliss was still up in the room getting ready. They'd be looking out for the two people on Sneed's list: Mildred the cook and Mrs Chambers. Betty was also keeping a lookout for Sonny. If his mother refused to answer questions, as Betty suspected she would, then perhaps they might wheedle something out of him instead. Meanwhile, a certain scarecrow would be lurking on the lower corridor and keeping a watchful eye on Lady Fortuna's and Mr Sneed's rooms. Once they came out, Fliss would follow them at a safe distance, and report their costume choices as well as where they went, what they did and who they spoke to before they entered the grand chamber for the ball. After that, at the first sniff of anything suspicious Betty would use the dolls to become invisible, watch and listen in, while Fliss and Charlie kept Granny and Clarissa distracted.

At first, everything worked better than Betty could have hoped for, starting with Granny and Clarissa. Initially Betty was alarmed to find they were not where they said they would be, which was in the dining room. It didn't take long to work out that they were actually in the drinking lounge. As Betty and Charlie peered round the door into a fog of smoke they instantly spotted Granny, who was in a long, hooded black cape with her pipe dangling from her lips. She was concentrating hard on a card game, but looking a bit bleary-eyed.

Opposite Granny sat Clarissa who was in a garish black and yellow bumblebee dress, complete with huge fuzzy wings. Both Granny and Clarissa wore black masks over their eyes, the only differences being that Granny's was skew-whiff and had slid down to cover one eye, and Clarissa's had two pom-pom feelers which bobbed about comically every time she moved. Unfortunately, she also had hiccups, and each hiccup sent the pom-poms pinging in every direction.

'Clarissa,' said Granny, slurring her words. 'You must be cheating.'

Clarissa narrowed her eyes. 'Are you calling me a cheat, Bunny?'

'Yes,' said Granny. 'I thought I just did.'

Clarissa hiccuped, which sent the bumblebee pom-poms bouncing about in front of her eyes again. She swatted at them crossly, then noticed Betty and Charlie.

'Oh,' she said uncertainly, eyeing Betty. 'Felicity, is that you in there?'

'No, it's me, Betty,' said Betty, feeling even more unlike herself in the shimmering feathered dress. 'Fliss is still getting ready upstairs. You, um, know what she's like.' She became aware that Granny was suddenly looking at her very hard.

'A peacock?' she said, her voice strained. 'You've dressed up as a . . . a peacock?'

'I didn't want to,' Betty muttered. She was already looking forward to the moment she could use the nesting dolls to become invisible. It wouldn't help with how uncomfortable the dress was on her, but at least then people wouldn't see her in it. 'It was the only thing that fitted. Fliss wanted—'

'*How* many times have I said to you,' Granny spluttered, 'that peacock feathers are *unlucky?*'

'Erm . . .' Betty racked her brains. Now she came to think of it, had there been something about peacock feathers in Granny's many superstitions? 'I don't know. Have you?' She couldn't recall any peacocks back in Crowstone. Meddling magpies and jumping jackdaws, certainly, and an old rhyming superstition Granny had often repeated about crows, but pesky peacocks? No.

'It's bad luck to bring them indoors,' said Granny, slapping her handful of cards face down, and pushing her black eye mask back into place. 'You'll have to get changed – you can't wear that.'

'There was nothing else,' said Betty hotly, her nerves humming like an angry swarm of wasps. Why did Granny have to tell her this now? She wished she didn't know, or that Bunny's superstitions didn't have that way of popping up everywhere – and worse, coming true. Even if there had

234

been another costume, there was no time left – the ball was about to start and Fliss was waiting by the ground-floor guest quarters ready to follow Lady Fortuna and Sneed. Everything was in place. Betty would just have to do her best to make sure that bad luck didn't derail them.

'I like your bumplebee outfit,' Charlie said to Clarissa, using a word she had never quite been able to shake off because Betty, Fliss and Granny had always found it too amusing to correct her. 'But what are you supposed to be, Granny?' She eyed Granny's black cloak. 'An executioner?'

'Close,' said Granny. She nodded at a pretend wooden scythe that was resting against a nearby umbrella stand. 'I'm the rim greaper. Whoops, tee hee! I mean, the Grim Reaper.'

A chill ran down Betty's spine. *The Grim Reaper? Granny was dressed up as Death?* This felt more unlucky than anything. Like it was ... what was it Granny sometimes said? 'Tempting fate', which meant daring things to go wrong.

'Make sure you get changed,' said Granny, with another wary glance at Betty's costume. She picked up her cards – which Clarissa had been trying to sneak a look at. 'We'll be along soon.' She lowered her voice. 'Once I've thrashed Clarissa.'

'Yes, Granny,' Betty said quietly, and she and Charlie left the lounge and headed towards the ballroom. There were people there already queuing to get in, in a line leading back from two grand white doors with gleaming silver handles. Against the whiteness of those doors and the walls, the colourful outfits almost made Betty's eyes ache. There were costumes of every fabric and colour from ruby red to shimmering gold, sequins to silk. Curious eyes blinked at each other, trying to work out who might be hidden behind a certain mask.

At the sound of clocks chiming the hour, the doors creaked open and the crowd shuffled forward, eager for their first glimpse of the ballroom. Betty and Charlie found themselves swept along like fish in a river, forced to swim with the tide. Betty hardly knew where to look first.

The chamber was dimly lit with golden glowing candles. Soft music was playing, and everywhere smelled of oranges, cloves and nutmeg. Beautiful garlands of ivy, holly and berries hung along the walls, and tiny glass snowflakes and icicles – like the ones at the winter market – were strung above their heads, tinkling like wind chimes. In the centre of the room was a stunning ice sculpture of a fairy-tale castle with a pale green moat that was some kind of drink. Next to it was the handsome ice sculptor who had pushed up his mask and was talking to another man whose face was covered in a wolf mask. Betty could just make out a skim of dark skin and grey hair, and guessed this was Finn Sharkey, the lake marshal.

'It's magical,' Charlie whispered.

The room continued to fill, with people pouring in through the doors. The music swelled, becoming louder over the chatting of voices and the tinkling of glasses.

People moved around, admiring costumes, inviting each other to dance. After a few minutes Betty spotted Granny and Clarissa entering the room. They waved and headed straight for the ice castle's moat, with Granny in the lead and Clarissa wobbling unsteadily behind on a wooden crutch. For a moment Betty felt herself relax into the magic of the evening. Her family was here, they were safe for now, and that was all that mattered.

Very soon after that, a scarecrow appeared in the doorway and made its way towards Betty and Charlie. Bits of straw trailed behind it, and it scratched itself bad-temperedly as it stopped before them and adjusted its floppy hat.

'All right, Fliss?' Charlie asked, with a barely concealed smirk.

'No.' Fliss's dark eyes burned like coal through the cut-out eyes in the straw mask. 'I am *not* all right. My one chance to attend a masked ball, and this is what I'm dressed as. A scarecrow! Not only that but it really pongs inside this thing.'

'It really pongs outside, too,' said Charlie, wrinkling her nose.

'And it's itchy, and there are bits of straw sticking in my ears and out of my hair,' Fliss glowered.

'I thought you'd be used to straw in your hair by now,' said Betty, unable to resist teasing her sister. 'You've spent enough time rolling about in it kissing people.'

'Be quiet,' snapped Fliss. 'That was once, and it wasn't even a good kiss.' She straightened her hat and fixed her gaze across the room, answering the question that was on Betty's lips. 'They're over there, under that huge chandelier. Lady Fortuna is in the green scaly dress, and Sneed is next to her in the top hat and the leafy green mask.'

'I see them,' Betty said, watching the pair closely. Fortuna's black hair hung loose and shining down her back. Her long, green dress was shinier still, shimmering with sequins. Her mask was also sequinned, the kind that people held up to their face on a long wand. Fortuna was laughing elegantly, moving the mask away from her face every so often to sip at her drink.

'She's putting on a show,' Betty murmured. 'Lowering the mask so everyone can see it's her.' They continued to watch as Fortuna and Sneed each took a glass from a passing servant with a tray of drinks, then began moving around the room, exchanging conversation and admiring people's costumes.

'Wish I was in her dress,' Fliss breathed. 'Even if it *does* look a bit like a dragon princess.'

'A Fliss scarecrow is ten times better than a Lady Fortuna dragon princess,' Betty said loyally, remembering the fortune teller's unkind words about her sister. 'She might have a fancier dress but you'd outshine her any day. Now, when you followed them did you see if they went anywhere, or spoke to anyone?'

Fliss shook her head, releasing a shower of straw. 'No, they came straight here from the rooms.'

'Good work, stinky,' said Charlie, patting Fliss on the back. The minutes wore on and Fortuna and Sneed continued to mingle. A couple of times, the girls passed by them, trying to listen in on their conversations. The second time, Sneed had stopped Finn Sharkey and was asking questions about his dogs – how fast they could run, and whether it was easy to control his sled in the thick snow.

Betty began to feel less certain of everything. What if the pair had already questioned Mrs Chambers and Mildred in some quiet corridor of Echo Hall, unseen by everyone? She tried to recall what Sneed had said about the ball and the costume switch: *a perfect recipe for confusion*. Had she missed something already? Was it too late? Or could she even have misheard him in the first place?

'Wait ... Where's he going?' Fliss said, as Sneed left Fortuna's side and headed off into the crowd.

'Getting another drink?' Betty supposed, noticing two empty glasses in his hands.

But instead of refilling the glasses, Sneed set them down on a tray and slipped out of the doors to the ballroom.

'I'll see where he goes,' said Betty at once. 'Stay here and watch Fortuna – if she leaves, follow her.' Her eyes firmly on Sneed, she wove her way through the tight knots of people, treading on toes and dress hems, muttering apologies. Sneed moved quickly and lightly, slithering through the crowd like a snake making a slippery getaway. Betty reached the door seconds after he had left and was astonished to find he was already a good way ahead of her. Waiting for a woman dressed as a swan to pass by, Betty took the nesting dolls out.

With a quick twiddle of the third doll containing Fliss's hair and Charlie's tooth she kept her sisters visible, while Betty herself vanished.

The front desk was empty, apart from Sneed who quickly glanced at the clock on the stairs. It was a couple of minutes to eight o'clock. Betty drew nearer, close enough to listen clearly to anything that was said, but Mrs Chambers was not at the desk. A little fire burned behind it in the fireplace, but the guard was up and there was no sign of anyone.

Betty watched and waited, expecting Sneed to call out or perhaps even ding the bell on the desk. He paused, checking his surroundings, satisfied that he appeared to be alone. Then he took something from his pocket – a small square of paper – and left it on the desk.

A *note?* If Betty could get a glimpse at it first, before Mrs Chambers arrived . . .

Sneed tapped the bell smartly, and in that *ding* Betty's hopes of getting to the note vanished. Quick footsteps sounded nearby – someone was coming. Sneed moved smoothly away from the front desk without looking back, but instead of heading to the ballroom he took the other corridor – the one leading to the rooms he and Fortuna were in.

What's he doing now? Betty wondered, torn between following him and waiting to see whether she could stay and read the note. Mrs Chambers appeared behind the desk, seeing no one. Betty expected confusion but instead a look of annoyance crossed her face, and Betty could guess what was going through her mind: people playing tricks, children most likely. Then she spotted the note.

She picked it up and read it once. It must have been short. Her hand began to tremble and her face drained of all colour.

She looks terrified, Betty thought, wondering what the note could possibly have said to have caused such a reaction. But in one swift movement Mrs Chambers tossed the scrap of paper over the top of the fireguard and into the flames. It flared up and was gone instantly. Mrs Chambers took a seat at the desk and sat very still, staring straight ahead.

Betty glanced away from her to the corridor where Sneed had disappeared. He would be in his room by now, but if she waited outside she could catch him leaving again and follow. Quickly and silently she went in the direction Sneed had gone, but before she turned the corner she heard voices. Sneed was not yet in his room. He was talking to someone – two people, in fact.

Betty crept closer. Sneed had removed his mask and was twiddling his moustache, which had gone flat and sweaty. His door was ajar with the key in it; evidently he had just unlocked it when he had been interrupted. The two old ladies speaking to him were dressed in flouncy, frilly dresses of purple and peach, and had lowered their masks to talk.

Betty recognised them at once from the dining room – she had sat at their table while she was invisible. The lady in peach was the one who had plonked her bag on Betty's lap.

'... We think there must be a ghostly presence that wishes to make contact with us,' she was saying. 'The bag was whisked right away before our very eyes! And so, we were hoping Lady Fortuna could fit us in before her visit is over?'

'I'm so sorry,' said Sneed, not sounding sorry at all, 'but Lady Fortuna is no longer taking bookings – she's been extremely busy and needs to rest. All those visions leave her mind very, um, cluttered.' He glanced at the door, his moustache limp with sweat. He looked strange, Betty thought. Worried, and almost sick, like he had a fever. 'Now, if you'll excuse me ...'

A series of bumps came from within the room. Betty turned towards it sharply. *What could that noise be?* The bumps continued, fast at first and then slower, slower ... followed by a loud THUD. Then silence.

'Did you hear that?' said the other lady, leaning towards the room excitedly. 'Something going bump in the night! Perhaps there are other ghosts here.'

'No, no,' said Sneed through gritted teeth. He wiped at his forehead which was also damp now. 'It's my ... um, window banging.'

Betty hadn't been planning to go into the room, not this time. But the look on Sneed's face was one of barely controlled panic. Something was very wrong – just *what* was he hiding? In a split second she stepped closer and gently pushed the door. It opened soundlessly, as though caught in a draught. She peered in but only saw half the room. It was still and in darkness; no sign of movement. The window was closed.

'The door!' one of the ladies squeaked. 'It's opening by itself!'

Betty took her chance and darted inside, holding her breath.

'Yes, yes,' Sneed babbled, grabbing the door. 'These old places are so quirky! Well, must be going. Goodnight!' He stepped inside and slammed the door, breathing hard as he locked it. His shoulders were heaving with shaky breaths. He took off the top hat, tossed it on the bed and wiped his forehead. Then, passing very close to Betty, who was pressed against the wardrobe, he lit a little round lamp and the room flooded with light.

'Just what the *heck* do you think you're doing?' he spat, his eyes bulging with anger.

Betty bit down on her lip, frozen with fright. Had Sneed somehow guessed she was in the room? But he was looking past Betty to the corner.

A chair was on its side on the floor. Betty could see its wooden legs and then two scuffed shoes and the hem of a black skirt, but the rest was obscured by the bed. Someone had been sitting in the chair as it had tipped. Why hadn't they got up – were they hurt?

Sneed crossed to the chair in three angry strides and pulled it up into its correct position, making a loud bang which masked Betty's shocked gasp.

The girl in the chair wore a black and white maid's uniform and had long, blonde curls which had come loose from under the cap and were hanging over her face. Betty was sure it was the same girl she'd seen last night in the corridor upstairs – the person she had chased who'd dropped the coal scuttle. Who'd been pretending to be Elora. Betty could see now why the girl hadn't got up from the floor. She hadn't been able to, for she was tied securely to the chair.

'That,' Sneed hissed, 'was stupid.' He grabbed the maid by the shoulder and shook hard. As he did so, her cap slid sideways, taking the blonde curls – *a wig!* – with it. The wig and cap landed on the floor, leaving only a copper-haired boy with a frightened expression.

Betty gawped, unable to believe her eyes.

It was Sonny.

Chapter Twenty
The Kidnapper

B ETTY'S HORRIFIED EYES WENT FROM SONNY
to Sneed, then back again, as she tried to piece
together what she was seeing.

Sonny?

Sonny was the fake Elora?

Sneed – and presumably Lady Fortuna – had captured
him. Had they thought they were chasing a ghost and
realised their mistake when they'd caught him? What were
they planning on doing with him now?

An image of a square of paper and Mrs Chambers' pale
face flashed in Betty's mind.

The note.

She hadn't seen what it said, but now thoughts were racing
through her head. Had the note informed Mrs Chambers
of what her son had been up to? *Surely not*, Betty thought.
Sneed could have easily marched him back to his mother
and revealed what had been going on. Yet the gag and the

245

cord binding Sonny to the chair told Betty this wasn't it. There was something else, something far more sinister than Betty had been prepared for. She had known that Sneed and Fortuna were swindlers and con artists, but she hadn't imagined that they might actually be dangerous.

She thought back to the noises she had heard from outside the room and understood what they had been: Sonny had been trying to attract the attention of the two women outside by rocking on the chair, and then he had overturned, making the loud crash.

Sneed snatched up the blonde wig and dumped it on the bedside table. Then he sat on the bed and turned the chair round so Sonny was facing him, silently watching him for a long moment. The anger he'd displayed moments before seemed to have vanished, and his usual smarmy, pleased-with-himself expression was back.

'You've made this very easy, boy,' he murmured at last. 'I knew this hall was haunted – I've seen things moving around with my own eyes. So naturally, when I saw a little ghostly maid wandering along the corridors, I followed. Imagine my surprise when I saw you stumble down that step and gasp out – not a very ghostly thing to do, was it? And unfortunately for you, I'm much quicker than I look.'

Betty thought back to her sighting of the 'ghost' yesterday evening. How many of the other sightings of Elora had been real, and how many had been faked by Sonny? The maid she'd seen on the first day, who'd seemingly vanished through the wall? And the face at the window? Had it been Sonny all along? *No.* She remembered, with a chill, the shadowy figure who'd been in the room with her when she awoke. The ice skate left on the bed ... Whatever Sonny's tricks were, he couldn't walk through locked doors.

'Now things are working out even better than I'd hoped they would,' Sneed continued. 'I'd had a little plan, you see. I'd prepared to plant some valuables of mine on the old cook in the kitchen – and your mother – just in case they needed any encouragement to answer my questions. No one likes to be accused of stealing, do they?' He chuckled, much to Sonny's confusion. 'But it turns out I didn't need to do that. Old Mildred was only too happy to have a chat with me earlier. Likes an audience, she does. And she had some *very* interesting things to say about your mother. So interesting, in fact, that it didn't even matter that I couldn't find her to speak to her myself. And now I have you.'

Sonny went very still. Betty could see the fear in his eyes as well as the questions. Sneed was intent on getting the crystal ball for Fortuna, but how far would he go to get the truth?

'So, now you can tell me what you know about your mother's life here,' Sneed went on. He leaned forward, placing his fingers on the gag in Sonny's mouth. 'Listen carefully: I'll give you one chance to speak, and only one. If you shout out for help, then we'll do this the hard way. Do you understand?'

Sonny nodded vigorously.

'Good.' Sneed roughly removed the gag from the boy's mouth and watched him warily, but Sonny made no attempt to call out.

'Firstly, I want to know *why*?' Sneed demanded.

Sonny hesitated. 'Wh-why . . . what?'

Sneed gestured to the wig and cap. 'Why all this? Boredom? A practical joke? I can't imagine there's much for a boy your age to do in a hall that's empty for most of the year. Is this your idea of fun, or is it something more?'

Betty waited, hardly able to breathe. She was as desperate to hear the answer as Sneed was. If it *was* a joke then it was a cruel one – especially if it had been Sonny whom she and her sisters had seen at the window.

Sonny's expression darkened, his coppery eyebrows knotting together in a scowl.

'No,' he said finally, his voice hoarse. 'Not a joke.'

'Then what?' Sneed said sharply, seeming oddly excited. 'Did your mother put you up to it? She did, didn't she?'

'My moth— what? No!'

'It's a clever idea,' Sneed rushed on. 'Using the story of the haunting to distract people – to scare them so that their attention is focused on the ghost, and away from the true secret of Echo Hall!'

'True secret?' Sonny asked. 'What are you talking about?'

'The crystal ball, of course,' Sneed hissed. 'It makes perfect sense! Build on the real haunting to try to scare people away.

Fewer people coming to the hall means fewer chances of the crystal ever being recovered!' He leaned closer to Sonny's face. 'That old cook told me your mother knew Elora Goode all those years ago. More than that, they were friends. Thick as thieves, that's how she described them. Always together, always whispering and giggling! If there was anyone Elora told her secrets to, it'd be her best friend, wouldn't it? And that's why I believe your mother could know something vital, some clue to the whereabouts of that crystal ball.'

Sonny shook his head, still scowling.

'My mother knew Elora, that's true. But she's never told me they were friends – not once. She has nothing to do with what I've been up to. Nothing! She doesn't know I do this. All the stories say that the crystal ball sank in the lake with the highwayman and I've never heard any different, so you're wasting your time. Just like all the other greedy treasure hunters who come looking for it.' He paused and gave Sneed a look of pure loathing. 'I couldn't care less about that crystal ball. What I *do* care about is my mother, and how hard she works.' He paused as his voice cracked. 'And how she's treated, every single day, by people like *you.*'

'Her superiors, you mean?' Sneed asked with a smirk. 'Your mother is here to take orders and keep guests happy.'

Sonny's fists clenched hard. If Betty wasn't hiding, she would have wanted to punch Sneed on the nose, too. *Superior?* Sneed was nobody's superior! *How dare he?* He was a lying, cheating swindler and a kidnapper!

'I've seen the way your sort talk to her,' Sonny whispered, fighting to keep his voice under control. 'Like she's nothing. Like she's the dirt on your shoes, and I'm sick of it!' He paused, his chin jutting out defiantly. 'So that's why it started. It was my way of giving people a scare. My way of getting them back, at first.'

Betty listened, allowing this to sink in. She remembered how angry *she* had felt when she had overheard Lady Fortuna saying mean things about Fliss, and how Betty had had that same desire to get back at her, to scare her. She could only imagine how Sonny must feel to see his mother treated horribly day in, day out.

'At . . . first?' Sneed enquired, looking amused.

'Later on it *was* to try to scare people away, but not because of the crystal ball.'

'Why, then?' Sneed repeated.

Sonny stared him straight in the eye. 'Because if no one comes here, then this lousy place will close for good and my mother and me will be forced to leave,' he said, his eyes filling with angry tears. 'Whatever she says, I know she hates it here as much as I do – but she won't leave. I don't know why.'

'Perhaps she's searching for that crystal,' Sneed mused, his eyes burning brightly. 'It would certainly be a treasure for a lowly servant like her.'

Betty thought of Mrs Chambers, always so sad-looking. Life at Echo Hall certainly seemed to have worn her down. Betty and her sisters had only known it to be busy there, and the market square full of life and movement. But the long months in between must have made the hall a bleak and lonely place to live for the rest of the year. No wonder Sonny wanted to escape it. Why wouldn't his mother agree? Could Sneed be right – could she be hanging on to search for the highwayman's loot, pinning all her hopes on a better life?

'You're wrong,' Sonny said, shaking his head. 'She doesn't care about riches. And she's good, my mother. The last thing she'd want is some stolen crystal ball.'

'Yes, well,' said Sneed, with a sneer. 'You didn't even know your mother was friends with Elora, which proves you don't know her as well as you think. But don't worry – you're going to be very, very helpful in what happens next.'

'What's that?' Sonny asked, his voice unsteady. 'I thought ... I thought if I told you what I know you'd let me go?'

'Who said anything about that?' Sneed got up and opened the wardrobe, selecting from inside a hanger which held a black dinner jacket with long coattails. He removed the green jacket he was wearing and put on the black one. From one of its pockets he removed something that looked like a large, hairy white doughnut and pulled it on to his head. It was a wig, Betty realised. A very good one that instantly hid Sneed's short red hair and gave him an untidy white mop. It even had a patch of fabric at its centre which gave it a convincing bald spot on the top.

Next, he pulled out a plain black mask, similar to the one

251

Granny had been wearing, and put it on. The effect was startling. With different hair and his distinctive red moustache hidden, Sneed was unrecognisable. Finally, he took something else out of the wardrobe: a black walking cane topped with a silver bird's head. Its beak was long, sharp and pointed. Sneed clasped his fingers over it and stooped, his back bent. He took a couple of limping steps, like an old, aching man. Betty watched, increasingly fearful. The amount of care and thought Sneed had put into his disguise frightened her.

He stood up straight and leaned the cane against the bedpost, pleased with himself.

'Just in case,' he said, chuckling softly.

'What are you going to do?' Sonny asked, his voice trembling.

'We're going on a little walk,' Sneed replied. 'And it'll be ... chilly, so I've made arrangements to wrap up on the way.'

'Chilly?' Sonny said uncertainly. 'You're taking me outside?'

'I've decided it's the best chance of refreshing your mother's memory,' said Sneed.

Dread curled around Betty like an icy draught. What was Sneed planning?

'You won't be able to get me out of the hall without anyone noticing,' said Sonny, bravely. 'Someone will see! I'll ... I'll make a noise. You can't walk me out of here tied up and with a gag on!'

'Quite right,' said Sneed, completely calm. 'You'll be untied. But you're forgetting that everyone else is at the masked ball.

It's loud and the corridors are deserted. However, if we do come across anyone, I warn you, if you try to run or call out, you will be *very* sorry.' He leaned in close to Sonny's face, lowering his voice. 'It's just you and your mother here, isn't it? We wouldn't want anything to happen to her . . . oh – or that dog of yours.'

Sonny went very still, the last of the colour draining from his face as Sneed's unspoken threat hung in the air.

'In any case,' Sneed continued, 'we'll be taking a different route out of here.'

'D-different?'

'You know exactly what I'm talking about,' Sneed hissed. 'I know there are parts of Echo Hall which aren't used by the guests – parts *you've* been using in your little charade! That's how you've moved around, isn't it, making it look as though you've vanished through walls?' He grinned nastily. 'Now it's time to do your little disappearing trick again – only this time, you won't be alone.'

Disappearing trick? Betty tensed at Sneed's revelations. So there *was* a way Sonny had been vanishing! No wonder his ghostly Elora had been so convincing.

Sneed pulled out a pocket watch and checked the time. 'Good,' he said. 'The dance will be in full swing by now. Time to go.' He snatched up the blonde Elora wig and cap and pulled them on to Sonny's head, roughly arranging the blonde curls, then began to loosen the knots that bound Sonny to the chair.

I need to find Mrs Chambers, Betty thought. *If I can tell her where Sonny is, then she can raise the alarm and rescue him.* She spied the key in the door and a daring plan came to her. If she was quick enough, she could get out of the door and lock both Sneed and Sonny in until help came. And she had to do it – *now* – because Sneed was hauling Sonny to his feet.

Betty crept towards the door, her heart racing wildly. She turned the key slowly, hoping it would be soundless . . . but the click was loud and unmistakable. Sneed's head twisted round like an owl's to stare at the door.

Betty did the only thing she could. She seized the key and flung the door open, stepped into the hallway and slammed it closed behind her, fumbling to get the key back in the lock on the other side. Her trembling fingers missed. She tried again, this time slotting it in place but before she could turn it the handle was pushed down from the other side. The door was wrenched open, forcing Betty to release it.

She was shaking, trying to still her breathing as Sneed came out of the room. He glanced up and down the empty corridor, looking as shocked as she felt.

'Wh-who's there?' he demanded in a hoarse whisper. 'Elora Goode – is that you?'

Betty stayed silent and frozen. If only she had been quick enough, Sneed would have been safely locked in the room. But it was too late, and she could see he was already beginning to gather his wits. He reached behind him and grabbed Sonny by the arm, pulling him out of the room.

'Move,' he ordered, locking the door and checking the corridor once more.

Sonny glanced about, eyes wide with panic. Betty could see hopelessness there, too. Just as Sneed had planned, they were alone. Sounds of music swelled from the ballroom, along with the occasional tinkle of laughter. No one would hear Sonny shout above that racket. No one would see where Sneed led him. No one except Betty.

With one hand firmly on Sonny's shoulder, Sneed marched him along the corridor in the opposite direction to the stairs. It looked almost identical to the corridor upstairs, with the same wooden panelling, and even the same brass lamps on the walls. Betty watched, hesitating. She knew she had to get to Sonny's mother as fast as possible, but something held her in place. She needed to see for herself what the 'disappearing trick' Sneed had spoken of really was, and she was the only witness to where Sneed would lead Sonny.

She did not have to wait long. She followed at a safe distance until Sonny and Sneed stopped just over halfway down the corridor. With a warning look at Sonny, Sneed stepped closer to the wall and pressed a finger into a circular shape in the wooden panelling. At once, the entire panelled section of the wall opened in on itself like a door. Beyond it was a black, unlit space. Betty knew what it was instantly, and at any other time a discovery like this would have thrilled her. But not now. Now, it scared her.

'It *was an old staircase,*' Mildred, the old lady in the

kitchens, had said. *'The servants used it years ago so they didn't get in the guests' way.'*

A swift shove sent Sonny through the gap. He gasped, stumbling a little, and the maid's cap slid off his head and on to the floor. Sneed, too busy checking the corridor was clear once more, did not notice the cap and followed straight after him. The panel closed behind them like they had never been there at all.

Betty blinked in shock, still unable to believe the enormity of what was happening.

Do something! she urged herself. And then she snapped into action. She grabbed the maid's cap up from the floor, not quite knowing why, only that it *felt* important.

And then she turned and ran, her feet pounding off the stone floors.

She had to find Mrs Chambers.

Chapter Twenty-one
The Hidden Staircase

BETTY SKIDDED TO A HALT IN FRONT OF MRS Chambers' desk. There was no sign of her or anyone else. The fire in the grate still glowed but hadn't been topped up. The desk was neat and organised but it had an air of stillness about it. Before now, the place had always felt busy even when empty, like Mrs Chambers had just popped away and was about to return. Perhaps it was her imagination or what she knew, but Betty could sense, deep down, that Sonny's mother wasn't coming back any time soon.

She's gone to find him, Betty thought. *And followed whatever instructions Sneed left for her.* And with her gone, and everyone else in the ballroom, there was no one who could help – except Betty.

A low rumbling groan reached her ears. For a moment she thought she had imagined it, but then she caught sight of a bushy grey tail on the rug next to the chair. Betty edged behind the desk and peered beneath it. Bonbon was stretched out underneath, his huge body only just fitting in. His large furry head was resting on his paws, but his icy blue eyes were wide open and alert. *Did he know Sonny was gone?* Betty wondered. A silver chain was attached to his collar at one end, and a leather strap on the other end was fastened to a hook underneath the desk. His head lifted as Betty neared him, and he raised his black nose in the air.

'It's all right, boy,' she murmured softly, not wanting to scare him. How would a dog react to someone he couldn't see? But to her surprise he thumped his tail in welcome and got to his feet, sniffing Betty's hand. She got a waft of warm dog's breath.

The cap, she realised. Sonny had been wearing it. That's what he could smell. She pushed it into her pocket and straightened up, trying to think. For all she knew, Sneed and Sonny had already left the hall. Was there anyone she could ask for help? Finn Sharkey, perhaps. He knew the area well and had the tools to navigate the snow, but finding him quickly in the crowded ballroom would be virtually impossible.

Betty turned and headed for the ballroom, trying to clear her panicked mind. Sneed could not have taken Sonny far – it had only been about two minutes since they had vanished through the concealed panel in the wall, and the snow would no doubt slow them down. Her focus shifted to Lady Fortuna. She must still be in the ballroom, unless she had given Fliss and Charlie the slip. The thought of this made her feel sick. The image of Sonny tied to the chair wouldn't leave her – and if Sneed was taking him outside, somewhere 'chilly' as he'd put it, then the boy would be in grave danger, not only from Sneed, but from the biting weather, too.

She reached the ballroom door. The dimly lit room was packed with people, picked out by the glow of candlelight and glittering chandeliers. The guests were a whirl of sequins and plush velvet, with only the whites of their eyes visible behind elaborate masks. It was dizzying to watch them, to feel the heat and noise coming from the room. The scent of oranges, cloves and berries was suddenly overpowering and Betty took a step back as the crowd parted and a woman in a shimmering green dress glided towards the doors.

Fortuna!

She moved smoothly through the doorway and left the ballroom, her mask lifted to her face. Betty took another step back as Lady Fortuna passed so close by her that she felt the draught from her swishing skirts. She watched, torn between following her and going into the ballroom to find her sisters. She knew it would be foolish and dangerous to follow her alone, but if she went to look for her sisters or the lake marshal she risked losing her.

A second passed, then two. Fortuna hurried further away. *I bet she's going to get changed,* Betty thought. *Just like Sneed did. Maybe there's still time . . .*

And then to her surprise and relief, two figures appeared at the ballroom entrance. A pirate and a scarecrow peered around the door, then stepped into the corridor an arm's length from Betty.

'There she is.' Fliss's voice was low and slightly muffled behind the sacking mask. 'Looks like she's heading for her room. Oh, Betty, where the heck are you?'

'I'm here,' Betty said, placing an invisible hand on Fliss's arm.

Fliss flinched, her hand flying to her chest. 'Betty! Thank goodness. You scared me.'

'Fortuna went that way,' Charlie added, her little voice fierce. 'We did what you said – we kept our eyes on her.'

'I know,' said Betty, feeling a flood of pride and love for her sisters. 'We have to follow her.'

'Where have you been?' asked Fliss, in a rush. 'Where's Sneed? Did you lose him?'

Betty shook her head before remembering her sisters couldn't see her. 'No. But we have to hurry – I'll explain everything on the way.'

'On the way where?' Fliss persisted, her voice dropping to a whisper. 'Where are we going?'

Betty waited until Fortuna vanished around the corner ahead. 'Go!' she said. 'Quickly, let's get to the front desk. We have a few minutes, if that.'

They moved soundlessly along the corridor after the fortune teller, arriving at the front desk moments later.

'I don't understand,' Fliss said urgently, casting a quick look in the direction Fortuna had gone. 'Shouldn't we be following her?'

'And shouldn't we all be invisible?' Charlie added.

'Yes, and we will be,' said Betty. Her mind was clearing now, the fog of panic dying back now she had found her sisters. She was not in this alone. A plan was coming to her, knitting together. She took the maid's cap out of her pocket and stepped behind the desk once more, holding it out to Bonbon. He was sitting up now, his ears pricked up and alert and his ice-blue eyes trained on Fliss and Charlie. He sniffed the cap gently, black nose twitching. Once again his tail began to wag.

'Bonbon!' Charlie exclaimed. 'What's that you've got, Betty?'

'It's Sonny's,' Betty replied. 'Sonny's been pretending to be Elora's ghost to frighten away guests – he wants the hall to close so he and his mother can move away.'

'Wait, *what?*' Fliss exclaimed. 'The fake ghost was Sonny?'

Betty nodded. 'Sneed kidnapped him and he's using him to make Mrs Chambers talk.'

'*Kidnapped?*' Charlie repeated in alarm.

'He thinks she might hold the key to where the crystal ball is,' Betty explained. She sank her hand into Bonbon's thick, soft coat and tugged her fingers through it. Several grey hairs came away and she pinched them in her fingers. With her other hand she took the nesting dolls out of her pocket.

'Charlie, open these up,' she said.

Charlie did as she was asked and separated the dolls, rendering Betty visible.

'What are you doing?' she asked, as Betty sprinkled a

261

couple of the dog's hairs into the third nesting doll along with her sisters' hair and tooth and the whisker of Hoppit.

'Taking Bonbon with us,' Betty said. 'I'm hoping he'll pick up Sonny's scent and lead us to him if we get lost. They could be anywhere out there, in that snow. But Charlie?' she said gently. 'I need you to do something for me.' She carefully took Charlie's little milk tooth out of the dolls and tucked it into her sister's hand. 'I need you to go back to the ballroom. Find Granny and Clarissa and Finn Sharkey, and tell them what's happening. They can send out a search party. Fliss and I will go after Fortuna.'

Charlie stared at her in disbelief. 'I want to come with you!' she said. 'Let me help! I'm brave, you *know* I am.'

'Yes,' Betty said softly. 'You are. Of course you are! But sometimes being brave isn't charging outside chasing someone down in the freezing cold. Sometimes being brave is asking for help – just like you did when I fell through the ice, remember?'

'But—' Charlie began.

'*Please*, Charlie,' Betty interrupted. 'There's no time. We're out of our depth here, and we can't do this alone. I'm not giving you the easy job; I'm giving you the safest one.'

'Betty's right,' Fliss added. 'Someone needs to raise the alarm.'

'But they could be anywhere,' Charlie said, her bottom lip trembling. 'You said they're outside in the freezing cold! How will Finn Sharkey know where—?'

'I know where they're going,' Betty cut in, remembering what Sneed had said. *Somewhere chilly . . . to refresh your mother's memory.* 'He said "somewhere chilly". At first I thought he meant Chill Hill, but everything about the crystal ball points to the lake. And if he thinks Mrs Chambers knows something, then my guess is he's taking her there, to where it all ended.' She paused, feeling the words sink in and becoming more and more certain of them. 'Elora's Tears.'

'All right,' Charlie said, sniffing back her tears. 'I'll get help. You can count on me.'

Betty gave her a quick, fierce hug. 'Go,' she whispered, watching as Charlie took off in the direction of the ballroom, the knitted squirrel and magpie dancing about on her small shoulders as though they were eager to get back to the great chamber. She turned back to Fliss, then crossed quickly to the lost property basket and rummaged through it. 'We'll need warm clothes and we have to hurry.' From the jumble of garments inside she pulled out several jumpers, scarves, the thickest hats she could find, some mismatched mittens and a filthy overcoat that looked as though it had been dragged through mud.

'You take the coat,' Fliss said, clearly unable to bear the thought of adding to her already hideous outfit. She removed the scarecrow mask and hat and tossed them under the desk before tugging on layers of jumpers.

Betty didn't argue. She pulled the clothing on over the

peacock dress, stuffing the chunky mittens into the coat pocket to put on later. Already she was trembling at the thought of going outside. Were they really going to do this? Would it be better to wait for help? She thought of Sonny, his terrified face. Of how Sneed seemed to have planned every detail. What was to stop him taking off with Sonny – or doing something worse to silence him? *No.* They had to go, and now. Betty unhooked Bonbon's leash and handed it to Fliss. Then she placed the nesting dolls one inside the other until only the outer one was left in her hand. With a final twist the two halves were aligned and Betty, Fliss, and Bonbon vanished from view.

'Come on,' Betty urged. Fliss followed, and Bonbon quickly took the lead, pulling eagerly against his silver chain, nose to the floor. Within a minute they were on the corridor, outside Fortuna's room, breathless and edgy with fear and anticipation.

'What if we've missed her?' Fliss whispered, her mittened hand tight around Bonbon's leash. He sniffed at the foot of Sneed's door, clearly picking up Sonny's scent. 'What if they've taken Sonny far away, someplace we can't get to? And should we be risking our lives for a boy we hardly know?'

Betty took a sharp breath, the question slicing through her thoughts. Why was she so intent on going after Sonny and Sneed? 'Because I need to know if it was Sonny who we saw at the window,' she said, and as she spoke the words she felt them even more strongly. She could not leave Wilderness, could not live with the possibility of another curse hanging over the Widdershins' heads. She gave Fliss a tight smile. 'And because ... because it's the right thing to do.'

The door opened, startling them both into silence. Lady Fortuna stepped out and locked it behind her. The glittery green dress was gone and in its place she wore plain, dark clothes and a thick, hooded black cloak. It was lined with something warm, either fleece or fur, and went right down to her leather boots. She checked both ways along the corridor before moving off, taking quick, confident strides in the direction Sneed had gone.

Sharing a single glance, Betty and Fliss followed, leaving a safe distance between Fortuna and themselves. Beneath the rise and fall of the ballroom music, Fortuna's footsteps made no sound on the stone floor, but still Betty found herself trying to match her own steps to the fortune teller's in case there was any sound to be masked.

Fortuna reached the wall where Sneed and Sonny had vanished. In seconds she had located the circular area of wood and pushed her long, elegant finger into it. Instantly the panel opened, and Fortuna slipped through it, closing it behind her with a soft click.

'Now what?' Fliss mouthed, staring with amazement at the secret entrance. She was jerked forward by Bonbon, who strained at his leash to sniff at the edge of the panel. 'How long do we wait before we go after her?'

Betty hesitated. Without knowing exactly what was

on the other side, it was impossible to guess. If they went through too quickly Fortuna could realise someone had seen her. Leave it too long and they might lose her altogether. She waited, counting to five, then ten. Then she reached out and pushed a finger into the notch in the woodwork. She felt something give, a slight *pop* as a catch was released, and the panel swung open once more.

They were in.

Betty stepped through first, breath held, eyes wide. It was black as ink on the other side of the wall, and the temperature dropped immediately. She half expected Fortuna's hand to seize her outstretched arm and dig her pointed, pale talons into Betty's skin, but nothing came. Fliss slipped after her, with Bonbon weaving between their legs. Betty put her hand down and found his warm, hairy head. She stroked his soft ears, trying to settle him, hearing the soft click of claws on stone.

Quietly, she pushed the panel back, but not all the way closed. Reaching under the smelly coat she found one of the feathers on the peacock dress and gave it a sharp pull. It came loose, and she let it fall from her fingers. When people came looking – and they would, they *had* to – then she would leave them a trail to follow.

The tiny gap allowed a chink of light through, and now her eyes were adjusting to the darkness Betty could make a few things out: a smooth stone floor and bare walls. Steps going down, and more going up to the next floor. Small oil lamps were fixed to the walls, but none were lit. Some were broken, their glass shades jagged like shards of ice. Everything about it felt lonely and unused. It smelled damp and stale, of dust and cobwebs, but something else lingered, too – something familiar. Betty tried to imagine it lit up and busy, used by servants rushing from place to place in the hall, but she found she couldn't. She wondered about the last time anyone besides Sonny had used it, and knew it had to have been a long time ago. Perhaps it was only used by ghosts now. The hairs on the back of her neck prickled as she remembered the things she'd overheard from the servants in the kitchen.

After Elora died there were stories about her ghost seen hurryin' down the stairs . . . And then one day, another young servant fell down them . . . he'd seen Elora weepin' . . .

'Look,' Fliss whispered, and through the gloom Betty saw her sister's hand outstretched, pointing. There was a small bunch of candles and a box of matches close to the entrance. *That's what the smell is,* Betty realised. *A struck match.* Fortuna must have lit a candle. Sure enough, when she leaned over to look down the stairwell, she saw a yellow light moving in the gloom.

'Should we light one, too?' Fliss asked. 'It's so dark in here!'

'No,' said Betty. 'She might see it if we do. We'll have to follow her and stay as close as we can without letting her hear us.'

They started down the steps, gripping the rail. One

wrong foot and either of them could tumble down the steps. The handrail was icy cold, and Betty felt her fingers drag through years of dust and grime. Only Bonbon forged ahead, surefooted. She was comforted by the dog's presence, his warm breath on the air. The clipping of his claws mingled with their own echoing footsteps. Her ears played tricks. It sounded like there were more of them in the passageway. For a moment it was easy to believe Charlie was there with them.

Charlie. Had she found Finn Sharkey yet, or told Granny what was going on?

The handrail curved under her hand, twisting lower and back on itself as they came to the bottom of the flight of steps.

'Careful,' she told Fliss. She nudged forward, searching for the next step. Her foot found air and for a moment she was off-balance, feeling as though she were on a see-saw that was plunging down. Fliss's cold hand grabbed hers in the darkness, holding her steady. Once more she was glad she wasn't alone.

They reached the bottom of the steps and found themselves in a narrow passageway, still unlit. Some way ahead they could see the glow of Fortuna's candle, the light allowing her to move more quickly than them.

'We must be in an old service passageway,' said Fliss, her voice low.

'Sneed spoke about this,' Betty replied. 'He'd seen old plans for the hall and said the staircase led to different

268

places – to the cellar and out to the stables.'

They followed the candlelight, picking up speed.

'Look,' Fliss whispered as, up ahead, a yellow square of light appeared. A dark figure flashed past it and then abruptly the light vanished, leaving them in total darkness.

'She's gone through a door,' Betty whispered, her heart thumping. She squeezed her sister's cold hand, and felt Fliss squeeze back. 'We can't be far from it. Keep going!'

'There!' Fliss spotted it suddenly, a faint line of light that was unmistakably coming from underneath a door. Seconds later they arrived at it and pushed it open to reveal a large cellar. It was dimly lit, but after the almost total darkness of the hidden corridor Betty felt as though she had walked into bright sunshine.

Rows of wooden barrels and shelves and shelves of wine bottles filled the cellar. The musty, damp scent of the place reminded Betty of her old home, the Poacher's Pocket. But overlaying this she could smell something else: the icy scent of snow. A set of steps led up to a trapdoor, left unlatched from the inside. Fresh chunks of snow lay on the steps, proof that someone had been this way very recently.

Betty went first, with Fliss and Bonbon behind her. The trapdoor was heavy but lifted easily, falling back with a *poomph!* into a wedge of snow. More snow showered down from above, falling on to the steps. Betty ducked out of the way, and heard Bonbon sneeze as some of it landed on his nose. Freezing air swirled round her cheeks, nipping her nose. Above them was a clear sky of darkest blue, winking with stars.

'Come on,' Betty whispered, climbing the last few steps out of the cellar. Her boots sank into crisp snow, but it wasn't as deep as she had feared it would be. Fliss joined her in the cold night, shivering, and Bonbon thrust his nose into a pile of snow, snorting and sneezing. Betty went to close the trapdoor, then stopped. Better to leave it open and keep marking their trail. She ripped another feather from the peacock dress and let it float down on to the steps, then reached into the pockets of the coat and pulled out the mismatched mittens she had stowed. It was only then, as she tugged them on, that she noticed something.

'Fliss,' she said, staring at her sister's hands. 'When we were in that passageway, did you . . . did you take off your mittens?'

Fliss looked at her strangely. 'No. I was holding the handrail with one hand and . . .'

'Holding Bonbon with the other,' Betty finished. Goosepimples shot up all over her. She remembered that cold, cold hand in the darkness, holding on to her own. It hadn't been Fliss's.

It hadn't been Fliss's.

'Then who . . . who was holding my hand?'

Chapter Twenty-two
Elora's Tears

BETTY'S VOICE WAS THIN AND SHRILL ON THE night air. The memory of those icy fingers wrapped around hers was as fresh as the snow under her feet. There had been no one else with them on the staircase, and yet they hadn't been alone.

'It was her,' Betty whispered. 'It was Elora, I know it was.'

Fliss gazed at her, colour seeping from her face. 'H-holding your hand?' she stammered. 'Do you think she was trying to hurt you? To pull you down the steps?'

'No.' The word came out before Betty even knew she was going to say it. 'No. It wasn't evil, she wasn't trying to hurt me. It was helping me, guiding me through the dark. That's why I thought it was you.' She felt shaky and light-headed, shocked but not afraid. It *hadn't* been trying to harm her, she was convinced of it. 'I think Elora's here with us.'

Shivershock.

271

The word came in her muffled ears, halfway between a thought and a noise.

'We have to get to the lake. That's where they're heading.'

'But *how?*' Fliss gestured to their surroundings. 'Everything's thick with snow! The roads are blocked!'

'There must be some way through,' said Betty. 'Look – some of it's been shovelled away, and it's not snowing now. The sky's clear. And if we can't make it to the lake, then I don't think Fortuna and Sneed will make it, either.'

'How are we supposed to know that?' Fliss asked unhappily. 'We don't even know whether they're travelling on foot, or ...'

'There'll be tracks,' Betty said, determinedly. 'That's one good thing about the snow. Look – there! Three sets of footprints.'

'You mean the only good thing,' Fliss muttered, staring at the trail that led away from the trapdoor.

Betty surveyed their surroundings. The high stone walls of Echo Hall were a short way behind them, and she saw some evidence of a garden: trees, another wall, a few canes poking out of snowdrifts. Ahead of them a path had been cleared through the snow, with great piles of it on either side. It reminded Betty of a maze she had once read about, only this maze was of snow, not leafy green trees. As they stepped on to the path she had the feeling of being swallowed into it. Where would it spit them out, she wondered?

A shadowy building stood to one side, close to the hall.

Beyond it were thick trees which stretched up and back, giving way to snow-capped mountains above.

'Ouch,' Fliss complained, as Bonbon strained at his leash, jerking her arm. 'He's so strong – I'm scared he'll pull me over!'

Bonbon gave a low *yip*, sniffing at the ground.

'He must have found Sonny's scent,' said Betty. 'Here, let me take him for a while.'

Fliss handed her the leash gratefully, and Betty gripped the leather strap tight. They began to move, following the sets of footprints in the snow. Their own feet made new tracks, boots squeaking through the powdery whiteness. The footprints led to the outside building, where a wooden door was set in a stone wall. Before they entered, Betty guessed it was a set of stables from the horsey smell. She opened the door carefully and peeped inside to find a dozen or so stables in two rows, with a path through the middle that led to two larger doors which had been flung open. On either side of them the horses were wide-eyed and restless in their stables, sensing their presence – even if they could not see Betty and Fliss.

'Something's wrong,' said Betty, not liking the restlessness of the horses or the way the stable doors were open wide. She moved inside the barn, closing the smaller door behind them, and tightened her grip on Bonbon's leash.

'Shouldn't there be someone watching the horses?' Fliss asked. 'Like a stablehand?'

'Looks like there was,' said Betty, noticing an upturned stool at the far end of the barn. A bottle of ale lay on its side nearby, its amber-coloured contents leaking out over the floor in tiny rivers between the cobbles. 'Someone was here all right, but there must have been a scuffle.' She glanced around, searching for other disturbances, and noticed one of the stable doors was open, too. 'I think one of the horses has been taken. If the stablehand saw then maybe there was a fight. They could have gone for help.'

She was pulled forward by Bonbon, who was wagging his tail wildly and heading in the direction of the stool. She allowed him to lead her, keen to see what he wanted. At the side of the last stable was a tack area, where reins and saddles and stirrups were kept. But it was something underneath these that had the dog's attention: a wooden sled, lined with fleece.

'Sonny's sled!' Betty exclaimed.

Bonbon gave another *yip* and wagged his tail again.

Betty spied the harness in the bottom of the sled. An idea came to her then, and her heart skipped as though she had just skidded on ice. 'What if . . . what if we took it? We'll have a better chance of catching them up, and it'll be safer, too.'

'Safer?' Fliss looked doubtful. 'I don't know, Betty. Sleds can go really, really fast.'

'And it's going to be really, really cold,' Betty argued. 'The faster we can travel, the better – especially if they've taken a horse.' She frowned. 'But why would they only take one?'

'Come on, quickly,' said Fliss, grabbing the harness. 'If we're doing this then let's move before someone comes.'

Betty removed the dog's leash and together she and Fliss fiddled with the leather straps and buckles until finally the harness was on Bonbon. Betty clipped the harness to the front of the sled. 'Come on, boy,' she told Bonbon, with a low whistle. She and Fliss shoved the sled over the stable floor and outside on to the snow. It was sturdy, heavier than it looked.

'I hope he's strong enough to take us both,' Fliss murmured, sinking her hand into the dog's fur.

'He managed with Granny and Clarissa,' said Betty, arranging the fleece in the sled. Her hands shook. She didn't doubt Bonbon's strength. Even through the dog's thick winter coat she could see how powerfully built he was. She was more concerned about never having operated a sled before – not one like this, in snow this treacherous. It would be all too easy to lose control.

Come on, Betty Widdershins, she told herself sternly. *If you can sail a boat you can sure as sugar steer a sled.*

She clambered in and gestured for Fliss to join her. Now they were outside she could see fresh tracks where something had dragged through the snow, and more animal prints: dogs and a single horse.

'Looks like they took a sled, too,' Betty said, recalling Sneed speaking to the lake marshal. 'Maybe someone is helping them – Sneed seemed interested in Finn Sharkey's dogs earlier, but I thought he was just killing time.' She felt a wave of despair. She had sent Charlie looking for Sharkey – but what if he was in on the deadly plan, and nowhere to be found in Echo Hall?

'Or maybe Sneed just stole it,' said Fliss, her eyes narrowing. 'And Fortuna went after him and Sonny on the horse.'

'Guess we're about to find out,' said Betty, fear prickling at her like icicles and her breath clouding the air. 'Ready?'

Fliss nodded. She wasn't, Betty knew, but it was now or never. She held on tightly to the sides of the sled, trying to remember if there were any special commands Sonny had used when they'd seen him on the lake, but all she could think of was, 'Bonbon, come on, boy!' and they surged forward as Bonbon took off, following the tracks in the snow.

The sled was going much faster than she had imagined it would. Betty felt herself pinned back, the air like ice on her cheeks. Her breath was whipped away and her eyes streamed as the sled cut through the crusted snow, beyond the stables and into the wooded area overlooking the back of the hall. Yellow light from the hall spilled across it in places, marking out pathways that had been shovelled clear. As the lights faded, the path through the trees loomed, and Betty had an eerie sense of fate being put in motion, like a row of falling dominoes. There was no other way for them to go except to follow the tracks in the snow and whatever scent Bonbon's powerful sense of smell was picking up.

Between the trees and under a canopy of frozen branches

they went, slowing as the path narrowed and became steeper. Here the snow hadn't been cleared, but it was less deep thanks to the shelter of the trees and a wind that had blown in their favour. 'Whoa, boy!' Betty called frantically, trying to help slow Bonbon through the darkness at first. She soon fell into silence. The dog did not need her commands. He knew every inch of this land, was every bit as wild as it was, and the invisible thread he was following to find Sonny held strong.

The ground changed, ice becoming more powdery. Above, Betty saw flashes of navy sky through zigzag branches lined with white. She turned to look back. The lights of Echo Hall became fireflies in the darkness. Beyond the trees the mountains stretched up, old and ancient, silent and watching it all. Then they were through the trees and on a thin lane that rimmed the mountainside.

'*Ooh-er*,' Fliss moaned, closing her eyes tight as they rose higher and the air became colder still. 'Meddling magpies, where is he taking us?'

Betty stared at the snowy scene around them rushing by. It was like a painted Yule card, or one of the snow globes they had seen at the market. Paths like white veins cut through the trees, the tiny hall now small as a dolls' house and the square before it. Only this time they were approaching it all from the opposite side. Then a road sliced down towards the square at a frozen, neck-breaking angle. *Chill Hill.*

They crossed it, finding the path on the other side which

led out on to a mountainside road. It was curving, compacted snow and ice beneath them that had been shielded from the worst of the snowstorm by the mountain. Betty thought the tracks were still present, but now they were harder to see, looking more like ridges in the ice. Below, over the treetops and coming ever closer, was Shivershock Lake, frozen white as milk.

'I don't see anyone on the lake,' Betty said, gasping, her eyes straining into the distance. 'It looks clear.' *Had she got it wrong?* She felt a stab of fear, a moment of dread. *What if it hadn't been the lake Sneed had aimed for . . . what if it had been Chill Hill after all?* Any mistake now would be costly to them all. It wasn't the same as getting a sum wrong in class. It was a matter of life or death.

Her doubts faded as Bonbon slowed, nose to the air, then picked up speed again. *No.* It wasn't Betty who'd led them this way – the dog was picking up clues no one could see. She imagined how ghostly they must look, a riderless sled pulled by an invisible dog, and her thoughts turned to the highwayman and the path he had ridden all those years ago. He must have come this way, she thought. Taking the back lanes out of Wilderness, lying in wait for the unsuspecting carriages to rumble along. There were so many places to hide within the dark trees. So many places to wait, and watch.

'Easy,' she commanded, and Bonbon obediently slowed. They were on a sheltered lane bordering the lake now, a steep fringe of trees between them and the frozen water. Here

Bonbon stopped, panting hard. On the opposite side of the lake stood Echo Hall, and Betty knew from its position that these trees had to be part of the deadly iced-up copse they had seen when they'd skated on the lake.

Elora's Tears. They were here.

The area was bigger than Betty had realised, stretching along the far side of the lake. There was no reaching it with the sled now. They'd have to go by foot, either round or through the trees. And given how impossibly frozen those trees were at the front, how they became a confusing grotto maze of ice, Betty knew going through wasn't an option.

'Wait,' Fliss murmured. 'There's something out there, on the water . . . a fallen tree?'

'We have to move closer,' said Betty, keeping her voice low. They might be unseen, but any of them could still be heard and she wasn't sure she trusted Bonbon to stay quiet now. His ears were pricked up high, his blue ice-chip eyes trained on something within the dark trees that neither Betty nor Fliss could see. 'Let's walk further along.'

They climbed out of the sled. Betty unclipped Bonbon's harness, keeping him close.

Her limbs felt numb, her mind fogged with cold and dread. *Was Sonny safe? Was he . . . alive?*

They walked along the lane, feet vanishing into deep, crusted snow as high as their knees, and almost reaching Bonbon's belly. After less than a minute, shadowy forms became visible on the lane ahead and the dog tugged at his harness, tail wagging. Betty's heart leapt.

Sonny?

No. The sounds of panting met her still muffled ears, and as they drew nearer the shadowy forms became a pack of dogs, harnessed together. Puzzlingly there was no sign of the sled. It was clear to see why they had stopped, though: a snowdrift the size of a wall was blocking the road. Trees were bent almost double with the weight of snow on their branches.

'That's Finn Sharkey's pack,' Betty whispered, recognising two of the dogs: one with its four white legs, another with black ears. Her dread rose like a breath on the air. So where were Sneed, Sonny and Fortuna – and the sled? Had it come loose, or fallen down through the trees? There were no signs it had left the road, no snapped branches she could see. Bonbon pulled harder, eager to greet the other dogs, but Betty resisted and held on tight. Finn's pack, she knew, could not see Bonbon and she didn't want to risk any excitable noises they might make.

'There's a track.' Fliss pointed to a gap that led down and around the copse of trees. It appeared to be an unmarked path that cut around the trees to the lake. 'Someone's been along it – see?'

Betty nodded. There were footprints – three sets. And something else that had been dragged, leaving thin lines like scars in the snow. It had to be the sled, although she couldn't imagine why they would take it and not the dogs. Carefully, she and Fliss left the road and began edging down the path, keeping close to the trees at the side for cover. Betty flexed her fingers, trying to bring warmth back into them against the biting cold. Every time she thought it wasn't possible to get any colder, Wilderness proved her wrong, and she noticed now that the clear night sky was filling with clouds.

Don't snow, she willed in her head. *Please, don't snow any more . . .*

The first flakes began when they were almost at the ice. Flakes tiny as confetti, drifting down through the air like dandelion seeds.

'Betty,' Fliss murmured fearfully. 'We can't stay out here if it gets bad. We'll have to go back or we – we might not make it.'

'We'll be all right if it stays like this.' Betty gritted her teeth, the icy air making her cheeks ache. 'We'll be all right . . .' *But would they?* She shuddered, remembering that cold hand on hers on the dark stairs.

When Elora's ghost's about, wrap up warm and don't go out.

Elora was here out in the snow, out in the night. Betty knew it as surely as she knew Granny liked whiskey.

The path opened out on to the lake shore, the frozen trees thick to their right. Betty and Fliss trod slowly, but there was no way to be completely silent. The snow betrayed them, leaving their own prints, each one with a crisp crunch. A voice sounded nearby. *Fortuna.*

'Did you hear that? Someone's coming!'

281

Betty froze, scanning the shore. Beneath the overhanging icy branches she spotted the slim, hooded figure of the fortune teller.

'Mother?' another voice called out, thin and afraid. This time it came from across the lake. Betty scanned the frozen surface, squinting through snowflakes catching in her eyelashes. She located the shape they had seen from the road above and mistaken for a fallen branch. And now Bonbon was pulling harder than ever, whining and straining to get on to the ice.

Finn Sharkey's sled was out on the lake, and Sonny was in it, alone. It wasn't far from the shore, and was scarily close to the area where Betty had gone through the ice. Even now, Betty could see a darker patch where the ice was thinner and had not yet frozen as solid as the rest. She felt a sharp spike of fear. Sneed was playing a very dangerous game indeed.

From the way Sonny sat, Betty guessed that once again his wrists and ankles were tied, preventing him from moving. Her relief at seeing him didn't last. He was alive – for now, but this was worse than she'd imagined. Much worse. The sight of the boy out there alone on the deserted, dark lake filled her with horror. *How could Sneed and Fortuna have put him there? Didn't they know what was beneath the ice?* she thought. *Not just the freezing water, but the Drowning Girl?* If Sonny went through it he'd die, whether it was from cold, shock or fear. And Betty knew how easily the ice could break, even when people believed it wasn't possible.

282

'Mother, is that you?' Sonny called again. His eyes were wide and terrified, his voice shaking with fear or cold, or both. 'Help me!'

'Shut up!' Fortuna hissed.

Bonbon let out a volley of barks now, determined to get the attention of his beloved Sonny. His claws scraped through ice and Betty would have toppled if Fliss hadn't grabbed on to the harness, too. It took both of them to hold the dog back.

Lady Fortuna looked round in alarm. Bonbon spotted her and his powerful body tensed. He gave a low warning growl.

'What do we do?' Fliss whispered urgently. 'We can't hold this dog off for much longer—'

A dark figure moved away from the trees, stepping out of the shadows. It was Sneed. Somewhere along the way he had discarded the white wig and mask, but curiously he was still holding the silver-topped cane that Betty had seen him with back at the hall.

'No one's there. One of Sharkey's dogs must have got loose,' he muttered, his eyes roving over the spot where Betty and Fliss stood. 'Doesn't matter.' He held up a hand to shield his eyes from the snowflakes. Betty glanced up at the sky. The clouds were gathering faster and thicker by the minute. 'Where *is* she?' he added impatiently, scanning the lake. 'She should have been here by now!'

Betty had been wondering the same thing: surely Mrs Chambers would have come as quickly as possible to her

283

son's rescue . . . unless she had tried to get help? She gazed at Sonny. He was shivering uncontrollably. They had to get him off that lake, somehow.

'I've got an idea,' said Betty, still struggling to hold the dog. 'If we let Bonbon go then he'll protect Sonny if Sneed or Fortuna tries to hurt him – and he could be the distraction we need.'

'To do what?' Fliss asked.

'Make Sonny disappear,' Betty replied, remembering the maid's cap in her pocket. It was too large to fit into the nesting dolls, but if she could rip off a tiny piece they could make Sonny vanish and get him to safety.

Fliss nodded, her cheeks flushed with the effort of holding the dog. 'Yes. Let's do it – now!'

They released the growling Bonbon. He made straight for Lady Fortuna, who had no time to react before she was set upon by the invisible dog. He sank his teeth into her long cloak and shook it, pulling her off balance. She screamed, a high, shrill sound that pierced even Betty's muffled ears.

'Get it off! Oh, Sneed, it's trying to kill me – a ghostly wolf!'

As Sneed swooped in to defend Fortuna from the unseen force, Betty took action. She pulled out the maid's cap and searched for a way to tear off a small piece. She'd been hoping for a frayed edge or loose thread, but there was nothing. She removed her mitten and began working at the white trim with her thumbnail. *There.* It began to loosen, but already the cold was seeping into her fingers. More snowflakes were tumbling down now, and the wind was picking up.

'Hurry, Betty!' Fliss urged. 'Quick – where are the dolls? Give them to me and I'll open them up!'

A yelp sounded as Sneed lashed out with the cane, striking Bonbon on the hind leg. Then another.

'Oh, no!' Fliss gasped with tears in her voice. 'Poor Bonbon! Blast it, the dolls are stuck! Why won't they open?'

'What trickery is this?' Sneed yelled, thrashing the stick wildly about him. 'There's something here, I can feel it but I can't see it!' Bonbon was ferocious and snarling now, unrecognisable as the friendly dog who'd trotted along at Sonny's side. He was fierce, wild. Possibly even deadly.

He caught the end of the cane in his snapping jaws, but Sneed held on. His mouth opened in shock and his horrid moustache formed a hairy ring around it. The commotion was so loud that none of them heard the hoofbeats from the road until the last minute.

Betty and Fliss scrambled back, ducking under the icicled branches as a huge black horse appeared and made its way steadily down the path at the side of the trees. Its rider was a black smudge in the growing snowfall, with a dark cape billowing out from broad shoulders. His face was shadowed by a tricorn hat, but as the horse drew nearer, Betty saw a black mask across the rider's eyes. A ghostly mist rose up around the horse, chilling her blood and making her numb fingers dig into Fliss's arm.

The highwayman.

Chapter Twenty-three
The Highwayman

TIME STOOD STILL. ALL BETTY COULD DO WAS stare, bewitched by the spectral figure before them. She was not alone. She heard Fliss's breathing coming fast and shallow, and saw her hands tighten on the nesting dolls. Fortuna and Sneed had been shocked into silence, too, and even Bonbon had stopped his attack, the only signs of movement from him the hot clouds of breath on the air.

The highwayman swept past them, rising up tall in his stirrups. He and the horse seemed to merge into one, a black phantom silhouette that was stark against the white snow. He raised one arm. There was a faint glimmer of light on metal . . . and then a pistol was pointing straight at Sneed.

'Stand and deliver.' The voice was a low growl, like an avalanche crashing down a mountain. 'The boy or your life!'

Betty shook her head, stunned. Had she heard right? The ghostly highwayman was trying to save Sonny? *The ghostly highwayman* . . . In a flash she remembered the mysterious hoofbeats they had heard on the very first night, when the carriage had left them at Clarissa's on Chill Hill. That had felt ghostly, haunted. And while this felt eerie and frightening, the spectre seemed too solid, too . . . *real*.

Because he *was* real.

'It's not a ghost,' Betty whispered, so faintly that she barely heard her own words. The snow was coming down faster now, each flake thicker than the last. They settled on the highway robber's shoulders and hat, and landed in the horse's mane. A horse which was snorting hot, living breaths into the chilled air and stamping so hard on the frozen ground that Betty could feel it from where she and Fliss stood in the shelter of the trees. The spooky vapour she had seen curling from them was not ghostly, but sweat and heat evaporating into mist.

'*Give me the boy!*' the highwayman repeated menacingly. The pistol stayed steady, unwavering in his hand.

'I-I don't understand,' Fliss whispered back. 'Could Mrs Chambers have sent someone from the ball out here to help? Who's behind that mask?'

Unexpectedly, Bonbon lurched away from Sneed and launched himself in the horse's direction. The horse, seeing nothing, but sensing *something*, reared up with a terrified whinny, and the unsuspecting highwayman was thrown violently from the saddle. He landed flat on his back with a sickening crunch. The silver pistol flew through the air and hit the ice with a *thwack*. At the moment of impact, a louder noise cracked through the air and there was a flash of light followed by smoke. The pistol had fired, making a clean hole in the frozen lake that was perhaps two strides from Sonny, who was still helpless on the sled. A crackling sound followed, like ice beginning to splinter.

The moment sped into a blur. The highwayman rolled with a deep groan, away from the horse's deadly hooves as they crashed back down. The startled horse turned and bolted back the way it had come, and Betty reached for Fliss to pull her even tighter under the icicled trees as it whipped past in a clatter of hoofbeats and flying spittle.

Bonbon reached the highwayman. He threw up his gloved hands in an attempt to shield his face but his movements were weaker now as a result of the fall.

'Oh, no,' Fliss cried. 'We have to help him!'

Her voice was drowned by Fortuna's. 'The pistol!' she screamed at Sneed. 'Get it!'

Sneed skidded on to the ice, using the cane for balance. He located the pistol and picked it up carefully, chuckling, and made his way back over the slippery ice to the shore.

Betty was glued to the spot. She wished she could do something, *anything*, but for once ideas and plans failed her. The sight of the highwayman had terrified her – but he had tried to help Sonny, so that had to be good, didn't it?

'Oh, I can't watch,' Fliss wailed as the highwayman's hands flailed around Bonbon in an impossible defence against a dog he couldn't see.

But Betty couldn't look away, even though a voice in her head was screaming, *Close your eyes! Don't watch!* She waited for the dog to attack. For ripped skin, red blood on the snow and terrible screams . . .

Bonbon gave an excited '*wuff!*' and licked the highwayman's face. His bushy tail wagged madly, sending showers of snow scattering from side to side.

'What the . . . ?' the highwayman groaned, bewildered. 'Bonbon?'

'Oh, my goodness,' Betty breathed, as she suddenly guessed the truth. The only person it could be . . .

Bonbon barked, louder this time, and nipped at the tricorn hat, pulling it away from the highwayman's head. Long, coppery hair fell free, tumbling over the ice.

'Mrs Chambers?' Fliss gasped in disbelief. 'It *can't* be!'

'Mother?' Sonny cried. His eyes were wide with confusion and relief. 'You came!'

Mrs Chambers coughed and struggled to her feet, fending off the dog's licks to gaze worriedly at her son. She looked taller, heavier, Betty thought. Beneath the black cape, the shoulders of the dark coat she wore were wide and square, padded with something to fill them out. Bonbon, sensing the 'game' was over, obediently sat at her side, panting, with his fierce eyes fixed on Sneed and Fortuna.

There was a moment of silence. An electric sort of silence, like the pause between a lightning flash and a crack of thunder. Then Lady Fortuna began to laugh. It began as a tinkle, like crystals hitting other crystals, but then it stretched into a cackle. Ugly and harsh, and mocking. Sneed chuckled too. He held the silver pistol, training it on Mrs Chambers. The snow whipped around them, settling in Bonbon's fur, betraying his invisible outline. Mrs Chambers touched her hand to her head, then touched the dog uncertainly.

'Oh,' Fortuna gasped, wiping her eyes. 'You had me going for a moment there!' She let her gaze travel up and down Mrs Chambers and her face twisted into a sneer. 'I really thought the ghostly story was true – but it was you. *You!*'

You. The word rang out over the frozen lake. Such a little word, and yet Betty could hear so many things in it. The contempt Lady Fortuna held for Mrs Chambers. The disbelief and outrage that someone like her should try to trick Fortuna by disguise.

'Yes,' Mrs Chambers said at last. 'It was me.' Her voice was quiet, but a different kind of quiet to how it was usually. She held herself differently, too. The weary, downtrodden woman on the front desk of Echo Hall was gone. This was someone strong and determined. Someone, Betty thought, who should not be underestimated.

'Like mother like son,' Sneed added, gesturing to Sonny mockingly. 'Elora and her lost love, the highwayman. Well, well! What a bizarre little dressing-up game, I must say.' He glanced at Lady Fortuna, who was still shaking with peals of laughter. 'I suppose you thought you'd just ride along here and scare us into handing over the boy without telling us a thing, didn't you?' He waved the pistol about madly and grinned. 'Well, that's not going to happen, Mrs Chambers. You're going to tell us what you know about your friend Elora and that crook she fell in love with, and what happened to his loot.' He tapped the cane against the frozen water. 'Otherwise Sonny is going to have a very tragic accident. And Wilderness will have another ghost to add to its collection.'

Mrs Chambers' gloved hands curled into fists so tight that Betty thought she heard the black leather creak. 'How *dare* you threaten my son?' she said, in a dangerously quiet voice. 'How dare you kidnap him and bring him out here, to this cursed lake?'

'How dare *you* answer back to us,' Lady Fortuna screamed, stepping closer to Sneed. Beneath the hood, her face was contorted with anger. 'Who do you think you are, anyway? You're no one, nothing! A useless servant!'

Fliss took a sharp breath next to Betty's ear, and Betty found that she, like Mrs Chambers, had clenched her hands into tight balls of anger at the fortune teller's cruelty.

To their surprise, it was Mrs Chambers' turn to laugh, a short, harsh bark that seemed to say: *Hah! You know nothing.*

'You weren't listening, were you?' she said, in that same quiet voice. 'You think you know who I am. People like you always do. I'm just the staff, a servant. The person who comes running when you ring that silly little bell on the desk.' She tore her eyes away from Fortuna and glanced at Sneed.

'DING! It makes you feel important, doesn't it? So full of your own importance that you don't see the truth, even now when it's right in front of you. Perhaps if I say it again you'll listen this time.' She spoke slowly, evenly. 'It was *me*.'

Betty stared at Mrs Chambers, her mind finally piecing things together. *The truth . . . right in front of them . . .*

'I always disliked my name,' Mrs Chambers went on. 'Jacqueline. I felt it was far too pretty for the likes of me. I preferred to go by my middle name, Robin. That had been my father's name, you see, and I loved that it was something he and I shared. It made me feel closer to him, especially after he was gone. I don't even know where the name Jack Frost came from, really. It was one of those strange coincidences that came about, purely because people believed I'd died on the coldest night.' She gave a wry smile. 'So, yes. I am Jacqueline Chambers, Jack Frost. Robin the robber. Not the highwayman, after all. The highway*woman*.'

Chapter Twenty-four
The Highway Robber and the Fortune Teller

Part Three: Madam Divina

THE FORTUNE TELLER HAD A BAD FEELING she couldn't shake off. It had started ever since she arrived in Wilderness two days earlier; not a physical feeling like a toothache or a churning tummy, but rather a sense of uneasiness gathering like a storm cloud.

Her crystal ball was not behaving itself. At first she wondered if she was imagining it. It could have just been her own hands, she told herself that first day. Her own hands making the crystal feel too hot, or too cold under her fingers. After all, the cold in this place was quite out of the ordinary. On the second day, however, just before her first fortune-telling session of the day, the crystal had rolled off its gilded stand and away from her.

'Come back here!' she muttered crossly, as the ball glided over the velvet tablecloth and darted out of her way each time she tried to grab it. It led her round and round the table, changing direction every time she thought she had caught up with it, and even loitered dangerously close to the edge of the table as if threatening to roll off and smash on the ground.

'We both know you're not going to do it,' Madam Divina scolded, but although she didn't show it, her heart skipped a beat. Eventually she caught the thing by tricking it, by pretending to turn her back and ignore it before throwing a black silk scarf over the smooth surface and scooping it up in her hands. The ball was not happy about this and immediately made itself so cold that Madam Divina thought her fingers might blister with it, even through the scarf. She decided to lock it away in its travelling case while she rubbed some warmth back into her hands. It meant delaying her first customer by twenty minutes, but Madam Divina decided it was necessary to teach the crystal ball a lesson. Sure enough, it was better behaved for the rest of the day, although there were a few moments where it filled with a sulky grey fog in between her customers.

Today, on the third and final morning of her visit to Wilderness, the ball would not co-operate. She awoke to find it a sullen black and was forced to cancel her morning sessions at a cost of several pieces of silver, which annoyed her greatly. Eventually, she sat down at the table with a sigh, clasping her hands together.

'All right,' she said. 'Out with it. There's something you don't want to show me, isn't there?'

The crystal remained stubbornly black, but a few swirls of grey began to appear within it. It was listening.

'I don't like it any more than you do,' said Madam Divina, her voice softening now. 'But you know the rules I follow.'

It was one rule, really. A very simple rule passed down from her mother – also a fortune teller – and that was to avoid telling her customers bad news. There could be warnings, yes. Gentle suggestions that a person should avoid a certain route, or a certain person, or to take extra care on a certain day . . . but it had to be done in a particular way. Madam Divina had become very good at this over her years of reading fortunes. It was a skill all the best fortune tellers had. People came to be thrilled, not frightened. Tantalised, not terrified. Seeing into the future was a privilege, and it was one Madam Divina took seriously. Besides, satisfied customers told people, who then told other people, which ensured a steady flow of work for her. It was good business, plain and simple. It buttered her bread and kept Madam Divina in the kind of comfortable lifestyle she had grown used to.

In her experience, people wanted to know about two things: love or money. And Madam Divina was only too happy to poke around in their futures to see what was coming their way. Even if a future was lacking in love or riches, Divina had a way of persuading her customer that good things still awaited, or reminded them of what they already had: good health, a new baby in the family, a new job opportunity. She made people grateful. She made them *happy*.

The crystal ball had shown her death on only a few occasions. Most recently, that of a very old man who was the father of one of her customers. The woman knew her father did not have long to live and was seeking reassurance that the old man's money would be left to her instead of her sister. Madam Divina, seeing that neither daughter would receive a penny, took great pleasure in telling her she would get all she deserved. The customer left happy, and Divina was content in the knowledge that she hadn't lied.

Other deaths she saw were expected: sick or elderly people whose passing would come as no shock to their loved ones, and so Madam Divina had no need to pass on the sad information. Instead she would make pointed remarks about changes ahead, and new beginnings. She focused on only the good, and up till now it had served her well.

'Come on, then,' she said, addressing the brooding black crystal. 'It's no use trying to hide it from me, whatever it is.'

The inside of the ball swirled, lightening from black to stormy grey. A flurry of snowflakes appeared within it, swirling round. Divina frowned. It had been snowing lightly since she had arrived in Wilderness, but this looked heavy. Dangerous. And through the whirling flakes there was a dark shape, someone on horseback galloping along a snowy road.

'A storm on the way,' Divina murmured, leaning closer to the glassy surface. The crystal cleared and for a moment she thought the vision was over, but then a new image appeared inside. Water, filling from bottom to top, water so cold that pieces of broken ice could be seen floating in it. Without warning a hand appeared, reaching through it to slam against the inside of the glass, its fingers blue with cold.

'Oh!' Madam Divina gasped, sitting back in her chair in shock.

The hand banged once, twice, then lay still before vanishing. The ball cleared, showing nothing more, but the fortune teller knew what she had seen. A drowning. The question was, *whose*?

The feeling of dread stayed with her throughout the day. She considered packing up her things and leaving while it was still light, but she could not do that. She had customers waiting, and they had expectations. And Madam Divina did not let people down.

So she put on her silver rings and necklaces, draped herself in velvet and tied scarves into her pretty, dark hair even though she didn't feel like it. None of these things was necessary, but Madam Divina knew that it was what people wanted. In order for them to feel special, she had to look a certain way even if she might have secretly preferred to sit in a woolly blanket wearing a pair of slippers.

They came together, two young girls. One slightly younger, with baby blue eyes and the softest, most beautiful-looking golden ringlets Madam Divina had ever seen. The other girl was older by a year or two, with dark, serious eyes and coppery hair. They were servants at Echo Hall, they said, like others who came to her every year. She knew the type; usually young, full of dreams and ambition.

'Tell us,' said the fair one, looking amused. Her smile was warm, but there was a touch of something cynical there, too. 'Will we be rich? Famous? Will we fall in love?'

Madam Divina peered into the crystal ball. She had begun to relax as the day had gone on and the ball had shown no more signs of misbehaving. And here were two young girls, usually her favourite kind of reading. They had their lives ahead of them, and surely plenty of good in store she could tell them about. The crystal, however, remained stubbornly empty.

Madam Divina frowned, giving it a light stroke. Its surface was ice cold and for a moment her fingers felt wet as she withdrew them. She saw a flash of gold, and jewels glittering . . .

'Yes,' she said, trying to disguise her surprise. 'I do see riches. Great wealth, in fact. But . . .' She frowned, uneasy. It would not do to make accusations and it was not her place, however certain she was – and she *was* certain – that these riches had not been honestly earned. Her uneasiness deepened and her fingers remained numb with cold. 'Fame, too,' she said, her eyes flickering from the blonde girl to the other. The dark-eyed girl who hadn't yet said a word. *Infamy.* Not fame. That was a better word for the feeling she was getting.

'As for love ...' She hesitated. There was love already, she saw that. A deep, everlasting love, the kind many people would never find. It was there already and would not be bettered for either girl. For one of them – she was not sure which – it would be the strongest they would ever know.

'Yes,' she finished weakly. 'The best kind of love, that goes beyond a lifetime.' She felt suddenly feverish, hot and cold all at once. *Very peculiar.* She needed this to finish, for these girls to go. Something wasn't right. 'I'm so sorry,' she began. 'I'm not feeling well. I'm afraid I have to ask you to—'

'I have a question.' It was the dark-eyed girl who had spoken, finally. Her eyes were trained on the crystal ball and there was a hungry look in them that Madam Divina didn't like. 'Is it true that you never tell people if you see something bad in their future?'

Madam Divina shifted in her seat. There was something cunning about this girl, something determined and ruthless. Even without the crystal ball, Madam Divina was gifted in reading a person's character, and everything about this girl screamed a warning.

'Yes,' she said, more curtly than she meant to. She trusted her instincts, and her instincts were telling her that this girl wanted the crystal ball for herself. Worse, she had the strongest feeling that the ball would soon be taken from her. Was this a trap?

'How old is it?' the girl continued. Her dark eyes sparkled, reflecting the glassy orb. 'Where did it come from?'

'Like I said, I'm afraid I have to end the reading here,' Madam Divina muttered. She pulled her scarf off, feeling it was damp with sweat. She instantly prickled with goosepimples, feeling shivery. 'No charge.'

'What's wrong?' the blonde girl asked, her blue eyes wide and concerned. '*Did* you see something bad?' She looked so innocent and sweet, and in that moment Madam Divina couldn't imagine why these two girls might be friends. They were so very ... *different.*

'No,' the fortune teller said, averting her gaze. 'Of course not.' A movement in the crystal ball caught her attention and she glanced at it. Cold sweat formed instantly on her top lip. The crystal ball showed water, just as it had before. Swirling with chunks of ice, freezing and deadly. She blinked and quickly seized the black cloth, throwing it over the crystal to hide it before the rest of the horrid vision appeared. *The hand.*

Because now she knew one of these girls would die – and soon.

She herded them outside, through the velvet curtains and into the bustle of the winter market. It was still busy, full of sounds of laughter and smells of cooking. In one direction she saw Echo Hall, no doubt preparing for its biggest event of the year: the masked ball. In the other, there was the lake covered with rosy-cheeked skaters. *Frozen surface, icy water beneath.*

'Stay away from that lake,' she said, the words slipping out before she could stop them. 'It's ... it's dangerous. Do you hear me? Stay away.'

She didn't wait to hear what the girls said, or what looks they might exchange with each other. She went back through her velvet curtains and sat quietly at the table, not daring to uncover the crystal ball. She had planned on leaving tomorrow, the same as every other visitor. Tomorrow, when it was light and others were leaving and the roads would be busy. But what if she left before, while everyone else was at the masked ball? She could go tonight. Because even though the thought of travelling those icy roads alone filled her with fear, she could not bear to spend another night in Wilderness with this awful vision hanging over her. And so it was decided – she would leave after dark.

Later, many years later, the vision would still haunt her along with that decision. If she had stayed until morning, the girl would have lived. She knew that, from all the stories of the highway robber. The unending stories, and questions about the robbery that followed her wherever she went. The same questions, over and over: *What did he say? Did you see his face? Did you fear for your life?* These were the questions she could answer. But there were two things she could never reveal, not to anyone.

When the carriage had skidded to a stop, and the door was flung open to reveal the barrel of a pistol pointing straight at her, Madam Divina had recognised those dark eyes behind the mask. Those dark, wanting eyes. Everything else –

the carefully disguised voice, the heavy padding sewn into the clothes – they all faded into nothing. She would remember those eyes as long as she lived, and the rage she had felt. The red-hot, searing rage that would melt a thousand frozen lakes when she'd heard the words:

'Stand and deliver! The crystal or your life!'

She had broken the rule, then. The one sacred rule of not delivering bad news. When she'd been forced to hand over the crystal she'd laughed, even *enjoyed* sharing it. Her anger made her cruel.

'Take it,' she said. 'For I have seen your future and it holds death.'

She was ashamed of that, of revealing that dreadful truth. She had seen fear in the highway robber's eyes. Just a flash of it, quickly replaced by sneering arrogance, but it had been there. What she was more ashamed of was that she was *glad* in that horrible, helpless moment where her most precious possession was being taken from her. She had seen death and she was *glad*. It was deserved.

She'd had no way of knowing that it was the other girl who would die.

And the second thing she was most ashamed of, the thing she would never, ever tell anyone as long as she lived, was that yes, she *had* known the identity of the highway robber. But it was the jeers and the mockery that stopped her from revealing it, to anyone.

'How come you didn't "see" it coming, this robbery?'

'Not much of a fortune teller, are you?'

They were already laughing at her. Her reputation was for ever in tatters. They only wanted the story now, not her fortunes. So how could she have told? How could she admit that the infamous robber who had taken everything from her, this fearsome villain who had terrorised Wilderness, was barely older than a child?

Chapter Twenty-five
Revenge

THE TRUTH SETTLED AROUND BETTY LIKE snow.

Mrs Chambers? *Sonny's mother was the highway robber of Wilderness?*

Jack Frost ... Jacqueline Frost. *Robin.*

'It can't ... She *can't* be,' Fliss breathed softly next to Betty's ear. 'It makes no sense!'

And yet, somewhere at the back of Betty's mind, she thought that perhaps, just *perhaps*, it did.

'You're lying!' Sneed shouted, his voice as sharp as a whip. 'Stop *lying*! Stop stalling, and tell us what you know, damn you!'

'I just did,' Robin answered quietly. 'I'm not lying. I'm sick of lies. *I* stole the crystal ball that night.'

'Then where is it?' Lady Fortuna demanded.

'Underneath you,' Robin replied. 'In the lake, just like the story said.'

'The same story that had everyone believe the highway robber was Elora's sweetheart?' hissed Lady Fortuna. 'The same story that said he was dead in the lake?'

'I had to protect my identity.' Robin's voice was quieter still, lost in the past. 'So after Elora died and people learned she was linked to the highway robber, the rumours began. That he was her secret sweetheart. It was safer for me to let them carry on believing that—'

'Shut up!' Sneed snarled, his face going purple with rage. He stepped closer, the cane raised in one hand and the pistol in the other still aimed at Mrs Chambers. 'If the robber knew where that crystal was he would have retrieved it, not left it for any fool to search for. What did you do with it? *Where is it?*'

'I told you, it's at the bottom of the lake!' Robin yelled. 'Which is exactly where it's been for the past thirty-seven years!'

A beat of silence followed. The pain in Robin's voice was enough to convince Betty. It was the kind of hurt and sadness that couldn't be faked. But was it enough for Fortuna and Sneed to believe it, too?

It was plainly enough for Sonny, who watched his mother with a pinched, disbelieving face. 'M-mother?' he said, in a small voice. 'It was really you?'

Robin nodded, her dark eyes full of shame. 'I'm sorry. I'm so, so sorry. I wish I could go back and change things, but I can't. Elora died because of my greed. My best friend is dead because of me.'

305

'All this time,' Fortuna whispered. Her eyebrows drew together, like a puppet's whose strings had been pulled. 'All this time, you've been at Echo Hall. Knowing what you did, knowing people were searching for that crystal ball.' Her eyes flashed with anger. 'I suppose that made you feel clever. *Powerful.*'

'No,' Robin spat. 'It made me afraid. Because I knew better than anyone the lengths people would go to in order to get their hands on it. I didn't want any more lives lost.'

'Well, now you don't have to worry any more,' said Lady Fortuna. 'Because after tonight, it will be gone. My mother's crystal – *my* crystal – is coming with me after all this time. And then I can be the one with the glory, the one with the fame!'

Robin laughed then, a harsh ugly sound. '*What?*'

'You heard,' Sneed snapped. 'We're not leaving without it!'

'You'll never find it,' Robin exclaimed. 'Did you honestly think it was possible?'

'Of course.' Sneed's voice brooked no argument. 'Because now we have you to tell us exactly where it went in.' He moved closer to the lake and gave the ice a sharp tap with the cane. 'It can't be that deep this close to the edge.'

'Don't bet on that,' Robin said darkly. 'It's deeper than you think, especially at night, when it's cold ... and there's no way of finding what you're looking for.' Her voice trailed off, and there was a haunted look in her eyes.

'Where did it go in?' Sneed demanded, impatient. 'If you

fell from the road up there then it couldn't have gone far, surely the crystal would only have rolled a little way. The lake wasn't even frozen at first, was it?'

Robin didn't answer. She was staring at the icy trees with a faraway look in her eyes.

'No.' Her voice was soft, like a breath on the wind. 'We knew the cold was coming, but I thought we'd escape the worst of it. I was sure I could. So young, so arrogant. So . . . *stupid*. We might have managed it, but it all went wrong.'

'So where—?' Sneed interrupted, but Robin continued as though he had never spoken. As though she were in a trance, forced to replay the terrible events of that night.

'Elora didn't want me to do it.' She smiled faintly. 'I thought I knew best, insisted that I could. She felt so guilty because she was the one who signalled to me from the window with a lamp to let me know Madam Divina was on her way. I did the rest. I lay in wait, ambushed the carriage, stole the crystal. All of it was so easy, like clockwork. Until the crystal . . . it somehow *slipped* out of my grasp as I rode away. Afterwards I knew I must have been mistaken, but I could have sworn the thing had rolled, like it hadn't wanted to be captured. Crazy as that sounds.' She blinked hard. 'I panicked, couldn't bear the thought of it smashing on the road. It was so beautiful, mesmerising. I lunged for it – *caught* it – but I came off the horse. Crashed through the trees and rolled down the bank. I hit my head as I landed and was knocked unconscious – for how long I don't know. Long enough for Elora to know something was wrong and come searching for me.

'When I came to it was snowing. I was shivering uncontrollably and could barely move my limbs but I forced myself, knowing I'd die if I didn't. The crystal was ahead of me, capped with snow. I grabbed it, then crawled between the trees and on to the lakeshore, and that's when I saw my hat. The wind had taken it and blown it out on to the water. Its surface had only just started to freeze. I didn't care – but then I saw something floating next to it.'

She paused, and a sob burst out of her. 'It was Elora's hair. Her perfect, golden hair. I knew then she must have seen my hat from the road and thought I was in the lake. She'd jumped in to try and save me. I ran in to drag her out. And the water, it went deep – so deep. I've never felt cold like it. I pulled her hard but she was tangled in something, some weed at the bottom, and with the cold . . . I guess she couldn't feel how to free herself. I made it about halfway back to the shore when I realised the crystal ball was weighing us both down. Added to my wet clothes and Elora it was too much, too heavy. I knew we'd never make it out. I was already succumbing to the cold the way Elora had. So I removed the crystal from my clothing and let it go. It sank instantly. *Gone.*

'I got her out,' Robin continued, her voice trembling now. 'I don't know how, but I did, even though I knew it was too late. She was already dead, I could see that, but I couldn't bear to leave her in the water and I wasn't strong enough

308

to lift her on to the horse to take her back. The snow was falling thicker then, and I was scared she'd be buried under it. I pulled her into the copse of trees – I thought they'd at least shelter her a bit, and make it easier to find her. When she was discovered they saw the icy tears on her cheeks and thought they were Elora's, that she'd frozen looking for me. But they were my tears, tears I'd cried for her. My best friend, lost for ever because of my selfishness and wickedness.' She turned to gaze at Sonny. 'And that's why I've stayed all this time, my darling. As a punishment. I know Elora hates me – that's why she haunts this place and Echo Hall. So if she can't leave, then why should I?'

'That's ... that's why we stayed?' Sonny asked. 'You thought you didn't deserve to leave, and start over?' He shook his head in shock and disbelief. 'Didn't you realise you were punishing me, too?'

Robin wept silently. The truth was finally out, her horrible tale told. Betty tried to imagine how it must feel to keep a secret like that all to herself, and for so many years. She couldn't. It was unthinkable. Tears burned her eyes. What a tragic death for Elora. What a tragic life for Mrs Chambers afterwards. 'Jumping jackdaws,' Betty whispered, numb with cold and shock. The highway robber had finally been unmasked. The living, breathing highway*woman* who hadn't died in the lake, after all. That had been Elora. *The Drowning Girl*. Betty tasted tears, hot and salty at the back of her throat. She heard Fliss sniffle beside her and saw her sister was crying, tears running down her face. Then Fliss gave a loud sob which cut through the snowy silence.

Robin whipped round, her eyes searching the seemingly empty space where Betty and Fliss stood. 'Elora?' she called, wiping her eyes. 'Is that you?'

The two sisters stood silently. Fliss bit her lip to prevent more sobs escaping. A slow movement on the ice caught Betty's eye, something zigzagging this way and that. A thin crack, continuing to spread from the bullet hole in the ice. It was growing closer and closer to Sonny.

'You mean to say,' Fortuna said, not moved in the least, 'that you dropped my mother's crystal in the lake *on purpose?*'

'Yes,' Robin answered through tears and gritted teeth. 'You heartless snake.'

'So, how do we get it?' said Sneed impatiently. 'If it's really where you say it is?'

'You don't. People have searched for the highway robber's treasure for years, sifted through the muck and silt at the bottom of the lake in this area and found nothing.'

'People?' Fortuna demanded. *'People?* We are not just people! I'm its rightful owner.'

Robin shook her head wearily. 'Not my problem. You wanted to know where the crystal was, I've told you. Now let my son go before we all freeze to death out here!'

Fortuna blinked. 'So that's it?' Her voice shook, but Betty couldn't tell whether it was from anger or cold. 'There's no ... no hope of finding it?'

310

'Not unless you want to smash through the ice and search for it yourself,' Robin snapped. 'And let me tell you, once you're in water that cold your thoughts turn to ice, too.'

'Perhaps in the summer, my beloved?' Sneed suggested. 'If we return, maybe then we'll have a better chance—'

'No.' Fortuna's voice was sharp. 'I'm finished with Wilderness. Besides, she's right. People have searched these waters for years and never found the crystal. My mother always said it had a will of its own – perhaps it doesn't *want* to be found.'

Sneed's shoulders sagged. 'So you believe her? That it's in the lake?'

'Yes.' Fortuna narrowed her eyes. 'Her story fits with something my mother said, something she knew and told only to me – that there was just one death that night, not two. Everyone else believed the highway robber was killed, but I knew that couldn't be right. My mother's visions were never wrong. So, yes. I'm done with Wilderness, and the crystal ball. I refuse to waste any more of my life on it the way my mother did.' She stared back at Echo Hall, then straight at Robin. 'But I'm not finished with you.'

Robin stiffened as she met the fortune teller's gaze. 'Not finished?'

Fortuna laughed bitterly. 'You think I'd let you walk away after what you did? You made my mother a joke and stole what's rightfully mine. And now you're going to pay!'

'I'm already paying.' Robin's voice was quiet now, full of

sadness. 'I've been paying every day since it happened. I lost my best friend – isn't that enough?'

'No,' Fortuna said chillingly. 'If I can't have the crystal ball, then I'll at least have my revenge.' She nodded at Sneed. 'Shoot her!'

'No!' Sonny cried out. He strained against his bonds, his eyes never leaving his mother.

Sneed looked appalled. The pistol wobbled in his hand. 'Wh-what? Now, hold on, my dear – we've done some questionable things, but you never said anything about *murder!*'

'You don't have to kill her,' Fortuna said, as calmly as if she were discussing what dress to wear for dinner. 'Just . . .' She waved a hand. 'Shoot her in the leg or something. Then we'll leave and the cold will finish her off.' An ugly cackle burst out of her. 'Who knows? Maybe the famous highway robber of Wilderness will be a ghost after all before the night is out.'

'She's mad,' Betty whispered, horrified. 'She really wants him to do it!'

'But the boy . . .' Sneed croaked. He was shaking now. 'We can't leave him out here alone in the snow. He'll die!'

'Don't,' Robin begged. 'My son is innocent. Don't punish him for my crimes.'

'I said, *shoot*.' Fortuna gave Sneed a venomous look. 'You said you loved me. Here's your chance to prove it!'

Sneed pointed the pistol at Robin, then lowered it. 'I . . . I can't,' he stammered.

312

The fortune teller shot him a look of contempt. 'Then give the pistol to me and I will.'

'Now, let's think about this for a moment,' Sneed began. 'We don't need to ...'

A horrible rushing sound began in Betty's ears, like water drowning out Sneed's voice. Her heart began to gallop. They could not simply stand by and watch – she had to *do* something! 'We have to help Sonny escape,' she whispered to Fliss. 'We can make him disappear and untie those ropes.'

'But what about Mrs Chambers?' Fliss replied.

'I don't know.' Dread uncurled in Betty's stomach as Sneed continued to stall. She glanced at the tiny yellow lights of Echo Hall. Had Charlie found Finn Sharkey yet and raised the alarm? And what good would it do if his dogs – and sled – were here? Would he still be able to help them? She couldn't count on it.

'We'll help Sonny and figure that out next.' She began working at the thread on Sonny's cap again. By now her fingers were so numb she could barely feel them.

'Give it to me, I've got sharper nails,' said Fliss. When the stubborn thread still refused to tear off, she took to it with her teeth. 'There,' she said, presenting Betty with a tiny piece of the white trim.

'Keep hold of it,' said Betty. 'We'll get to Sonny and untie the ropes first – if he vanishes too quickly it could cause Robin – or Sneed – to panic. We have to keep them calm.'

Fliss gulped as they crept away from the trees and towards

the lake. 'We told Granny we wouldn't go back on the ice.'

'As soon as we get Sonny free we'll be off it,' Betty promised. Together they stepped on to the ice, hand in hand.

'I said *give me the pistol!*' Fortuna shrieked.

'No!' shouted Robin. 'Mr Sneed, don't get yourself in any deeper. Let me have it and I promise this will all be over. You go your way and I'll go mine. You keep quiet about my secret, and I'll keep quiet about you kidnapping my son.'

Sneed's hand continued to tremble. He hesitated.

'Don't listen to her,' Fortuna spat. 'She's nothing but a thief. *Now give it to me!*'

In one bumbling movement Sneed handed the pistol to Fortuna. She pointed it straight at Robin without a moment's consideration and, unlike Sneed's, her aim appeared scarily steady. She was still on the shore, perhaps ten or twelve paces away from Mrs Chambers, but now she began closing the gap, and forcing Robin to step on to the ice.

'Betty,' Fliss whispered, as they advanced closer to the sled. 'This is dangerous! The pistol – she's getting closer! And look at the cracks!'

'Then you go back to the shore,' Betty whispered back fearfully. 'But we can't leave Sonny tied up. The ice surely can't hold much longer, and if it breaks he won't stand a chance!'

'I'm not leaving you,' Fliss said fiercely.

'Enough, Fortuna,' Robin demanded, glancing in panic towards her son. 'We both know you've never fired a pistol

314

any more than you've ever cleaned your own shoes. Now, hand that over before you shoot yourself in the foot – or worse.'

A gunshot cracked the air, so unexpectedly that Betty bit her tongue. Fortuna had fired, deliberately aiming at the ice. A second black hole had appeared – and it was only a short way from the first. Robin leapt back further on to the frozen lake, positioning herself between the fortune teller and her son. Sonny let out a frightened whimper. Even Sneed looked stunned.

'What were you saying?' Fortuna asked dangerously.

'Meddling magpies!' Fliss whispered, clutching her chest. 'She did it!'

Without warning, Robin charged at Fortuna, grabbing for the pistol. It was a clumsy skid across the ice to the shore which saw the two women topple over and crash on to the ground. Then the pair of them were rolling and shrieking, wrestling to overpower the other, with a bumbling Sneed trying to intervene and Bonbon snapping and snarling as he leapt to Robin's defence.

'Hurry!' Betty urged. They had almost reached Sonny. The layer of snow on the ice made it easier to grip under their boots, but Betty was wary that any slip could be disastrous. Especially after last time.

It won't happen again, she told herself. *That was just a freak accident. It's colder now. The ice can't break a second time . . .*

But she didn't believe it. The ice had broken once before,

and now there were two bullet holes and numerous cracks in it. She pushed the thought away, concentrating on keeping her balance until they reached the sled. Sonny was shivering and crying inside it, twisting against the ropes and calling for his mother as the fight for the pistol continued. Betty glanced back and her tummy lurched to see that the struggle had taken the two women on to the ice. They were rolling about, thrashing and shrieking. Mrs Chambers was strong and heavier, but Fortuna was fast, like a viper, and neither could seem to get the better of the other for long.

'Sonny,' Betty said gently, afraid of startling him. 'Don't be scared.'

Sonny whipped round, looking this way and that for the mysterious voice.

'Listen carefully,' Betty persisted, speaking faster now. 'It's me, Betty Widdershins – my sister Fliss is here, too. We're going to help you escape, just keep still for a moment.' She leaned into the sled and began working at the knots binding Sonny's ankles, and felt him flinch at the unexpected touch of someone invisible.

'Why can't I see you?' Sonny whispered, his eyes darting nervously.

'We've a … a sort of a … something that can make us vanish,' Fliss babbled. 'And it's a long story.' She removed her mittens and began picking at the ties around Sonny's wrists, haste making her clumsy.

316

'A sort of something?' Sonny asked, his eyes widening as the knots began to loosen.

'Magic,' said Betty in a rush. 'And I'm guessing if you believe in ghosts, you'll believe in magic.'

Sonny gave a faint nod of understanding, his eyes glued to his mother. 'Is that what made Bonbon disappear?'

'Yes,' said Betty. 'But in a moment we'll be visible, just for a second. Then we're going to make you vanish.' Her fingers ached with cold as she tackled the final knot. Sneed had done them tight, too tight. She glanced at the ice under her feet, watching as a hairline crack ran across it. *There!* The rope slid free.

Sonny groaned faintly, circling his ankles. A moment later, Fliss had freed his hands.

'Get ready,' Betty told Fliss. They ducked down behind the sled.

Betty pulled the nesting dolls apart, first the outer, then the second, then the third.

'Wolf!' Sneed shrieked suddenly, as Bonbon became visible. 'The ghost dog – it's a wolf! Oh, wait, no – it's that great thing of the boy's!'

Quickly, Betty pushed the piece of trim into the third nesting doll and replaced the set one inside the other. Twisting the halves of the outer doll to align, she shoved the dolls into the coat pocket and pulled Sonny out of the sled and on to the ice, tugging him towards the lake shore.

'It's gone again!' Sneed squeaked as Bonbon vanished.

317

'What is going *on* here?' Then he gasped. 'Where's the boy?'

Instantly Mrs Chambers and Lady Fortuna stopped wrestling to glance at the sled, their hands clamped around the pistol.

'Sonny?' yelled Mrs Chambers, releasing the pistol and staggering to her feet towards the sled. 'Where are you?'

'I'm safe!' Sonny yelled back. 'Just get away from—'

'Aha!' Fortuna grabbed the pistol, using the moment's distraction to her advantage. She smiled wickedly and took aim at Robin. Easing herself to her feet she drew closer, determined not to miss this time.

'No!' Mrs Chambers gasped. '*Don't!*'

A *crack* rang through the air as the gun went off again. *Please not Mrs Chambers or Bonbon*, Betty begged silently, as she, Fliss and Sonny rushed over the ice. *Please not—*

Then she realised Robin had gone down, and was clutching her leg. Fortuna had shot her, and now loomed over her, raising the pistol a final time.

An awful, familiar groaning noise reached Betty's ears. Had she not heard it before, she might have thought it was a person. This time she knew straight away what it was. The lake, groaning as though it were a living thing, in pain.

The ice, breaking.

She turned to Fliss and Sonny, knowing it was already too late.

'*Run!*'

Chapter Twenty-six
The Crystal Ball

A T FIRST BETTY THOUGHT THEY MIGHT make it. A thick vein-like crack splintered the ice, shattering it from the sled to the shore. Water seeped through the crack, wetting the surface.

'Keep going!' she panted, as Sonny and Fliss turned, stricken, to stare at Mrs Chambers, still lying on the ice with Lady Fortuna poised over her. Snow whipped around their heads, blinding them. There was a huge *SNAP!* and an enormous chunk of ice shifted like a raft beneath Mrs Chambers and Lady Fortuna. Almost in slow motion it tipped, swinging like a trapdoor to reveal black water beneath, and the two women slid straight in, vanishing beneath the water.

'Fortuna!' yelled Sneed in horror. He had made it to the shore now, and was trying to use the cane to keep Bonbon's snapping jaws at bay, but Bonbon wrenched it from his grasp.

'No!' Sonny bolted towards the black hole in the ice.

'*Mother!*' Alerted by his cry, Bonbon turned away from Sneed and began whining and pacing up and down the lakeshore, his eyes on his master.

'Sonny!' yelled Betty. 'Wait, it's not safe!' She stood motionless on the lake as Fliss continued to the shore, torn between running after him and racing to safety.

'Betty!' Fliss hollered, beckoning from the shore. 'Look!' She gestured frantically across the lake. Tiny lights moved in the darkness from the direction of Echo Hall. Slow and steady. People on foot, moving towards them around the edge of the lake. 'Charlie must have raised the alarm! There are people out searching!'

Charlie. Betty's heart leapt with hope. Her brave little sister hadn't let them down. Help was on the way – but would it arrive fast enough, with the water that cold? With people trapped in the blackness under the ice?

A slinking movement caught her eye. Sneed was skulking away into the icy fringes of Elora's Tears. His face was a deathly pale and his eyes were everywhere, clearly bewildered by the voices of unseen people. *He's given up,* Betty thought. *He doesn't think they can be saved, so he's trying to save himself.*

'Betty Widdershins!' Fliss yelled again. 'Get off that lake this instant!'

Betty took a hesitant step towards her sister, remembering the feel of the icy water on her skin, in her ears, up her nose. She didn't think she could take that again.

'Sonny!' she tried again. 'Come off the ice – help's on the way!'

If Sonny heard her he made no sign. He reached the black hole, lying flat on the ice next to the jagged break to search the hidden depths. He paddled it with his hands, gasping at the iciness of it. Ice broke away beneath him. From the shore Bonbon began to bark, loud and fast. Leading the search party towards them.

'*Betty!*' Fliss yelled again, brandishing something. *Sneed's cane.* Betty glanced at her, then turned back to see Sonny disappearing as the ice gave way.

'No!' Betty cried.

'Here,' Fliss shouted, running on to the lake. She threw the cane towards Betty. 'Use this! It'll give Sonny something to grab—' Suddenly her feet went from under her and for a terrifying moment Betty thought she was about to go through the ice, too. Instead she came down heavily on her left arm, landing with a piercing cry.

'Fliss!' Betty yelled. 'Are you hurt?'

'My arm!' Fliss groaned. 'I – I can't move it!'

'Stay there!' Betty told her, spotting Sneed's cane abandoned a short way from the sled. The sled itself was tilting now, water rippling around its base. Terror gripped her. *If I can just get it*, she thought. *It'll give Sonny something to reach for if he surfaces.*

If.

A hand broke the water surface, then a face emerged. *Sonny.*

321

There was no time to go for the cane. Betty slid towards him, her arm outstretched. 'Take my hand!' she gasped.

His fingers slid over hers, grasping uselessly. They were already numb with cold. His lips were blue. She grabbed his hand and pulled with all her strength. It was not enough.

'The dolls!' Fliss shrieked suddenly, from somewhere behind. 'No one will be able to see—'

Her words were cut off as Sonny's weight pulled Betty, too far, and too fast. She went in headfirst, the water like cold knives slicing every part of her.

I won't get out this time, she thought, closing her eyes in the dark. *No one could survive this twice. No one is that lucky.* She felt Sonny's hands grappling for her, and wished he wouldn't because she knew now she couldn't help him. She couldn't help either of them.

She reached up, the heavy old coat billowing around her, and found ice above her head. She forced her eyes open, and they stung with stirred up silt and grit. Below, everything was black, but the icy surface above was pale. She closed her eyes again. Saw snowflakes, and heard words in a jumble.

When Elora's ghost's about, wrap up warm and don't go out . . .

They say seeing her leads to a death in the family. The death of a loved one.

The prophecy was true. Betty was going to die under the ice with three people she hardly knew . . . and no one would find her because . . .

Fliss's last words echoed in her head. *The dolls! No one will be able to see—*

No one would be able to see her. Or Sonny, or Fliss. They were all invisible and could only see each other. Betty's chest was tight with the need to breathe. Soon she would have no choice but to suck the icy water into her lungs. And then that would be the end. There was just one thing she could do, for all of them. She reached down, numb fingers jabbing at the coat pocket. Finding the dolls, buoyant with the air inside them. Her hands tangled in fabric before finding smooth wood. With both hands and jerking movements she managed to twist the two halves of the outer doll. *There.* It was done. The dolls slipped from her fingers, falling through the water with a peacock feather floating next to them.

Gone, thought Betty. *Like me.*

A light had started to glow around her, a warm light that was something between white and golden. It made Betty think of sunshine, or candlelight. *So this is what it's like to die*, she thought. *I might as well see it. After all, it'll be the last thing I ever do.* She forced her eyes open for the final time.

What she saw was not death.

What she saw was three other people floating in deep, deep water that was no longer dark but lit up with the white-gold light: Lady Fortuna, with her black hair billowing around her and her eyes like dark pits of malice; Mrs Chambers, frantically banging against the ice above; Sonny, hands outstretched, touching nothing.

323

Wait ... Not three people. There was another, Betty realised. A girl below them all, with golden hair that seemed to radiate the strange underwater light. Weeds moved around her in a slow dance. Mrs Chambers gazed at her, and a stream of shocked bubbles escaped her lips. *Elora*.

Below her, within the weeds and the years of thick silt, lost things were lit up by the golden light. An ice skate, half rotted away. A silver pistol, dropped only moments before. A curved, shining surface ... a clear orb sucked into the mud. Lady Fortuna's eyes widened as they homed in on it. *The crystal ball*.

Don't, Betty tried to say as the fortune teller grasped for it, kicking feebly. *You'll never reach it*. Fortuna's lips were already blue, her once-pretty face contorted by greed. She seemed to have no awareness of anyone else in the water, consumed only by the sight of her lost treasure. She sank, a mass of black hair and a swirling cloak, just a raggedy outline against the brilliant white glow.

The phantom Elora surged towards Mrs Chambers and Sonny, and for a moment her light dimmed. *They've gone*, thought Betty. *Elora has taken them so she doesn't have to be alone any more, down here in the dark. I guess she's going to take me, too.*

Cold fingers wrapped around Betty's wrist. The light was back, brighter than ever. Golden hair swirled in the water before her, and there was a face she was almost too terrified to look into. The hands were pulling her through the water, urgent and insistent. The same hands she had felt on her ankle the first time she had gone through the ice. Pulling her, pulling her ... not down, but up. Up to air, and the break in the ice. Just before she hit the cold air she saw a face: a sweet, kind face full of love. Elora Goode did not want revenge. Of that, Betty was sure.

She was also sure she could hear her name being called, but Elora was trying to tell her something. She could see her lips moving, but the light was fading now, the lake falling away to blackness. Betty hit the surface, gasping for air and flailing.

'Grab this!' someone was saying. 'Betty! Grab hold of it!'

Fliss.

Her sister was flat on the ice, Sneed's cane in her good hand reaching towards her.

With her last ounce of strength Betty flung out her arm and tried to grab the cane. Missed, and tried again. Words whispered in her head. One word: *forgive.*

Elora's voice?

Forgive.

Betty grabbed the cane and held on, hearing Fliss groaning with effort as she pulled it clear from the water. Warm hands lifted her from above. Cold hands pushed her from below. Betty slithered out of the water to land on the ice. There were lights, loud voices, confusion all around.

'We've got three out! One's been shot and someone's still in there – that fortune teller,' they said. Finn Sharkey's voice was shouting instructions: 'Another one here with a broken arm, and someone else – a Rupert Sneed – still missing . . . Wait – who's that over by Elora's Tears?'

Betty rolled on to her side, gasping and shivering. She looked up into Fliss's warm brown eyes, so full of love and relief. Strong arms went round her, hauling her up and away, off the ice and into blankets. Then Charlie's sweet voice ringing out from across the ice: 'My sisters! My *sisters!*'

And finally, Granny, her wrinkled, worried face lit up by a lamp, still wearing her black eye mask. Granny, dressed as the Grim Reaper – or Death.

But Betty was alive, alive, alive.

She closed her eyes and burrowed into the warm blankets. As she did she felt a *pop!* followed by a warm trickle of lake water leaving her ear from somewhere deep inside. It was gone, clear at last. She could hear again, properly now. What a wonderful thing that was.

And wonderful, too, that somewhere close by a dog was barking joyfully.

Afterwards, people would talk about how the winter storm had stopped as rapidly as it had started that night. By the time the search party had reached the lake the sky was clear and lit with stars, with no sign of snow. Nor did snow return to Wilderness until the following winter, and only then it was a light dusting.

They spoke too, of the disappearance of Lady Fortuna – the

only person not to have been pulled from the lake that night. Driven mad, the rumours said, by the desire to locate her mother's missing crystal ball. Driven to kidnap, and willing to kill for it. Some claimed to have seen her ghost, black hair billowing like a sail under the water of the lake. Others said she walked the corridors of Echo Hall, muttering to herself about the highway robber who had stolen the crystal ball all those years ago – and whose identity would forever remain a mystery.

Over time, the two tales merged into one and the ghost story of Wilderness changed into something different. There were no more sightings of a ghostly maid at Echo Hall, or echoing hoofbeats on icy nights on Chill Hill, or reports of a drowning girl. Instead, the whispers were only of the phantom fortune teller. The crystal ball, however, was never seen again. Only those who had lived that night knew the truth.

On the night itself, the masked ball came to an abrupt end for the first time in its almost fifty-year history. A doctor was summoned, fires were stoked, and endless blankets were wrapped around the three people who had survived the icy water of Shivershock Lake, and the fourth with a broken arm. An infirmary of sorts was set up in an empty room on the ground floor with four beds and several chairs.

For hours Betty drifted in and out of sleep. She dreamed of golden-haired girls and wicked fortune tellers and awoke every so often to soft fussing words from Granny and

Clarissa, and impatient demands from Charlie.

'Why ain't she awake, yet? When? *When?*'

When she awoke properly she found the room was dim, lit by a single lamp and the glow of the warm fire. She wiggled her toes and fingers. All still there, thank goodness. Her hand was being held by someone: Granny, who was dozing in a chair next to her with Charlie fast asleep on her lap. On the other side was Fliss, eyes closed, mouth wide open and her bruised and broken left arm in a sling.

And opposite, dark eyes that were wide awake, burning into hers. Betty gulped and stared back at the highway robber of Wilderness.

'You followed us out there,' Mrs Chambers said quietly, her gaze unwavering. Her leg was heavily bandaged, and resting on a small table. 'I'm grateful to you, and your sisters. You tried to help us. Even after you'd heard what I said. Who I am, and . . . what I did.'

Betty nodded silently. There was no point in trying to deny it. 'Yes.' Her voice was dry and croaky. 'I heard. I know who you are – or who you were. But it's clear you're not that person any more.'

'No.' Mrs Chambers turned to Sonny, asleep next to her. 'I . . . no.'

'There was also another reason,' Betty admitted. 'We saw Elora from the window of room nine and we'd heard about the stories . . . of a sighting of her causing the death of a loved one. We already suspected that Elora was the Drowning Girl,

328

and we thought that if we got to the bottom of it then the haunting would stop and—'

'Elora would never have hurt anyone.' Mrs Chambers sighed and looked away from Betty for the first time to stare into the flames of the fire. 'That part of the story was never true – just silly rumours made up after someone happened to die after her ghost was seen. In places like this, a story can grow and take on a life of its own. I tried to control it, feeding the parts that benefitted me—'

'Like the highway robber being a man?'

Betty turned. It was Fliss who had spoken, soft and sad. Her eyelids were red and heavy as she fought to come out of sleep.

'Yes. It was the safest way for me never to be found out,' Mrs Chambers said. 'People assumed the robber was a man from the very start.' She smiled wryly. 'It didn't take much to convince them it was true. I practised disguising my voice and sewed padding into a large coat to fill it out. With my face covered, people were easily fooled.' She blinked fiercely as tears swam in her eyes. 'One thing was true, though. I loved Elora, just as much as she loved me. She was the best friend I ever had. More like a sister than a friend, in fact.'

Betty glanced at Fliss, and then Charlie, finding that her own eyes were now blurred with tears. 'Yes,' she whispered. 'I understand.'

'Will you stay at Echo Hall, even now?' Fliss asked.

Mrs Chambers shook her head. 'No. I think . . . I think

the reason Elora haunted this place and the lake was because *I* was haunted by what I'd caused. I think somewhere deep down I knew she would have forgiven me, long ago. And when we were down there, under that lake ... I heard her. Telling me that she forgave me.'

'So did I,' said Betty softly, remembering the voice in her head. *Forgive.*

'I just didn't believe I deserved it,' said Mrs Chambers. 'In a way, staying here was a way of remaining close to what was left of her. But now I think, I *hope*, I'm ready to move on and remember her the way she would have wanted.' She tapped her heart. 'In here.' She glanced at Sonny, a look loaded with guilt and love. 'And I need to move on for my boy's sake, too.'

She fell silent. Betty watched the sleeping Sonny, and thought about how desperate he must have been to act the way he had. At least now he would get his wish: a new start for them both.

Someone knocked gently on the door, and then Finn Sharkey poked his head around and peered at them.

'Good – you're awake,' he said, relieved. 'I've got someone here who's very restless and keen to see you all now the doctor's gone!'

Bonbon burst into the room panting heavily, tail swishing everywhere like a daft brush. He looked more like a huge puppy than a wolf now, and Betty wondered how she could ever have found him menacing as he stuck his wet nose in

Mrs Chambers' hand, then rolled on his back in front of the warm fire.

'Quick update for you,' Finn added. 'Rupert Sneed confessed to kidnapping Sonny and paying an ex-servant for information and blueprints of the hall, as well as stealing master keys to some of the rooms, including number nine. He's currently in the holding cell down by the kitchens until a warden arrives.' He paused, frowning. 'He seems quite confused. Keeps babbling about people and dogs appearing and disappearing, as if by magic. Perhaps it's the shock, or maybe the cold just got to him.'

'Maybe,' said Mrs Chambers, her dark eyes devoid of an ounce of pity. She reached across to the sleeping Sonny and gently touched his cheek. Finn nodded and left the room, closing the door quietly behind him.

'People appearing and disappearing, as if by magic,' Mrs Chambers said thoughtfully. 'Yes. I seem to recall something like that, too.' She looked from Betty to Fliss, waiting expectantly.

'We had a set of wooden nesting dolls,' Betty explained, keeping a firm eye on Granny to make sure she really was asleep and not listening. 'They were enchanted, and allowed us to make ourselves, and other people, vanish.' She swallowed hard, fresh tears springing to her eyes. 'But they . . . they sank in the lake. I couldn't keep hold of them.'

She allowed herself to cry, weeping hot tears that felt endless. The dolls had been important to all of the sisters, but to Betty especially. They'd been the sisters' pinch of magic, their key to adventures. Now they were gone, at the bottom of Shivershock Lake to join all the other lost things. She wondered if anyone would ever find them one day, or whether time and winters would slowly destroy them and wear them down to nothing. She rubbed the tears away savagely, unable to bear thinking about it. They were gone, but what she had left was what mattered. Her family.

'Magic,' said Mrs Chambers, finally. She settled back to stare into the flames once more. 'A magical, mesmerising crystal ball. An enchanted set of nesting dolls. They sound like just the kind of thing a highway robber might have wanted to steal, once upon a time.'

She gave Betty a kindly, secretive smile.

'But not any more.'

Epilogue

'AND WE ARE NEVER, *EVER* GOING TO THAT godforsaken place again!' Granny concluded, banging down her bag on the kitchen table so forcefully that a cup nearly jumped out of its saucer. 'Oh, Barney! What a time we've had. Kidnappings, falling through ice, and now a broken arm. It's been never-ending!' She threw her coat over the back of a chair and began poking tobacco into her pipe as Barney Widdershins heaved the girls' trunk over the threshold of Blackbird Cottage.

Betty gazed around the kitchen, drinking in the familiar smells, creaks and noises of home. It was good to be back in Pendlewick, better than she ever could have imagined.

'Look!' Charlie exclaimed, as Oi strutted towards them curiously, tail flicking from side to side. 'He's missed us!' She scooped up the scraggy black cat in her arms and then released him just as quickly after he emitted a furious *yowl!*

'Missed the smell of rat, more like,' said Betty with a snort.

'Imaginary rat, you mean,' Fliss added quickly, with a sideways glance at Granny. 'Oh, it's so lovely to be home, safe and sound!'

'Bit poky, if you ask me,' said Clarissa, peering down her nose at the kitchen.

'Good thing no one did, then,' Father muttered under his breath. He winked at Betty, then gave Fliss a gentle hug.

'And I must say I'm starting to feel queasy, what with these wonky floors,' Clarissa added, plonking herself down at the table. 'I feel like I've been on the whiskey all week. No wonder Bunny chose this place.'

'How long did you say you were planning on staying?' Barney enquired politely.

'And which room is she in?' asked Charlie, pointedly.

'Clarissa,' said Clarissa. 'Not "she". And Bunny said I can stay till my ankle's better.'

'You'll have to go in Fliss's room,' said Granny, puffing out contented clouds of smoke. 'You can't manage the stairs with a broken ankle.'

'Oh,' said Clarissa, suddenly looking uncomfortable. She cleared her throat, and Betty watched her with interest, reminded of a similar shifty look on their cousin's face when they had just arrived in Wilderness. 'See, the thing is, Bunny – you did jump the mark a bit when you rushed all the way to me. I said in my letter that I *thought* it was broken. I mean, it really was *very* painful. But in fact, I had it checked over just before you arrived and it turns out it was a minor sprain! Isn't that lucky?'

Granny coughed and gave Clarissa a thunderous look. For a moment Betty could have sworn there was angry smoke coming out of her grandmother's ears.

'*Lucky?*' she said at last. 'I dragged these poor girls out to the middle of nowhere and waited on you hand and foot, and your ankle isn't even broken! Why on earth didn't you say something sooner?'

'Well,' Clarissa waffled. 'It was so lovely to see you all, and such a treat to be fussed over . . .'

'Right, you're upstairs,' Granny boomed, her mouth puckering up into a squiggle of cross lines.

'Upstairs?' Clarissa protested. 'With my ankle?'

'The exercise'll do it good,' Granny snapped. 'You can have Charlie's room. Charlie, you bunk in with Betty.'

'Yippee!' crowed Charlie. She gave Clarissa a cheeky grin. 'It's nice in my bed. Lots of rat fluff to keep it warm.'

Clarissa bared her teeth and muttered, 'Charming. I'll just carry my own bags up, shall I?'

'Good idea,' said Granny, with a glint in her eye. 'After you've put the kettle on and made us all a nice cup of tea. Perhaps it's a good thing you're here for a few days now that Fliss will be resting up with that broken arm.'

Later that evening after they had eaten, and had hot baths, and Charlie had excitedly finished telling Father all about their time in Wilderness (including Finn Sharkey's assurance that Mr Sneed and his rotten moustache would be going to prison for a very long time) the three sisters sat upstairs in Betty's room talking quietly as they unpacked their trunk.

Fliss fidgeted on the bed, trying to get comfortable. Betty had seen her silently wince at every bump in the road on the journey back, although she hadn't complained once.

'Cheer up, Fliss,' she said. 'Look on the bright side: at least it was your arm that got broken this time instead of your heart.'

'Oh, ha ha, very funny,' Fliss said, rolling her eyes. 'I still can't believe it, though. All those years people believed the story of the highwayman – and even thought he had died. But in the end, it was a love story, wasn't it? Just a different kind of love.'

Betty nodded, stuffing a pile of stockings back into a drawer without checking for ladders.

'And don't you think it's strange how Lady Fortuna predicted a broken arm?' Fliss went on. 'I mean, I thought you said she was a fraud?'

'She was,' Betty answered. 'She probably didn't even realise it was going to come true. What's weirder is that we were worrying about a death in the family, and we sort of got it.' She waited, but her sisters stared at her, equally baffled. 'Granny! She was the Grim Reaper at the ball. So there was a death in the family after all, get it?'

'Bats and broomsticks,' Fliss said with a shudder, looking

well and truly spooked. 'It just goes to show, we really should be superstitious!'

'Or when you look for certain things you're sure to find them,' said Betty, trying very hard not to snort.

'What shall we do with these?' Charlie asked, unwrapping the pretty decorations they had bought at the winter market on their first day. She handed Fliss her delicate glass snowflake and then lifted her own silver wolf to the light. 'It does look like Bonbon, doesn't it?' She eyed Betty's little sled enviously. 'Can I borrow that? I reckon Hoppit could fit into it for a ride.'

'Nope,' said Betty, grinning good-naturedly. 'It's too fragile – you'll break it. And anyway, he's getting so fat he won't fit. You're feeding him too much.'

'Ain't!' Charlie protested indignantly. 'He's just got a healthy appletite!' She stroked her thumb over the silver wolf thoughtfully. 'I know! We can pretend these three objects have magical powers. Now we don't have the dolls . . .'

She trailed off, seeing Betty's face fall. 'Sorry, Betty. It was just an idea.'

'It's all right,' Betty muttered, rubbing her nose as she took another jumper out and shoved it into her wardrobe. The decorations were lovely, but she could never pretend they were magical, however much she wanted to, because she'd had magic, *real* magic, and now it was gone. She still couldn't believe she would never see the dolls again, never use them to get up to mischief. She turned and grabbed a heavy scarf from the trunk. 'They're gone—'

She gave a soft cry and the scarf fell to the floor.

'Betty?' Fliss prompted. 'What's wrong?'

'I don't understand,' Betty whispered, staring into the trunk, her heart racing. For there, tucked neatly into one of Betty's shoes, were the nesting dolls. 'How . . . ?'

'Jumping jackdaws,' Charlie exclaimed, leaping on the bed. The glass decorations tinkled in her hand. 'I thought you said you dropped them in the lake?'

'I did,' Betty said croakily. 'I know I did!' Tentatively she reached for them, half afraid they would disappear – or that they were some other set of nesting dolls, even though she knew that made no sense. It made even less sense that they were here, in her hands, when they should be at the bottom of Shivershock Lake. But here they were. Nervously, she pulled them apart, afraid one would be missing, or broken, but they were all there. As real and solid and perfect as the day she had first unwrapped them. She undid the third doll with shaking fingers. Out came the tiniest trickle of ice-cold water and the final tiny doll which did not open. The hairs, scrap of fabric and pinches of fur had washed away.

'She brought them back to us,' Betty whispered, laughing even though tears were streaming down her face. 'Elora must have brought them back!' She placed the dolls inside each other then paused before fitting together the final two outer pieces. Slowly, she brought the upper part of the largest doll to her ear.

'What are you doing?' Charlie asked, puzzled. 'I thought

338

you only did that with seashells to hear the sea?'

'I'm listening,' said Betty, though she wasn't quite sure why. Perhaps it was the trickle of cold lake water that had given her the idea. For a moment she imagined she heard the soft rush of water, or a whispered voice ... but the harder she listened, the more it just sounded like silence. Elora was gone, but the Widdershins' pinch of magic was not.

Betty carefully twisted the outer dolls together, the set complete.

'There,' she murmured, placing them on the chest of drawers. 'Ready for next time.'

'Whoop whoop!' cheered Charlie.

'There won't *be* a next time, I hope,' Fliss protested, alarmed.

'Oh, there will,' said Betty, winking at her sisters. 'I'm sure of it.'

Acknowledgements

HUGEST thanks to my excellent editor, Lucy Rogers, who's been with me on every step, seasick boat trip, and sled ride of the Widdershins' adventures. Meddling magpies, you're good. Thanks also to the S&S children's books team: Laura Hough, Olivia Horrox, and Lucy Pearse for all your Widdershinsy work, and to Leena Lane and Emma Young who have saved me from many embarrassing bloopers.

Big thanks to incredible illustrator Melissa Castrillón. You somehow surpass yourself with every magical cover. What a huge talent you are. Thanks also to designers Jesse Green, Sean Williams and Sorrel Packham.

As always I'm grateful to my agent Julia Churchill, and the Rights team at A.M. Heath for all you do.

A wet lick and a cold nose in the hand thanks goes to Krystal Avery, who came up with the lovely name 'Bonbon' in the Twitter competition.

Thanks to my family for being helpful, supportive and

putting up with me in general when my head's usually in the clouds.

Last but never least, thanks to the booksellers, librarians, teachers, and bloggers who've championed the 'Pinch of Magic Adventures' and above all, YOU, the reader, for being here!

Team Widdershins!

Q&A with Michelle Harrison

Is there anything in particular that inspired *A Storm of Sisters?*

One of my favourite poems is *The Highwayman* by Alfred Noyes. It's a wonderful – but very sad – ghostly tale of a doomed robber and his secret love, Bess. The story of Robin and Elora was loosely inspired by this, but took its own path.

Which Widdershins sister is most like you, and do you have a favourite?

I'd say I'm most like Charlie because I've got a soft spot for animals and I have a very sweet tooth! Charlie is also my favourite sister. I love her mixed-up words and how cheeky she is.

Have you ever had your fortune told?

Yes, three times by 'professional' fortune tellers, but only one of them was any good.

Do icy tree grottos like Elora's Tears really exist?

Yes. I was lucky enough to find one in a country lane just before I began A *Storm of Sisters*. The moment I saw it I knew I wanted my next book to be set in deepest winter.

If you had to pick between the Widdershins' nesting dolls and Madam Fortuna's crystal ball, which would you choose?

The dolls. I'd love to sneak around being invisible and playing tricks like Betty does. The crystal ball would be a bit of a burden, and I'm not sure I'd be able to resist poking around in people's futures . . .

Michelle Harrison grew up in Essex and is the youngest of three sisters. Her first novel, *The Thirteen Treasures*, won the Waterstones Children's Book Prize. She also won the Calderdale Book of the Year Award for *The Other Alice*. Her work has been translated into over 20 languages. A *Storm of Sisters* is the fourth adventure in the bestselling Pinch of Magic series.

Before she was published, Michelle's jobs included working in a bar, a bakery, and an art gallery. She was then a Waterstones bookseller before becoming an editorial assistant in children's books at a publisher in Oxford. She now writes full time and lives with her partner, her son Jack, and cats.

www.michelleharrisonbooks.com
Find Michelle on Twitter @MHarrison13
and Instagram @elvesden